TOOTH & NAIL

Tooth & Nail

The Withrow Chronicles
Book II

Michael G. Williams

Falstaff Books

Cover Design by Natania Barron

Print Formatting by Susan H. Roddey, Clicking Keys
www.clickingkeys.com

ISBN: 978-1-946926-10-4

For more information on this or other Falstaff Books publications, visit www.FalstaffBooks.com.

Published by Falstaff Books
Charlotte, North Carolina
Printed in U.S.A

To my sister Maria, whose work and life are an inspiration to all who know her.

To the the Scourge of Nibelheim, the Heroes of Wayhaven, the Flatliners and the Tinker Trading Company, for the stories we tell together that I cherish so much.

PART I

CHAPTER 1

1951: HARDISONVILLE, NORTH CAROLINA, JUST SOUTH OF ASHEVILLE

I was standing outside the Hardisonville Country Club wearing a chrome-plated tuxedo, old-fashioned spats, and a look of general distaste, when my closest friend from high school dashed through the last scattered dregs of a storm to greet me. It was the night of our ten-year reunion and a late autumn rain had rolled across the mountains like a crashing wave two nights before.

"Withrow Surrett. Well I'll be damned." His thin face wore lines of age before its time and his eyes looked tired. I was pleased to see they sparked with the same intelligence and urgency they'd had when he was the resident bookworm of our tiny and eminently forgettable school. His ginger hair was hiding more white than I'd have expected, and his posture was a little bent, but as the only vampire in town I was probably safe assuming no one else would ever notice these details. They were well outside the realm of mortal perception and we have a unique sensitivity to seeing signs of age in the world around us. Clyde wore a basic blue suit and a long brown raincoat and he couldn't have looked any more the part of out-of-town cop if he'd been wearing a sandwich board sign advertising free suspicious glances.

"You're looking well."

I held out one hand and we shook for a long time, grinning at one another. Clyde was a good friend to anyone who'd be kind in return, but he and I had formed a close bond as two of the weirder people in school: he the lanky redhead tripping over tree roots because he had his nose in a book, and I the fat boy who doodled all the time and spoke only at gunpoint. It was a time when being weird was usually slapped out of a kid, but neither of us had gotten the message. He went on to a specific definition of great things, as expected, and I vanished before the ink on my diploma was dry. No one had heard from me in a decade – including Clyde – and I'd have kept it that way if I could. The dead are supposed to stay down, after all, but Agatha had a job for me and I had to take it. When the boss says jump, you jump. "That's kind of you, Clyde, but enough about me. How's life as a bracelet salesman?"

"Never as good as it ought to be." He shrugged. "And at the same time there's always more business than one would hope." His turn to deflect the question; this wouldn't be easy. "I didn't expect to see you here. What changed your mind?"

I told Agatha I'd need a good reason to be there, that anyone who'd known me would want to know why the hell I'd show up now when I'd skipped out on every other hometown obligation, large and small. She told me to get creative. "Traveling through. I was delivering a piece to a collector in Atlanta and thought it would be a gas to time it so I got to attend." It was plausible enough but it didn't draw attention to any off-limits topics. It wasn't hugely creative, but neither should any cover story be. An effective alibi is supposed to make the listener stop thinking about it, not elicit further interest.

Clyde's eyebrows quirked up and he gave an impressed nod. "A collector? There's someone in Atlanta who admires your work enough to have you deliver it in person?" Clyde had the police investigator tone down pat and it worked. It was really just him giving me the business for a subtle laugh, I knew, but dealing with a cop was an extremely risky bit of tap dancing and always has been, in all times and all places. We have it knocked into us repeatedly, over and over and over again in the first years after we're turned, to avoid cops at all costs. Agatha had made it clear that she would be staying a thousand miles away from every variety of fuzz, normally, but this was a situation in which one of her people just happened to have a cop friend from back in the day. It was a unique opportunity to soak him in the punch bowl then squeeze some information out.

My throat caught. I chuckled, though, after a gap of less than a human heartbeat. I was supposed to be the predator here. I needed to remember that. This was the new life I'd chosen: that in every future interaction with a simple human being, they were to be the ones who ought to fear me. I cleared my throat. "I was just transporting it for a client." Clyde looked interested so I waved it off. "I've been putting the art degree to good use doing a little art dealing and authentication. Before you ask, I promise this piece wasn't stolen and anyway once I crossed state lines I was out of your jurisdiction."

"Okay, Signore Peruggia, I'll put the gun down if you come out with your hands up." Clyde laughed and I laughed and he chucked me on the shoulder. Our patter didn't make a damned bit of sense to me but I didn't know if that was because we were two old friends whose affection was never based on comedy routines to begin with or because we were two old friends trying to figure out if, and how badly, one of us had offended the other by disappearing in a puff of smoke without so much as a bye. Clyde's tone changed and he said, looking me up and down, "I guess the art world pays well these days."

"No, but all the best advice columns say to dress for success." I shrugged it off. I'd rumbled up an hour after sunset in a gray Oldsmobile given to me last year by Agatha's people. The tux was courtesy my maker as well, and so was the ten dollar haircut – nearly a hundred these days – I'd been given by some barber she'd had wheeled up from Atlanta by one of her boys. The suit had been purpose-made, tailored to fit my generously distributed three hundred and fifty pounds without a single wrinkle or crease. After all, I was guaranteed I'd be shaped this way for the rest of my unnatural life so I might as well look good in it, Agatha said. It was all a little over the top and I'd protested that Clyde wasn't the type to be impressed by some fancy nest or granddad's stompers, but I was still too low in the organization to override direct orders. I chewed the last shot of smoke in my aging cigarette then flicked it off into some shadows. "Shall we? I bet there are at least a dozen people in there who won't remember who I am."

"They'll remember," Clyde said. "But they might have forgotten your sunny personality."

The country club was a rambling two-level manse wearing its aspirations of a better town on its prominent sleeves. It sat perched on a bluff's edge overlooking the carefully manicured grave of an old wooded valley. I couldn't help but feel it was a waste of real estate but I'd never been an athlete. For all I knew, golf was the singular apex of human experience. I doubted it, though. The sorts of persons drawn to make serious investments in it were not usually my preferred company except as the occasional meal.

The building itself was framed in massive timbers hewn into rectangles and stained the color of last night's coffee. Everywhere that wasn't a dead tree was a plate glass window or an unexpected angle. The silhouette's whole effect was of a Viking ship turned upside down for winter storage. It was beautiful, actually, but I hated everything about it. Country clubs were – are – full of people who think manual labor is evidence of congenital deficiency. Getting their hands dirty was a personal failure and I despised them for that. I wasn't exactly living off the land or even mowing the lawn on Saturday afternoons but I had known already, at 24 years of life and four of death, that the predation of humans on one another could be far more casual in its brutality and vastly more cruel than anything I might do to one of my victims. Oh, I stalked prey and attacked them and drank their blood and had, on occasion, left them dead – certainly dying – but they'd seen my face and known the final moments of their own fate and I'd done it without spending years lording it over them. I hunted them, sure, but I never denigrated them for becoming my prey. That counted for something, I believed. I still do.

Inside were a few hundred yards of expensive yellow wallpaper, ten pounds of carpet padding per square foot and a couple functionaries waiting for something interesting to happen so they could disapprove. I was overdressed and Clyde was under-styled so the maitre d' knew what we were here for. He shuffled the deck of his facial muscles in a way one could choose to read as an obsequious smile but he clearly felt events of this sort were beneath the Club. I liked that just fine and gave him a big grin. I stretched it all across my fat face and said, "I can't wait to get downstairs. I hear this joint has a great buffet." The host's features fumbled the ball and I showed him the sides of some molars in genuine enjoyment while waving him silent. "Come on, Chuckles, just get us downstairs and cut us loose." He said something unmemorable and led us across an expanse of dining room to the downstairs banquet hall with a minimum of further interaction. Halfway down the steps I realized Clyde was trying not to laugh and doing a pretty decent job. Phase one of my assignment – reconnect with Clyde and put him at ease – was going just fine. The rest was going to go a lot easier after I'd gotten a couple of cocktails in him. Any additional rounds of insults I got to unload on bystanders would just be a few bonus pins I could knock down in the last frame.

As casual as I could possibly ever have asked, I opened my mouth and kicked off the next gambit. "Let me buy you a drink, Clyde, while you tell me what you've been up to lately. I hear you're an agent with the State Bureau of Investigation."

Three hours later I was crossing a clearing two steps behind Clyde, ruining my ridiculous shoes in the mud and taking care to seem to wobble a little, when he stopped and held one hand half-way up to bring me to a halt. "I don't mean to be a drag, Withrow," he sighed, "But before I show you the site I need to remind you that this is supposed to be off limits. I shouldn't be letting you see this."

He had, though, because I'd made him. He didn't know that, but I'd forced him do it just as surely as if I'd put a gun to his back. I'd looked into his eyes and told him to do it and he had as though it had been his own idea. My supernatural vampire hoodoo still had the wrapping paper on, though, and he had lots of competing and counterbalanced motivations when it came to things like this. Even though I'd compelled him to do it by inserting specific directives, he resisted. I could see it in his eyes: somewhere back there his brain was turning my commands and his own instincts against one another like grist in a mill. I couldn't take any of that away; I could just add a few new cards to the catalogue.

"Indulge your eccentric artist friend and his dark interests," I said, spreading my hands a little. "I have to draw inspiration from all of life. How many chances to see a real crime scene will I get?" Tone and content mattered a lot when I tried to reinforce the hoodoo conversationally like this. I wanted something that wouldn't require a lot of thought on his part. "You know how we sensitive types are."

"You're about as sensitive as a severed limb," Clyde growled. He was annoyed, but not particularly with me. I didn't know all the details of my assignment but Agatha had me briefed on the minimum amount of necessary information: a murder, thus far unsolved, that we needed to make sure the authorities didn't link to anyone with exceptional canines. Clyde had taken it over from the local species of citation wavers. If he was still as tenacious when it came to professional pursuits as he had been with his academics ten years before, it was driving him crazy not to have an answer.

"Okay," I laughed, "But I am an artist nonetheless. I might want to memorialize these poor bastards." This mind-shaping business was new to me and it felt like juggling hot bowling balls. I decided to give it a little supernatural extra after all. My eyes met his and I commanded him. "Trust me," I said.

Clyde watched my face for a minute and then nodded. "Sorry. I do trust you. It's just... well. Just don't tell anybody I did this, OK?"

"Cross my heart," I said with a faint smile. I flicked the dog-end of my cigarette off into the shadows that draped everything but the single, stretched circle made by Clyde's cheap flashlight. Lights back then were nothing, just a bulb in a silvered dome we could point at things. Clyde couldn't see a damned thing by that light but I could see just fine. I'd aimed the coffin nail for a puddle eight feet away and bulls-eyed it. I sniffed the air once as the breeze shifted slightly and something turned over in my guts. It was weak, mostly washed away by the two days of rain, but I could smell it: blood, buckets of it, along with other smells of flesh and entrails and rot and, very faintly, the smell of a predator, a beast of the shadows. The rain had come at just the wrong time; it had encouraged everything terrible that hangs out in a body waiting for it to die. "We're close now, aren't we?"

Clyde narrowed his eyes for a moment and then nodded his head jerkily to one side. "Ten yards that way. We can go look at it in the flashlight but I can't let you stomp around. There are going to be five eggheads out here with protractors and slide-rules and a few local coon hounds for the next week trying to count every footstep for half a mile."

"That's fine," I said, though it wasn't really. I wanted to turn all my senses against the place where those people had been murdered, but that would be impossible.

We walked that direction and about five yards away Clyde pointed the flashlight at two matted spots on the ground. "The kid and the granny," he sighed. "Looks like there was a fight from all the knocked down weeds a little ways over there." He bobbed the flashlight off into the dark in such a way it might have indicated a spot twenty feet or two hundred from where we stood. "Don't know who got them, but we've got stories about an outsider hanging around with them for a few days. Real reclusive guy, secretive. Supposedly he was a song chaser, the academic types who crawl around the woods trying to find someone knowledgeable in old hillbilly music and asking to record them. Word is he is—or was—some professor from up North, but what if he wasn't? Neighbors say the kid had been shut up in that house with him for at least two weeks. Lots of late night drives, lots of sleeping in all day."

I grunted and rubbed my chin; I was too busy flaring my nostrils and taking deep, quiet breaths to say much. I could still smell a predator, still faint, but it was a little stronger here and it was unquestionably real. None of my kind would have smelled that and failed to recognize it. On the other hand, no human could possibly detect it. To have something to say, though, after a few moments I turned back to Clyde and kept his topic going. "The granny?"

"Nobody saw her around the place." Clyde reached up to rub one eye with the palm of his free hand, then gummed a cigarette out of a pack in his jacket. His tie was out of place, his hair oil slipping, bags under his eyes. He hadn't slept much in the couple of days since the SBI had moved in on the case. The locals had messed it up beyond repair, Clyde had told me. The mud was mostly from kids coming out in the sedan to do slow doughnuts around the place and pretend they'd seen something grizzly or funny or new. "She lived out in the middle of nowhere, towards Pisgah Forest. No neighbors close enough to know anything useful. No power, no radio, just an old Victrola and some brittle records."

I clicked my cheeks against my teeth. "What's your gut tell you?"

Clyde thought for a long time, watching the tip of his cigarette burn. Without the flashlight I could have seen well enough by that tiny red glow to find the crushed plants where the bodies had lain for days; with only the sliver of waning moon still rising I could have read a book. The experience wasn't completely new to me at that point, but I hadn't spent a lot of time around people—you know, regular humans—since the Big Bite and I kept finding it startling to realize how weak Clyde was compared to me: how limited he was in abilities and how terribly vulnerable he was to factors as inevitable as night. "I don't know," he finally said. "They say eventually you get a knack for that kind of thing, but I don't guess it's bitten me yet."

"You must think something..." I tried not to sound too eager.

"Truth? Conventional wisdom says it's the outsider. Natural choice, isn't he? Shows up, hides from everybody, probably drains a small fortune out of the kid by one con or another, then dumps the body out here and leaves town. He and the kid left the house together three nights ago, never came back. The kid was rich. Inherited everything when he was too young to know anything about what to do with it."

"And the granny? What's she?"

Clyde shook his head, took a drag, let it waft out his nose and the corners of his mouth while he spoke. I lit another just watching him. "Accomplice? Maybe she tried to warn the kid. Maybe she used to be his babysitter and she stopped by to say hello at the wrong time." He shook his head again. "Can't say. Regardless of who it was, I figure he'll turn up again. That's why I come out here a lot. He'd have to come back sometime. Too much attention on this one, he's going to come back to make sure he didn't leave anything untidy that might point to him. If I were the murdering sort, I wouldn't exactly worry too much about the local Sheriff catching me but the SBI's a different story. If he's worried, he'll want to double-check everything. If he's arrogant, he'll want to gloat."

I smiled a little; I'd heard that tone before behind many of Clyde's hypotheticals. "You don't think it's the outsider, do you?"

Clyde stood silent for a few seconds then shook his head at the ground. "No, I don't." He took a long drag. "Song chasers go way up the mountain sometimes and it isn't always a pretty business. They go out at night because it's quieter then, and sometimes the only way to hear the old songs is to sneak up on a house where some mountaineer – who shoots anyone lacking their same last name – is singing them. No, the outsider is the easy answer. My personal opinion..." Clyde paused, looked up at the sky, looked around in the direction of the trees that ringed the clearing some fifty yards away in any direction, went on. "It wouldn't be popular around here, but I suspect he ran these folks across the wrong bunch of hillbillies somewhere and got himself in trouble: maybe some old moonshiner, maybe somebody who married both his sisters. I don't know." Clyde shrugged halfway before clearing his throat and then straightening his back and his hat at the same time. "There were some things we found that were unusual. Things that point up the mountain to some backwards place more than anywhere else. Anyway, I expect it's a lot simpler than some complicated con and a stranger. That's too neat and too messy all at the same time. Wouldn't be able to build much of a career at it, killing rich orphans and old women, would he? Meantime, it's too convenient for some of our fine citizens to point at an outsider and remain certain of their own purity." He spat suddenly, at the ground, the shadows. "A couple years of police work has taught me about purity."

I let him stand there without saying a word. He was headed away from the personal conclusions that I knew would endanger him – regardless of whether he was right – and I didn't see any need to get out and push along the way. Finally Clyde turned back to face me and put on something like a smile. "Anyway," he drawled, "We'll get 'em sooner or later."

I ran the details through my head again and sighed. I could afford to talk to him as my old friend, for just a moment, rather than prey. "I have to tell you, my instincts are different on this one. I don't think you'll ever know who did it or why. I don't know who did it, Clyde, but I don't think you will, either. It's so random, there's nothing to tie it together. I wouldn't know where to begin." I smiled a little. "Not that I'm questioning your skills as a detective."

"Thanks." Clyde produced a soft, dark chuckle: two parts maybe to one part is-that-so. "But I'm pretty sure I'm right." He nodded to himself. "Pretty sure." He enunciated each syllable distinctly, as though a separate word: pret tee sure. We stood in silence for a couple of minutes, finished our cigarettes and eventually turned our attention to those two depressions again. After a few forevers had gone by, Clyde spoke. "You really are looking well," he said.

I smirked, unseen in the dark. "Clean living." Clyde snorted loudly and I tsk'ed him. "Now, now. Judge not. How's Edith?"

Clyde produced the most unguarded, honest expression I'd seen all night: a broad smile. "She's great," he said. "It's our third anniversary in seven weeks. Christmas, you know." He looked over. "We missed you at the wedding."

"Sorry." I chewed my lower lip for a second. "Business."

"I imagine your line of work does demand a lot of travel." Clyde didn't sound too wounded, which was kind of him. "Edith hasn't seen you at all since graduation. She said to let you know you're welcome any Sunday for lunch."

"Maybe this winter. Depending on the time."

Clyde nodded and looked away again. "It's been ten and a half years since we graduated from high school and nobody in this town has seen you since the day after we walked the stage. You didn't even show up for your family's funerals – didn't even have funerals in the first place." His voice was dragging a hundred questions around behind it. I'd have hated to be some perp hearing him wind up like that in an interrogation room somewhere.

I sighed a little. I'd figured he would get there eventually. "Yes, I did. I just didn't tell anyone about them. I wanted privacy."

"And the community wanted to say goodbye." Clyde wasn't angry. He was just sad. He coughed finally and shook it off. "None of my business. Sorry."

"No offense taken." My voice was low. I didn't want to talk about it. I didn't want to think about it. One day I'd have to open up that corner of my mind and look inside but not yet. I had plenty to think about, wonder about, to keep that far from the front burner. "Thanks for bringing me out here. I hope it doesn't get back to anybody. I just wanted to see for myself."

"Don't mention it." Clyde gestured with the flashlight and I went first, retracing my steps back to the cars. When we arrived, I walked over to mine with the keys already in my hand. He stopped halfway to his and the light swung around as he spoke. "Don't think anyone hates your or thinks you're too classy for them just because you went away. People get over things. They grow up. Sometimes I..." He paused and dug out another cigarette, lighting it. "Well, sometimes I think I know how you felt or maybe how you feel now, coming back here. I spent a long time at headquarters just training. I've seen enough of the local underbelly through fresh eyes to feel like I can't really just walk out my front door in the morning and fit into the rest of the world. I..." He paused again, took a drag. I said nothing, indicated nothing, just listened. "I'm wasting your time," he finally sighed.

"No," I said, quick off the starting block. "You're the best friend I've got in this town – hell, this end of the state. You can tell me. I know what you mean. I went off to college and now this place feels like a pair of shoes I grew out of: beat up, worn down and I can't go anywhere without it hurting a little. If you need to talk, I've got a phone."

"Thanks. If nothing else, call us the next time you're in town. Maybe by then you can babysit for us." He and Susan had been going together for four years when they got married. They were perfect for each other. I'd tried to set them up when we were seniors but it didn't take for a couple years. Edith was too smart for this town, always had been; so was Clyde. I couldn't believe it when I found out he'd bothered to go get educated and had wound up back here as the long arm of the law no one liked to see. The State Bureau of Investigation didn't help with cases back then. They just showed up and took them away from incompetent locals. "Just... whatever your situation is, stay in touch."

"Will do." I smiled, touched the brim of my hat – too small, too cheap, like all of mine were when hats were *de rigueur* and now it was crushing that haircut Agatha had paid so much money for me to have – and got into the car and drove away.

I went fifteen miles, watching my mirrors the whole time, cutting across dirt roads, doubling back. Finally I pulled into an Esso way down out towards nowhere and stepped into the phone booth. Beyond the meager lights of the gas station I could see apple trees by the tens of thousands spreading away in all directions, the sharp edges of leaves outlined in starlight. "Operator," I murmured into the receiver, "I need to place a long distance call to Atlanta, charges reversed." It took a minute or two to get the call set up. When a voice came on the other line I kept my report simple and by the book:

"Suspected activity, natives blind."

"There will be a telegram to you tomorrow evening, Mr. Surrett." Agatha's help were all very crisp, very professional. I outranked them, but only nominally. I hung up the phone, got back into the gray sedan and set off for my motel. I had nothing but time to kill. Back then it felt like I'd never be out of time, that time just stretched out in front of me like so much endless highway I'd never have to leave or share or think about.

That was over half a century ago. I was young and stupid.

Now I'm old and none the smarter.

Chapter 2

"Sudoku is probably the single greatest thing that ever happened to vampires."

That's what I was telling my cousin Roderick when I pulled the Firebird into the driveway in Hardisonville on my first return there in what felt like a hundred years. I couldn't believe the things technology made available to me. Here I was, driving along in my car with a cellular phone on speaker, and I could just chat away with Roderick as though he were right there in the cabin with me. In truth, he sounded like he was at the other end of a tin can telephone, but he had explained to me that we – all of us, society or however you want to call it – had tacitly accepted degraded performance in one area for dramatically enhanced utility. It felt backwards to me, but the phone itself felt a little bit like magic.

"No way," Roderick purred. "Infomercials: humans preying on other humans in the middle of the night. I think it's cute. it's like watching kittens wrestle." Roderick purrs everything, unless he's angry. His voice is a little hypnotic in a weird way and I've never been able to tell whether he cultivated that quality or it just happened on its own.

"You think infomercials are the best thing that ever happened to us? *Ever?*" I reached up and back and scratched Smiles behind the ears. He's a hundred fifty pounds of Doberman I feed a little of my blood now and then to keep permanently young and stronger than a team of horses. At the moment, he was curled up on a towel I'd draped across the back seat with his head poking between the front seats so he could keep an eye on me and the road.

"On second thought," Roderick mused, "I'm going to say it was skin cancer. It made them so paranoid. Pallor has never looked healthier."

I couldn't help but laugh. "Where are you staying, by the way?"

"I'm in Asheville. I can't find a decent place to stay in the countryside."

"Lots of good hotels around," I said, "But suit yourself. Been in long?"

"I got here three nights ago, actually. You know, Asheville has a very rich history." He emphasized 'rich' as if it were a suggestive curse word. "Hauntings, murders, suicides, ghostly hitch hikers, a headless horseman, all kinds of fun."

Roderick is... well, I don't know what to say about him. He likes trouble. He likes to pry and poke. He likes to find all the buttons on a person or a place and press them to see what happens. Roderick is a psychopath. Probably.

The thing about my cousin is that he really is my cousin. That's not some weird *la familia* vampire bullshit. He's my father's middle brother's youngest son's only child. He was born about twenty years after I was but through a weird set of coincidences we both got turned. He never knew his maker like I know mine, though. He was an orphan. I think that's part of what made him how he is. He lives in Seattle – grew up there – and the local boss, name of Emily, keeps an eye on him for me. I've been to visit. It was weird, but I extended the invitation in return. He may be a freak but he's family. None of us gets to choose the one we wake up in. "I see you've done some research," I replied, neutral. I paused, then: "I'm glad you're here."

"I promised I'd come visit." He said it too simply for it to be the whole truth, but that's just par for the course for us. "Emily sends all her love."

"Tell her same back, if you talk to her."

"When shall I come by?"

"I've got an appointment," I said. "I'll call you later tonight, maybe tomorrow. That okay?"

"Of course, cousin." Roderick sounded calm and that was always good. "I'll talk to you then."

He hung up and so did I.

I only go back to Hardisonville every autumn, now. No need to stick around a lot; it's not like there are many of us up there. I'd been up on my victory lap – that's what Roderick called it – after I'd burned Bob the Third down to a pile of bubbling fat and taken over fifteen years earlier, but there weren't many bloodsuckers up here to whom I needed to pass the news of the old boss' demise. I now simply resolved to make my visits to Clyde coincide with my friendly little check-ins on the tiny handful of us who can blend in across a rural population that sparse. In a little place like Hardison County, a single sloppy vampire can really do a number on a town. It doesn't matter that they – humans – so vastly outnumber us; we so vastly overpower them, after all. Their refusal to believe in us works to our advantage but their ready inducement to mass hysteria works to theirs. To live as a vampire in such a place requires a tremendous amount of restraint combined with a little con artistry or a loyal servant or some other means of minimizing one's own direct impact.

I'd rung up and gotten a week's subscription to the local newspaper before I came up to visit the old place so I'd have something to read, some source material for catching up on local events, puzzles to work on. Crosswords are good but Sudoku is better. That's part of the deal with living forever, or at least a very long time: we have to work hard to stay nimble. The body doesn't age of its own accord, doesn't weaken – quite the opposite – but the mind decays fast if one doesn't keep exercising it. I'd found chasing numbers around on a grid was satisfying and it stretched some corners of the brain I hadn't had to use in a while. I've tried buying the big books but they don't work for me. I don't want to become an expert. I want something to do when I get done reading the newspaper. Doing a book of puzzles feels too much like jogging in place. Doing the puzzle in the paper, the one all the humans find themselves stuck on over a bowl of oatmeal in the morning light, now that feels real.

I'd had to leave Raleigh right at sundown and stopped twice to buy gas on the way, cruising into Hardisonville around 11:15. The Firebird tears through that stuff, just eats it up. I should get something cheaper to run but nothing today feels as solid as a big slab of steel from the '70s. Sure, the paint is faded and the panels are dinged and the seats are sagging and half-crushed, but it's my Firebird. Even if I wanted rid of it, I couldn't show up on a car lot at lunch to close a deal on the paperwork for a new one. Maybe I could line things up to walk in after dark, pay cash, whatever: it can be done but it draws attention. It earns the notice of the IRS, of the bank, of the salesman on the lot. Things like that have to be very carefully planned and executed or else you're always stuck on the lookout for a moron you can get past without a million little questions. Sometimes it seems like it would be easier to do everything at a remove, through a slave, but I'm always trying not to give in to that eternal temptation to just go completely off the grid and withdraw from legal life. No, that way is madness. I know how it works for vampires who do that. They get proxies—butlers, assistants, interns, "nieces" whose names are on the deeds—to do all the legwork for them but it never pans out. Even if they try at first to do most of it themselves, to keep an ear to the ground of common experience, slowly over time they draw further and further back – or get pushed further away – until they're just out there somewhere in the shadows, one too-curious patrolman or one nosy neighbor or one ambitious servant away from having everything taken in the fluorescent glare of bureaucracy or the silent swipe of petty theft. I like to keep things simple but most of all I like to keep things *me*.

I've made concessions, of course. No man in his eighties looks like me: hair thick and curly and dark black, face more or less unlined except by the little creases even an immortal acquires from worry or thought or, perhaps, from too much Sudoku. I was turned at twenty-four but I look thirty or thirty-five; I always looked older than I was. I'm my own grandson on paper but it doesn't much matter given that when I sign for something I put down my name, *Withrow Surrett*, just as bold as I please. I've had to give up one public career to pantomime being a failure at another. For a while, I was a lay-about trust fund baby and now—in theory—I'm a failed writer selling off a collection of his grandfather's paintings one at a time. That bothers me sometimes, but not as much as it would bother me to hide altogether. Agatha doesn't like it, of course. She thinks it makes me conspicuous, but to hell with that. I am who I am. I didn't accept immortality so that I could become someone else; I did this so I could be here when the world of the living finally meets my standards.

I gathered up the stack of newspapers from around the blue delivery box at the end of the drive then turned and walked all the way back up the steep drive to the front door of the house. It was just pouring the rain in great sheets that night, a real drencher blowing up and over the mountains from the southwest, but I hadn't thought to bring an umbrella. Don't much care for them, to be honest. I'd rather feel the rain than insulate myself. I fished around for my keys, came up with them, and tried a couple of different ones before I got one that would turn the lock. House keys, they all look alike these days. No personality at all. Lightning was cracking far off, jagged veins of day on the other sides of mountains revealed in silhouette.

Smiles followed me out of the car, down the drive and back up. He was the first one into the house and into the dry where he promptly sprayed the foyer with a rapid and thorough shake. I closed the door behind me but didn't turn on the lights in the hall or anywhere else in the house. I could see just fine by the light of the VCR, blinking 12:00 at me every two seconds. I checked my watch: late but not so late I'd missed him. Clyde still went out to that field on this night every year, rain or shine.

I went out to meet him every time.

I got Smiles set up with a bowl of kibble and started turning on lights around the house, checking to see if any bulbs blew. I only turn the power on for a month every time I come up to visit so there are always a few surprises waiting for me. The wrapping on the pipes in the crawl space needed some work – something had gnawed at them over the summer – and the water ran a little dark for the first few seconds after blowing the air out. Old house, old pipes.

Around midnight I locked the place back up, left on a couple of lights in the living room and climbed back into the car. Smiles would be OK on his own for a bit; it never hurts to let the neighborhood hear and see your huge-ass dog when you're out of town for extended periods. If all the lights were with me, I'd get out to see Clyde by half past and that would be right on time by our usual schedule. The rain was still coming down, and I'd drenched myself peeking into the crawl space and checking the storm windows, but I didn't much care. I turned on the heater in the Firebird and cranked some music and hit US 64 through town.

Hardisonville had changed a lot over time. New houses everywhere while old houses were torn down and replaced. Whole sections of woods I'd once driven past on this route were gone and McMansion-y boxes had been stacked two inches apart all across the nude slopes left in their places. It reminded me of the Reinholdts back home. Their kids were off in college now and their house was up for sale. I wished I could buy it and finally bulldoze the goddamn thing but the neighborhood association they started probably had a rule against that.

I scowled and turned the music up higher. There was a Chinese restaurant in Hardisonville now. Nothing wrong with Chinese food, don't get me wrong, but the time was it couldn't support one "home-style" restaurant because people thought eating out was decadent. Everything had changed so much in my absence. Everything had a sign in front of it now that started with the word "Historic." What they didn't tear down they turned into a museum. The anonymity of one neighborhood compared to another was grating. I used to be able to date the neighborhoods, the developments, the farmhouses, one by one as I drove by. Now they all looked the same. For all the new growth, it felt like a place with the life drained out.

Hardison County, if you see it on a map, looks like a square that's stood up to stretch. It's higher, mountain-wise, on the western and northwestern ends than it is on the southeastern. In the northwest it's a bunch of dairy farms and a few little commuter enclaves that twenty or thirty or sixty years ago were nothing but a gas station and a couple of churches. In the southeastern corner it's apple trees. In amongst it all, though, are housing developments that weren't there five or ten years ago. Property values are through the roof. The county is growing. Gods only know what people there actually do for a living. Some work in Asheville, some hoof it all the way down to Greenville or Spartanburg, maybe, but most of the people moving in are retirees.

The dead and dying circle the countryside looking for an empty roost. The number one industry in that part of the world is health care and most of that is "retirement" care: buildings full of people who never get out of bed and a professional staff waiting for them to die. The rest homes all have waitlists. If you don't want to idle your engine at home until a bed opens up then you go to some hole in the wall rank with the last days of hard living. There is nothing good in those places. I've only ever been to a couple of them and I could not believe people would do this to themselves, to one another, charge money for it, do the landscaping for it, approve the permits for it. Everything about it made me want to turn and run and never look back. Those places terrify me. The times I've been to one, I've gone straight out into the night, found someone terrible and drained them while they screamed. I would turn them to the sky and eat the last bit of their life with their eyes staring into the darkness, their feet kicking in protest. I killed fast and mean to wipe away the images of all that slow death creeping up on prepackaged corpses. Better to take a life that fights not to go than to institutionalize the process of dragging death out for years like that.

US 64 used to be the main artery through Hardison County, running roughly from the northwest to the southeast. I took it for ten or fifteen minutes into the heart of town then turned right along the way and set off back up and down the mountains to the southwestern corner of the county. I couldn't get it out of my head the whole way there that the rest homes had come here to spawn, like flies laying eggs in dead flesh. A part of me believed that if they expanded long enough sooner or later they'd all grow together to encompass the county; that eventually the county itself would be a patient comprising geography and bad luck; that all the people in it would just be there to attend to that one county-sized patient, waiting for it to die.

Rain gushed down from the sky so hard that finally even I pulled off at a convenience store – twenty four hour gas stations were one of the few advantages I could see of the county growing fat on the blood of the dead – and bought an umbrella. It was a simple, cheap, black number with manual everything. It was funny to note a manual umbrella cost more than one with buttons and spring-loaded doodads. Whatever. I climbed back into the car and started back down the road and up the mountain towards my appointment. I'd be a little late, it looked like, and Clyde certainly wasn't getting any younger. I hoped he didn't think I'd forgotten or abandoned him.

By 12:40 I'd reached the turn-off for the clearing. I arced around from the main highway on a road now paved—used to be dirt, and I wondered who'd paved it and what newly-minted mansion I'd find if I kept going past the field itself – until I reached the little gap in the trees where I had to pull in and park before walking the rest of the way.

Clyde's car was still there. It was two inches deep in mud. I'd have to help him get it out; not at all a difficult job for me, but he was going to be damned lucky to have a vampire there to help him. My Firebird, well, I could about carry it out myself on one shoulder if I had to. I still had a winch on the front, the 1970's answer to SUVs before there were SUVs. You never know what you'll get into out in the country. I killed the engine and sat in silence, listening to the rain pound the roof. He was probably half-soaked out there already. I grabbed the umbrella, climbed out and gave my eyes a moment to adjust. I could just barely see ahead of me thanks to the blood gurgling around these old veins. A mortal would have been blind.

I squelched through the mud and the high grass, brown and bent by the autumn and approaching winter, through the trees. Twenty yards, thirty, forty. The trees used to be thinner here, the brush smaller. Whoever inherited the land didn't take care of it like their predecessor had. The first time Clyde and I had been out here, it had been neatly trimmed, a fence on the far side carefully mended, no rust on the barbed wire, fresh nails in some of the posts. Now the fence had probably fallen down. The undergrowth was thicker; there were briers pushing in over most of the ground. There were a few irregular paths through but they were deer trails, nothing more. This had become a forgotten place.

I started off through the undergrowth and stopped short a few feet in. I'd have sworn I smelled, for just a moment, blood. Fresh. Well, fairly fresh. Spilled tonight, I'd have wagered, but then, just like that, it was gone. I stood stock still, sniffing the air in silence, but couldn't pick anything up through the rain. Finally I kept going. Maybe Clyde had snagged an arm on one of these brier bushes. Whatever. I'd fed on the way out of Raleigh; I wouldn't be a danger to anyone who smelled of a couple cuts tonight.

I stepped out of the trees and into the dark field. What little moon there should have been was entirely shut out by the clouds. Even I was having trouble with anything at much of a distance. I reached into my pockets and produced an LED flashlight, bright enough for me to walk confidently and to see that there was something, someone – Clyde, I guessed – out in the middle of the field, more or less where I'd expect him to be. I walked closer and, the closer I got, the less it looked right. He was sitting down on the ground – no, make that laying down on the ground. I shoved the flashlight in a pocket and took off running towards him.

Clyde was white as a sheet and lying facedown on the ground. I didn't need to be a vampire to tell he was dead. Anyone would have looked at that form and known it was a corpse. One thin – no, frail – arm was up over his head, the other under him. He wore a long, heavy coat, galoshes over his shoes, thick corduroy pants, and a flannel shirt. He looked like a retired lumberjack. His hair was thin and patchy. His scalp was splotched with age, and his face was lined.

His eyes were open wide. He'd died in absolute terror of what killed him.

My last mortal friend was dead and he looked very, very old.

I spent a half-minute just standing there over him, staring. It took some time for the vampire instincts to kick in. He'd been dead for a few hours at most. He'd been drained of all blood – I could only catch the faintest of whiffs when the wind was right and there wasn't any spilled on the ground. Even in the rain there'd be some left under him if he'd bled out here. He'd been killed somewhere else, drained and brought here in his own car, then left behind; or he'd been killed by someone who met or followed him here and then drained cleanly before being ditched. A part of me – the part of me that always hunts – started to make me turn around and go back, look for his footprints, smell his car. The part of me that remembered an old friend from high school kept staring at him, though. He must have been – gods, we'd graduated together. He was eighty-three years old.

Same age as me.

I reached down and wrapped my right hand in one corner of my coat, then gripped his shoulder and turned him very slowly. The neck had been slit with something sharp. It hadn't happened here. If it had, there'd still be blood no matter how big a barrel the killer had held under him when he made the slice. He probably didn't live long enough to bleed to death; he probably drowned before that. Leaning closer, I could smell the blood when I tilted his head back a little, dead blood, pooled in his lungs. My stomach turned. He didn't even have appeal as food for the very worst part of me. Clyde was just a dead thing now. His mouth was open, the skin stretched tight around his eyes. They were mad, with the whites showing as big as Kennedy half-dollars. His eyebrows were up, stretched high. Water had pooled in the lines and crevices of his face and ran out of his eyes like great tears when I moved him.

I rolled him back over, putting him as he had been, stood up, turned my back, drew a slow, shaky breath and let out one long, quivering, sudden, strangled sob. Before I could do anything, I dropped the umbrella, raised both hands to my face and bent double to weep openly, angrily, shaking my whole oversized body up and down its length. My back spasmed and my shoulders jerked against and away from themselves. I cried out. I wailed like an animal until the anger underneath the tears sprang up all of a sudden and I stood straight, threw my head back, and cried out high and horrible and piercing. Rain fell in my mouth, up my nose and pattered against the eyelids I'd squeezed shut. All I could hear was rain and wind and myself screaming and in the distance the occasional car on the old country highway I'd taken to get here. I hated everyone in those cars, everything about them, every imagined happy facet of the lives they were on their way to living out there. I hated whatever they were doing that they weren't here weeping with me. I threw my arms out and screamed again, first shrilly then descending into a yell, then a groan, then a serrated sigh as I finally squatted and then sat in the rain and the mud, water soaking the coat under me in an instant.

I sat beside my dead friend and I cried for long minutes, weeping out all the years I could remember.

Clyde was dead – murdered – and I already missed him.

When I looked at my watch, it was past one o'clock in the morning. I'd sat there and shaken and cried out and sobbed for the better part of twenty minutes and I could tell I wasn't done yet. Still, I had to get moving at some point. I had to leave. I had to get out of there before someone found me with him. I had to go home, clean up and get my brain working. I had to find out who had done this to him and why. I had to track them down and put my hands around their neck and make them stare me in the face – my real face, the one with the fangs – and make them wish they'd never been born. The prowling thing in a vampire's gut never really sleeps and a lot of bad emotions can make it come out. The worst one is anger.

I was so very, very angry.

I needed that anger, though, because his throat had been slit but he hadn't been beheaded and as terrible as it was to see him dead like this, it was worse to consider that he might start moving again of his own accord. Better to tear his head off now than to risk letting him turn into a Steeplechase – the polite new term for the walking dead we'd had crop up once a few years ago. It still happened every now and then, maybe once in a million deaths, and I couldn't stand the thought of it happening to Clyde. I reached over, turned my head so I wouldn't watch myself do it, and then tore his head from his body in one move. It was as light as a feather. I barely had to try.

I stood up, hefting all three hundred fifty pounds of myself back onto my legs, and set off to the car. I got halfway there when I remembered the umbrella, turned around, went back for it. It had blown a few feet away. I kicked myself for leaving footprints all over the area where the body – where Clyde – was. I was fucking up a crime scene in a major way and tomorrow or the next day or sometime there would be cops crawling all over this place. I went back, trying to mangle my own prints, but all I did was make new ones on top of the old ones. I cried out again in anger, started stabbing my old footprints with the butt end of the umbrella to deform them, backtracked all the way to the car like that. I got in, gunned the engine hard, then got back out after a moment and walked over to Clyde's car. I could see the keys in the ignition. I could see a couple of paperbacks on the front seat, a half-full ashtray, a cassette sticking out of a tape player. Clyde was driving the same car he'd had the last dozen times I'd been here: an early '90s sedan of American make. It was a sensible car – a little get up and go, a little space, generous weight, average gas mileage. It was an old man's car.

The cassette was probably a book. He liked books on tape. I'd meant to bring him one and forgotten.

I put my hand back in the fold of my coat and tried the door. It was unlocked. There was a scent there besides Clyde's. I didn't recognize it, but I stood there snuffling the air for a long time to make sure I had it down good. I'd know it the next time I smelled it, of that much I was sure. It was a human smell, and I would be able to catch it from the other end of a shopping mall.

I slammed Clyde's car door shut so hard the window rattled and then climbed back into the old Firebird. I floored it a couple of times to rev the engine, then put it in low and backed very slowly out of the mud and onto the blacktop. I got out and went back through messing up my tire tracks as I'd done with my footprints. The cops would know someone had been here and that they didn't want to be spotted. I hadn't spotted any tracks in the mud – such as those of Clyde's killer – but he'd been dead so long the rain had probably done away with his killer's tracks already. Maybe mine would be gone by the time someone found him, I thought. Maybe all this is just wasted effort, just something to do with the time I'd have spent talking to him.

Or maybe I was going to call the cops, against my better judgment.

I got back into the car, cranked the stereo as hard as it would go and took off into the night to ask myself that last question over and over again while I drove around, hit dirt roads and doubled back again and again.

By the time I'd gotten fifteen miles away, I was in the southeast of the county, out among the apple farms. Countless years later the gas station was still there. There was still a pay phone. I thought about it, but there were probably also security cameras.

I kept driving.

On the way back home, I passed the old Appleton high school. It'd been abandoned at some point. Appleton was a "community", not a real town. The old school was just a shell of a building, windows boarded, some of the boards missing and any others that were reachable covered in the slightly crude country facsimile of a real city's graffiti. It was childish: the autographs of a teen population that saw no reason to leave anything standing when they left.

There were two phone booths on one wall. On a whim I stopped and got out to check them. One was just barely hanging by some wires, but the other produced a dial tone. I stood there with the phone in my hand, then hung it back up, shoved my hands into a coat pockets, wrestled the receiver back off, wiped it down, managed to get it between my face and my shoulder. I dialed 911 with fingers made extra thick by the trench coat and when the operator picked up I spoke in a flat monotone.

"There's a body. He's dead." I gave quick directions then paused. The operator asked if I needed medical attention, if I was still there. After long seconds of silence I said, "I didn't do it."

I hung up the phone, got back in my car and drove away. It was stupid to attract the cops to where I'd just been, stupid to call them myself, stupid to do anything about it at all other than melt back into the shadows. But... it was Clyde. He wasn't just someone. He was my friend. He'd been a cop, himself. I couldn't leave him out there. I couldn't bed down for the day and pretend I hadn't seen him. I couldn't know he was dead and do nothing.

I drove home in silence, listening to the rain and the wiper blades.

No music.

No nothing.

Not even tears.

Officially, my name is Withrow Surrett III. As I said, there never was a junior, much less III. It's a pain in the ass these days to get the paperwork done, but the fixers love it. It used to be a lot easier: a birth certificate by a country doc who was a drunk; that kind of thing. It has always been easy to find prey in the great wash of humanity, whether needed for blood or for graft. These days everything's in a computer somewhere. You need a fixer to do "records insertion" in all the right places. You spend most of one legal adult life building a trail for the next one, then assume that one and start all over again. I've been Withrow Surrett III for nearly fifteen years and I'm already behind on building a life for Me IV.

Anyway, that's a part of why I should have just melted away and not drawn attention. Attention is the very last thing any of us wants. The records might not hold up on close examination. The paperwork might not have ever been done in the first place if you didn't ride the fixer pretty hard. Then there are the usual concerns, the ones you probably thought of first: getting stuck in a cell with a window; getting caught feeding; getting jumped by a rent-a-cop in the bushes out behind a nightclub when you're half crazy from starvation; being unpleasantly surprised when you show up in a photograph on display in a historical exhibit down at Town Hall; that kind of stupid stuff. All that used to happen a lot but it's mostly the oldsters who get caught with their pants down in those circumstances. If you got turned in the 20th century you're pretty good at living in the modern world. If you're pre-World War I, you're pretty screwed if you're not a fast learner, especially if you've been taking a dirt nap for a while. I've heard tell of vampires who bedded down in immigrant communities peopled entirely by their personal herds and never been seen again. I'm forced to wonder if they sometimes hear the heavy machinery of urban redevelopment rumble by up top and stir in their sleep. I try to imagine what would happen if any of them found their coffins unearthed in the middle of the afternoon. It wouldn't be pretty. It would probably get labeled terrorism and hushed up.

People: always the same, always ready to bury a problem and forget it existed.

You're probably wondering right about now why on Earth I was out meeting a friend from high school, then, if I was so shy about the long arm of the law. Clyde, well, he was a friend I couldn't easily escape. He asked around about me if I wasn't seen much. His job as a fancy state cop left my maker shy about eliminating him, I think. He knew, eventually. He couldn't help noticing that I was staying late 20's and he was pushing retirement, could he? We never much talked about it. We did talk, mind you, but not much. I don't know if he ever told Edith. He'd always tell me she said hello. I was so proud of setting the two of them up, and I guess over the years maybe they turned into something I felt I'd done that was good in the midst of all I've had to do that wasn't.

Enough of that, though; more than enough. I'd thought myself half to death by the time I pulled up in the driveway back in Hardisonville and parked the Firebird right in front of the front door so I wouldn't have far to go in the rain. I hadn't minded it earlier but now I couldn't be fussed with it. I'd been too wet tonight, too cold, too old and too much had changed. I wanted to be inside. I wanted to turn on the old baseboard heat and pull up a chair by the window and read a week's worth of newspapers and not think about my friend.

The newspapers – the *Times-Report* – didn't hold a lot of comfort for me. I couldn't focus myself enough to do any puzzles, not even the crossword, and when I flipped to the front page of the paper from a week before all that had greeted me had been news of a single-car accident up around the country club. I looked at the pictures, taken as they were from a discreet distance, and sighed at all that death and destruction. Big deal. Another day in the mortal world: something burned, someone suffered, somewhere was the setting for starvation and sadness. I read a little further down and then arched an eyebrow at a detail mentioned in the story: Dwayne Sherill, *retired SBI agent*.

That made me sit up straight in my chair. *Not a good week to be SBI*, some colder, more calculating part of me thought to itself. I kept reading and saw a pretty generic quote along the lines of "He was a great officer, a great friend," all the usual stupid bullshit and arched the other eyebrow at to whom it was credited: Clyde Wilfred. My friend Clyde had been this guy's partner.

I whistled long and low and then set that paper aside and moved on to the one after it. No especially scary headlines in this one. I read it for a while, then moved on to the next. In its obituaries section I saw something that made me actually stand up from my chair in silent surprise: Edith Wilfred, 83. Cardiac arrest. Clyde's wife died four days before the night I arrived.

Now was not the time to stand around wondering at coincidences. I flipped open my phone and dialed the last number that called me.

"Cousin?" Roderick sounded amused by something.

"Cousin," I said. "I think you'd best come over tonight."

Roderick didn't hesitate or ask why. "I'll be there in thirty minutes. I'll bring an overnight bag."

Roderick arrived in twenty minutes. He was driving a flashy little sports car manufactured someplace with a lot of sun and beaches. It was a rental and it probably cost a fortune a day. Back home in Seattle, he drives a Caddie from the '60s. It's a convertible coupe, gold colored, overstuffed leather seats. It looks like a jar of honey spilled in the middle of the road. Roderick is sort of trapped in 1969. Lucky for him, that's in fashion again. I told him the short version of finding Clyde out in the field.

"What's a Steeplechase?" He wasn't looking at me, but he was clearly synthesizing that he'd heard.

"The state senator who got the law through was named Steeplechase."

"That's from the zombie thing?" His head turned towards me but not all the way.

"Right. They give a tax credit to people who'll cremate the dearly departed instead of embalming them and hoping for the best." I shrugged. "Can't require it, because of religious freedom bullshit, but they can incentivize the hell out of what they want people to do. The cremation becomes a massive write-off on your state taxes. Pays for itself, basically, and nobody has ever turned into a zombie once they were a pile of ash. Sometimes the fundamentalists don't do it, though, because they think death is just a dirt nap while they wait for Judgment Day and they'll need their bodies in heaven or some shit. Some people opt to have Dear Auntie discreetly beheaded by the mortician and hide the wound with a high collar. That seems to work just as well."

"Are there still zombies, then?"

"There haven't been in a long time, but right after that first time there were a few who were found in, like, people's attics and shit, being tended to. Sort of. For all anybody can tend to a dead person who just won't get back down no matter how much you cajole them." I shuddered. The talk shows all had their rounds of interviews with Keepers after the fact. It was too much to watch. Mostly they were just sad, desperate people trying to hide something unable to be hidden. I marveled that Roderick had never heard this. How disconnected was he? On the other hand, I suppose we're all disconnected from the world of the living: it's just a question of where our experience fails to overlap theirs. Maybe his was talk shows.

We were silent for a while and then Roderick went on.

"Your last living friend?" Roderick was facing a window in the musty old living room of the random, sufficiently private house I'd bought in the 1970's to use as my local home base. There were huge windows overlooking a back yard I'd let go to waste. I'd left the house dark for no real reason other than that I didn't need the light and I wanted to be able to look out into the night. He turned and leaned his back against the glass. Smiles was curled on the old couch, snuffling in his sleep. I sat at the writing desk against one wall, the chair turned around and my bulk leaning forward against its back. Roderick's face was mostly invisible in the shadows. "That's a long time to wait for your Last Gasp."

"Just lucky, I reckon."

Roderick quirked up one side of his mouth. I could see the jut of his smiling cheek.

"Don't give me a bunch of shit," I growled.

"I've no idea what you mean, cousin."

"You were about to suggest I'd be luckier if it had happened ages ago."

Roderick produced a noise like a soft chuckle. "Blood does know its own."

I was silent for a little bit before I drew a confessional breath. "So here's the thing. I called the cops to report Clyde's body." I put up a hand when Roderick opened his mouth. "I was careful. Trust me. Regardless, they're going to be all over this. His partner? Tragic accident. Wife? Old age. Throat slit and his body dumped at the scene of the most famous crime he investigated?" I trailed off then swallowed in what I hoped was silence. "Sheriff's deputies are probably there now. The crime scene investigator has been paged. They start with the dogs first, then they bring in a photographer, then some bright lights and the lab guys." I stood up, tucked my hands in my pockets and made for the door onto the screened back porch. I wanted to feel some breeze, and a cold, wet autumn was happy to give me that and then some. "They're going to draw the same conclusion I jumped to, and I assume you did, too." I opened the door, stepped through, and settled into my chair. Roderick followed, leaning on one of the posts that hold up the roof of the porch. Roderick does that a lot: leaning. "They're going to assume this is connected to a murder Clyde investigated fifty years ago."

"The problem?" Roderick had produced a cigarette from somewhere with an illusionist's flourish. Almost all vampires smoke. I don't know why. Fire's one of the few ways to take us out, and maybe that's what fascinates us. I eventually gave it up when it became so socially suspect it drew more attention than it was worth. Agatha rides my ass about using my real name, of course, but at least I don't sit around in tweed knickers smoking cheroots and asking about the buggy whip business.

"That murder was committed by a vampire. I felt it in my bones then and I'm just as sure now."

"Some signature makes you think that? Some tell-tale sign?" Roderick never speaks with smoke in his lungs. He would take a drag, then exhale long and focused, then breathe in again and speak. He is not a natural multitasker.

"No." I shook my head. "Well, yes. I smelled vampire at the time, but more importantly, it's a question of physics and fitness. Anyone who could kill three people then would be at least seventy-something now. No one that old could slit Clyde's throat, carry him out there and get back out without his car." I shrugged.

"And you'd like to solve the mystery Clyde never could?" Roderick's voice was soft.

I shifted in my seat and made a noise of contempt in my throat, though I didn't indicate for what. "No. There's a vampire out there I don't know about and it's my job to know them all." I lifted one shoulder. "It's my state. This is my yard. *All* of it is my yard. It's that simple."

Roderick watched me for a few moments and then smiled. "Sure."

I looked over at Roderick and wondered what was going on in his mind, but that wasn't a power I had developed. Yet.

Chapter 3

"Nice night for it, eh?" Deputy Hendricks was standing with his thumb hitched in his belt and a potbelly still in its infancy poking over the buckle. He'd been the first officer on the scene and had put up tape everywhere at first, then realized he was going to run out of black and yellow CRIME SCENE DO NOT CROSS way before he got all the way around the clearing so it was down to a few stakes in the ground in a ten yard perimeter around the body. He had tramped and stomped all over everything before anyone else had arrived, so that H'Diane, her huge flashlight trained at the mud, could tell she wouldn't find a good goddamned thing on the ground. She turned the light up towards him briefly then swung it in an arc.

"As good as any," she said. God, but she was nervous. This was her first crime scene as a detective in her first job as a detective. She'd been a cop long enough to know the drill, been the first one on the scene more than once, knew better than to walk everywhere and screw up everything like this. That had been a long time ago, though, in a city with a – she stopped herself.

These are real cops, too, she thought. *I can't think of them as nothing but bumpkins if I'm ever going to cut it in this job.*

"The wagon's twenty minutes out." She drew a breath and started to run through her personal checklist. "I need a media containment area somewhere out of sight of the body in case anyone catches wind of this. I need someone directing traffic down at the main road and I need someone to call the dog handler."

"Smith and Jeffers are on their way," Hendricks drawled in reply.

"Great, go down to the main road and pick a spot for their cars, then start handing out assignments. I want total coverage of the site. I want twenty minutes in this clearing and then I want a deputy with a drawn sidearm patrolling the edge of the trees. Anybody caught spying, book them for trespass and see if they piss down their own leg."

Hendricks arched an eyebrow. This lady detective was different beyond being some Chinese type. He reached up to scratch under his Sheriff's Department cap and opened his mouth. "We'd need to call in some extra deputies if you want all that."

"So somebody manages to do sixty in a fifty-five tonight," H'Diane shot back. "Don't you read the paper?"

Hendricks blinked owlishly at her.

"This guy," H'Diane said, and she pointed at the body of Clyde Wilfred, "Is one of us."

"All due respect," Hendricks said after a moment, "But he weren't with the Sheriff's Department. He was SBI."

"Which makes him a cop." H'Diane kept her voice even. "I want to do this right." She paused, and tried another tactic. "He lived here all his life."

Hendricks ran that through his own personal loyalty determination subroutine and then nodded slowly. "I'll head on down to the highway, wave Smith and Jeffers in, hand out some assignments. You alright up here by yourself for a few minutes?"

"Yes." H'Diane tried not to get angry. Getting angry her first time out wouldn't make her any friends, and this was a department where everything was based on friendship and subtle tests of loyalty. "Thank you, Deputy Hendricks."

"Just, y'know, if this feller gets back up in a bit..." Hendricks gave her a look with both his eyebrows raised a little.

"Thank you, Deputy, but someone seems to have taken care of that for us already."

Hendricks nodded and started to stroll away, one hand still hooked in his belt, one hand swaying. He looked like Elvis, H'Diane thought to herself. Old Elvis, but Elvis. Weird.

Twenty minutes later, she had gone over the crime scene as thoroughly as she could while standing back ten feet from the body. Her flashlight was a monstrous sun in her hand, blinding white light so bright it bleached everything in its beam; she ran it slowly back and forth over the form of Clyde Wilfred and then the ground around him in a slow spiral that ran out to her own feet over time. There were mangled prints, no blood, not even the smell of blood. No stains on his shirt, very little dried at the gaping wounds on his throat, one a cut and one a tear. He hadn't been hung up and bled or there'd be crusts in his hair. On the other hand, it had pissed down rain for hours and just let up in the last forty minutes or so. It might have all washed away. It was cold that night, her breath misting in front of her, thick gloves on her hands, so that would screw with the time of death. Being planted out here all night was no better than being shoved in a refrigerator. They'd need a full autopsy to sort that out.

Deputy Smith – young kid, eager, helpful, H'Diane liked him – walked up making plenty of noise so she'd know he was there. "Got an ID?" he called.

"I recognize him from the paper," H'Diane called back, "But I haven't gone into his wallet yet. Waiting on the photographer."

"That's me, ma'am. Detective. I mean, Detective." He produced a big old Polaroid from a bag. "Got the digital, too, if you want that instead."

"Plenty of both," she replied. "Document everything. If you need the lights set up, radio down to Jeffers. I assume he's setting up the media area?"

Smith nodded and pointed off into the night. "Other side of the private road, no sight lines to here."

"Good work," she nodded. She didn't smile. H'Diane had a feeling detectives shouldn't smile next to dead bodies. She kept walking in a slow circle around the body. There was some mottled skin around the wrists and neck. The face was locked in an expression of fear. You can, of course, attempt to rearrange someone's expression after death but the killer had either not even tried or was the master of it. They were in a hurry, they were sadistic or both. She pondered that one in silence, crouched close to the ground, looking into his glassy eyes, when she heard someone clear her throat behind her.

H'Diane stood and turned. "Jeffers," she said halfway around, "I'm going to need a perimeter patrol—" but she stopped when she saw that it was LaVonde. LaVonde smiled a little, produced a miniature digital tape recorder and held it out.

"Comment for the *Citizen-Times?*"

LaVonde and H'Diane had been together for four years. Four weird years that started with them running into each other at the scene of a meth lab that had been burned in a murder/arson. LaVonde liked to joke that it was their first date. H'Diane figured she'd probably been awakened by the phone but hadn't counted on her staying awake, hearing her side of the conversation, and coming down here to write a story.

H'Diane wasn't out at work. Well, not yet. It was one of those weird things about being a woman, a cop, a professional, a lesbian, an out gay woman in the twenty first century: you don't really *come out* anymore. It just happens in time. Or...it doesn't. Sometimes it feels as though there's no real way to engineer either outcome without seeming like you have an agenda or a problem with yourself. The world had changed so much in H'Diane's life and so much of it was scary still, but a lot of it also seemed to be for the better. This was one of those things. Being out at work didn't have to feel like a very special episode of *Law & Order* anymore. On the other hand, that it didn't *have to* meant the 'phobes could make sure it was kind of frowned upon to force one anyway.

H'Diane sighed a little, drew a breath. Smith, bless his heart, he just didn't know what to think. There was a sort of electric tension in the air between the new detective and the reporter. He just stood there for a second. "We're setting up a media area," he blurted out, pointing... well, somewhere else. LaVonde looked at him for a moment, then very obviously leaned her head to one side to peek around H'Diane at the corpse.

"A murder?"

H'Diane didn't let herself smile. "Deputy Smith," she said, very calm, "Please show Ms. Burke to the media area." She turned back. She didn't cross her arms, didn't shift her weight to one hip, just stood there with her hands by her side and her face as blank as a bedroom wall in an empty house. "The Sheriff's Department will issue comment, as appropriate, as soon as we can."

LaVonde smiled. She couldn't help it. She didn't say anything, though, just nodded once, clicked off the recorder, put it in her jacket pocket. "Deputy Smith," though she pitched it more softly so it didn't quite mock H'Diane. "Please do as the detective asked."

"Yes... ma'am?" Smith scratched his forehead, cap lifted, then tugged it back on and started squelching away through the mud.

Do they all do the cap thing? H'Diane smiled, finally, when they were far enough away that they wouldn't hear her face crack. She was going to kill LaVonde for this. They had talked about it already, after all.

In the end, the Sheriff himself showed up, lights going, siren blaring, like a clown car late for the circus. He got out and did a meaningful and photo-friendly walk around the site. There were only a few media people there at that hour, with the sun just about to rise. By six in the morning there would be TV trucks down the road but the owners of the property wouldn't let them on their land to broadcast so all they had were shots of grey, autumnal countryside and news readers repeating the same "breaking" news over and over again. LaVonde went back home and wrote up a story to go on the *Citizen-Times* site, then started on something longer for the print edition.

H'Diane stayed at the scene to brief the Sheriff, then the dog team, then observe them working. They caught a scent and spooked immediately. They didn't at all like what they'd picked up. They followed it out of the clearing, through some brush and to some tire tracks that had either been driven over or messed around with to disguise the treads. They sniffed it around the victim's car, too, and the handlers thought they'd picked up a different scent in the cars but it didn't lead much of anywhere. The rain had ruined a lot of the tracking they could do. The handlers weren't any happier to be out in the middle of nowhere at goddamn o'clock in the morning, either, and continued sweeps of the woods around the scene didn't turn up a damned thing.

H'Diane—Detective Bing—went straight to the station, drank three cups of coffee and started going over crime scene photos. The coroner was working the body, the scene evidence was being bagged and tagged to go to the Asheville SBI office, the digital photos were coming out of the printer and the Polaroids were up on the wall in a conference room. She did a quick debrief with each of the deputies, focusing on Hendricks as the first one on the scene. She didn't tear him a whole new one for having fucked up the scene by walking all over it so much as she pointed out where, exactly, the new one would be torn if he messed it up again. She did some reading on the victim's history, re-read all the stories about his partner being killed in a car crash and his wife dying of a heart attack, assigned some deputies on day shift to start interviewing the neighbors.

Then she finally—*finally*—got the recording of the 911 call.

"I didn't do it," the voice drawled. She wound it back, played it again.

"I didn't do it."

"I didn't do it."

"I didn't do it."

She started making notes. Male, sounded to be, well, his voice was odd. He sounded sort of *young*, but not young, not a kid. There was something in it, though; there was something old there. He was so calm as he said it, but H'Diane knew the sound of creepy calm, the sound of someone who'd just shot their whole family dead and called 911 so there would be someone to find and bury them after the shooter killed himself, and it wasn't that. Was it? She shook her head and listened to the whole thing again. He'd been there. He knew exactly where it was. He drove a long way across the county to use a pay phone that wasn't supposed to work anymore—caller ID and modern telecommunications infrastructure long ago put the lie to the television trope that a call has to run for a while before it can be traced—and then called it in as pretty as you please. Of course there weren't security cameras at Appleton. The place hadn't been a school in fifteen years at least, according to Deputy Smith. It was a place where kids went to get high because the county couldn't afford to tear it down.

H'Diane played the recording for what seemed like an hour. White, male, young but not that young, knew what happened, left the scene and didn't want trouble with the law. Someone who'd found the body with its throat slit and cared enough – about the deceased, about himself, about the neighbors, somebody – to tear the head off to make sure he didn't turn into a Steeplechase. Someone strong enough to do that with their bare hands. H'Diane had been at the top of her class when she finished that degree in Criminal Justice and trained to be a detective. Most leads dissolve in the first forty-eight hours after a case. Investigators have to work fast and be thorough if they can track down enough information to actually produce an arrest or, to be honest, even a serious questioning.

She needed to find out who made that call, and fast, before he was gone forever.

"You know that's where that old murder happened, right?" This was LaVonde's greeting to H'Diane when she walked in the door that night feeling stiff, sore, too caffeinated, too tired.

"Yeah, my day was a bitch," she sighed. They kissed hello, then H'Diane slid into a chair at the kitchen table.

LaVonde waited a moment before diving right back in. "That old murder. Fifty-five years ago. The double homicide down off Green River Road." She pulled open the phone book, an absurdly quaint item she refused to surrender to her smartphone. Nobody was in any shape to cook and delivery pizza seemed like a good idea to the desperate. LaVonde paused in flipping pages and then said, pointedly, "Where we were this morning?"

"Triple homicide?"

"Yes, sugar, triple homicide. Did no one in the department mention this to you?"

H'Diane blinked and shook her head.

LaVonde scowled a little, but not unkindly. "Figures," she said. "Bunch of good ol' boy crackers. Wanted to know if you'd figure it out yourself."

"Great, so what's the story?"

LaVonde picked up the phone, dialed, ordered, and hung up. In that time, H'Diane sat there, stretched back, and leaned against the wall, crossing her feet at the ankles. The cold outside felt like it could creep right in through the walls and she hunched her shoulders closer and crossed her arms.

"Con man comes into town, shacks up with a rich orphan, lures the kid and a little old lady from out near Brevard into the woods somehow and kills them both. Never seen again. Hell, hardly seen when he was playing Daddy May I with the kid." H'Diane arched one eyebrow and LaVonde arched hers back in confirmation. "That was the rumor at the time. Anyway, their bodies were found right there. Same spot. Clyde Wilfred was the lead investigator. It was the first case he and Dwayne Sherrill worked together in their time at the SBI. Still technically an open case but no one's pursued anything in decades." LaVonde shrugged. "Might be of interest to you so I printed some scans from the morgue at the *Citizen-Times*."

"And nobody told me at the station," H'Diane mumbled.

"Don't think of it as them trying to trip you up, honey," LaVonde cooed as she walked over to plant a kiss on H'Diane's sharp cheek. "Think of it as them believing you're smart enough to figure it out on your own."

"Sure," H'Diane sighed, but she reached for the printouts and started reading. Much later, pizza half-eaten, she set the papers aside and turned to LaVonde. "You can't write about this case, you know."

"I know," LaVonde sighed. "Conflict of interest. But I'm an editor now. I don't get to write about it anyway." H'Diane cocked an eyebrow: there was no such animal as an editor who did not also write for their paper. LaVonde had the good grace to look a little mollified to be caught in such an obvious lie. "Okay," LaVonde went on, "I won't write about it."

That doesn't mean I can't investigate. Or encourage. It was written on her face but H'Diane said nothing.

"You know, Clyde Wilfred has a son." LaVonde added it as mildly as she possibly could.

"No comment." H'Diane smiled a little as she replied.

"From what I've heard, nobody can find him..."

"No comment." This time, H'Diane didn't smile as much.

Chapter 4

Roderick had asked me if I was going to call Agatha in on this. No, I'd told him. I have to handle this myself. I had no desire to sew those apron strings back together.

"Maybe I can help?" Roderick asked.

"Maybe," I'd said. No promises. No guarantees.

The thing is, I took over North Carolina a few years back. The old boss, Bob the Third, he was this good ol' boy from a long line of Bobs just like himself. They'd run the state – him and his maker before him and his before *him* – for so long nobody was around who remembered a pre-Bob era at all. At least, no one who'd admit to being that old. You might expect that age would be a status symbol amongst our kind, and for some it is, especially in Europe. Here in the States the current vogue is to seem as young and precocious as possible. I'd had reason to believe Agatha was at least a hundred, maybe a hundred fifty years old as a vampire, plus twenty or thirty years tacked on at the beginning, but she'd never say. Asking point blank would be the worst possible offense, so no dice there. Anyway, the deal is, a lot of us like to claim a youth long lost to us, especially the ones who stake out some territory as their own and make themselves boss. I think it's in part because we're American vampires and American culture has been youth-oriented since at least the second half of the nineteenth century and youth-obsessed since at least the 1920's.

Anyway, I just barely make the cut on having been born in that era of youth-oriented culture and you know what? I'm fed up with it. Vampires have adopted it as some sort of peg to hang their hat on like demure society types, so eager to prove a virility that's been lost to them for as long as they can remember. When the Big Flush & Fill happens, we're stuck. That's it. We learn new stuff, sure. I can drive an automatic, I can use a cellular phone, I can do a Sudoku puzzle. I'm not *young*, though. I'm not who I was then. I don't have the same capacity to learn and adapt that I used to have, and that's the thing with proxies and thralls and servants and fixers: they don't help with that. I suspect they accelerate the loss of those abilities. They free up people like Agatha from the complicated work of learning how the world functions these days so that she can devote her time to *pretending* to understand. She mimics. She apes. She doesn't deeply comprehend. It drives me crazy.

So what does this have to do with Roderick? Roderick got stuck – got turned – in 1969. Like I said, lucky for him that's back in fashion right now, but what happens when it isn't? More important to me at the time was this: what did it mean about him *now*? Three days before he got turned, he was arrested in a drug bust. His daddy got him out – we had money despite what you'd think from my mother's compulsive penny-pinching, sure, but my father's brother had *money* – and then turned up dead the same night Roderick became a vampire. I've always had to wonder about that. It's traditional for our families to get eliminated after we're turned. Their sudden absence from the scene prevents a lot of uncomfortable questions. It doesn't happen as much these days as it used to, but it still does sometimes. It's something that's getting harder to do, I suspect, in the age of forensic science. Regardless, I'm left wondering this: did Roderick kill his father? I've never known a thing about his mother, and he already had no relatives left except for me, but he didn't know I was still around in any meaningful sense. Did his maker – whoever that was – do it for him? Was it coincidence? And if it was Roderick, well, let's just say he's always been a little screwy. Tie that in with the culture of rebellion in which he'd gone native at the time he got turned and you get somebody who might be a fearsome vampire, indeed. There's a theory that goes around, a sort of vampiric old wives' tale, that the emotional or psychological state in which we get turned also sticks around forever in some way: leaves an imprint, if you will. I don't buy it because if that were true we'd all be screaming paranoiac everything-phobes all the time. Being turned is the most terrifying experience a body can ever have. Still, I look at Roderick – or at another vampire with some overwhelming sense of oddity about them – and I wonder.

And that's why Emily, the local boss in Seattle, keeps an eye on him for me.

Just as an aside, vampires hate the idea of mortal relatives both being turned. It's kind of perverted, somehow. That biological tie lingering after biology stops being an issue and mortal ties and meanings are supposedly washed away? It makes us uncomfortable. Maybe that's why I'm always sort of scared to hang with Roderick and always sort of eager. It gives Agatha the creeps that he's still around and that we're still in touch. That discomfort on her part, despite, or perhaps in addition to, everything else, is an excellent reason to have these little family reunions every once in a while. It never hurts to remind her I'm my own vampire now.

As to the question of what to do about Clyde's murder and the chance a vampire had done it, I was fairly in the dark. I could come up with all sorts of situations to explain it: a vengeful child of the murderer from back then, a vampire who'd done the deed and was trying to clean house for some reason or another, someone who wasn't at all related but got put away by Clyde and Dwayne back in their past. The only thing I could do was start nosing around without tipping my hand. Last Gasp is supposed to be a tender time for my kind, half meditation and half Bar Mitzvah, as we experience the severing of the very last tie we had to our mortal lives. There's more to it than that – a lot more, and I wasn't sure I believed half of what I'd been told – but it boils down to entering the last phase of a vampire's transformation. There are crazy stories of vampires gaining special powers, of being able to feel it deep inside when the last person who knew them as a human, as a creature of daylight, passes from the world. There's a lot of big talk. I hadn't felt any of that when Clyde died and the discovery of his death had generated feelings that were purely human. That wasn't a word I expected to use much again, but it was true. If a vampire did this, there was just as good a chance that they did it purely to throw me off balance, psychologically And if they did that then they must be making a play for power of their own. I couldn't imagine who would know about Clyde, but it was a possibility I had to consider.

Yes, now was a good time to start visiting other vampires – which is why I was here anyway – and to seem very, very nonchalant. First on the list: a kid named Marty Macintosh.

Marty lived in some anonymous apartment complex in Arden. Arden is a non-town between Hardisonville and Asheville, a series of shopping centers and apartment developments on a multi-lane highway. It was where the first megaplex went in, long years ago. When that happened, followed by a Wal-Mart next door, I knew it was over for Arden. Forever could pass and it would stay a bunch of rental condos and strip malls. Way back in the day, Arden had grown up around the railroad tracks that ran south out of Asheville towards the upstate and everything else downhill from the city. It had been a place where factories went up and warehouses were built. The presence of industry was long since a thing of the past. Now it's endless suburbia. The passenger trains went first and then most of the shipping lines. The tracks are grass-covered skeletons these days. Sometimes a train will rattle past on them but it's a rare thing and it sounds like a ghost drumming skeletal fingers against an old desk.

I drove north on NC 280, still finding it weird to take the new Boylston Highway through what used to be fields and meadows, a straight shot rather than the old way around on Airport Road past the state research farm. What had to be the last plane of the night was coming in for a landing at Asheville Regional as I scooted around the turn at the end of the runway. It was a big jet covered in lights. I remembered when the biggest, best plane that flew into or out of there was a refitted puddle-jumper that had started life as a Yugoslav transport plane in World War II.

That's one of the hard things about being a vampire; our eyes are so good we sometimes see the past superimposed on the present and all that clutter gets in the way of seeing the future.

I drove on past the airport and past where there's a Target and a Best Buy now – just so damned insane to me – and where the Huddle House used to be until it got turned into a Starbucks. The road ran along beside a branch line of those railroad tracks until it hit US 25 and turned left/north into Arden. I was halfway to Biltmore when I saw that damned megaplex and knew I was nearly there. It'd been a couple of years since I'd last seen Marty – he wasn't there last time – and I'd lost the directions I got out of Bob's files after he died, but I'm pretty good at remembering that sort of thing so I caught the next left after the Asheville Racquet Club and then took the series of twisting turns that put me in the back corner of a complex of apartment blocks called Tournament Landing.

It's funny, names like that. I read a story – a news story – about a guy who made up a housing development name generator on a webpage somewhere, just as a gag. It would spit out combinations like Deer Hunt Trails and Creek's Edge Estate and whatnot based on a simple formula of, if I remember correctly, (Animal or Geographic Feature) plus (Activity or Geological Feature) plus (Landscaping Term). Clever enough idea to get a chuckle, sure, but then he started getting calls from real developers who wanted to know if they could use the names they'd generated playing around with it. When a real estate mogul is ready to let some webpage somewhere name their new neighborhood rather than name it something meaningful to the land or the people on it, I don't know what to think.

I pulled up and parked in a Visitors space then stepped into the shadows to begin a perimeter of Marty's building. I had not, of course, announced my imminent arrival. It wasn't necessarily meant to be a pop quiz, and I wasn't looking for some special reason to find Marty with his metaphorical pants around his ankles, but I like to catch them when they're their real, natural selves. It gives me a better chance to decide what I think of them based on who they really are, what they're really like. Marty had a lot going for him in that department already, to be honest. He's not particularly social but he's got it together enough to maintain a lease on an apartment in a building full of mortals and not attract attention. That's good work, in my book. On the other hand, he doesn't seem like he's been a vampire more than fifteen years. It might just be that he's still in the habits of the living or this era has changed little enough in that time to suit him so that he doesn't stand out much yet.

There was a light on in his bedroom but nowhere else and I didn't hear any moans or screaming, which almost always counts as "so far, so good." I stepped up to one of the windows and tried to peek inside but he had the same full-window blinds most vampires use if they don't have a more permanent lair. If his senses were worth a damn then he might hear me out there, too, but I'm as good at staying quiet as any of us, so we might balance each other out. The back porch – just slightly above ground level due to a weird dip in the landscaping, low wall, easily leapt in a hurry with zero risk of injury to one of us but high enough that a human would think twice about running straight for it – was tidy, one chair, one table, one ashtray with about a thousand cigarette butts sticking up out of it in a mounded heap. There was a book face down on the small table, smudges of ash half-wiped from the back cover. No dust jacket and lots of small print on the back so I lifted myself just slightly onto the exterior of the porch railing and leaned over to look at it: *Advanced Understandings of Statistics—Theory and Application.* It was a late-80's printing of a textbook; no change there.

I went on around now to the front door and rapped slowly and distinctly with three even knocks. I could hear some music inside, muffled by the door – reinforced, and I'd bet it was a homemade job his apartment complex management didn't know about. It was being played very softly to begin with so that a mortal didn't stand a chance of complaining about it but I had no trouble making out the words: *and then thought this'll never end, this'll never end, this'll never stop.*

After half a minute – all of us are good with the passage of time, at least in terms of measuring it – I saw the light coming through the peephole dim and heard a gasp, then heard a hand clap over the mouth that had gasped. I lifted one hand and waved and tried to smile. I'm no good at smiling: the Grinch with fangs when I try to look casual. The peephole stayed dark, then light again, then the music stopped.

I stopped trying to smile and reached out to knock with another three simple raps, faster this time. The peephole flickered, like maybe he thought about putting his eye to it then decided against it. Everything was very quiet on the inside. I leaned against the door jam and put my face in the corner where the door opens.

"Marty," I said, so quiet that I knew he would be able to hear me but no one else would, "I believe you probably remember me. I'm Withrow Surrett. I ask that you open the door, invite me into your home and allow us to spend a little time together."

Silence on the other side of the door, though after a moment I could hear breathing. He was so young he still breathed out of habit.

"Marty," and now my voice was much quieter, "I can hear you. I know you can hear me."

More mostly-silence.

"Marty?" I cleared my throat and spoke even more quietly. I could hear his breathing get closer as he put his ear right to the door to hear me. "What's the square root of nineteen thousand eight hundred twenty four?"

The breathing stopped. After seven seconds, the locks started to turn. The knob turned. I stood back to show a little respect. The door cracked just a half-inch. "One hundred forty point seven nine seven seven two seven two five four three eight four three—"

I held up a hand and stopped him. "Good enough. I took another step back, then bowed very slightly at the waist. "Withrow Surrett. Is this the home of the one known as Marty Macintosh?"

Marty hesitated, still only looking at me with one eye before he stepped back, closed the door, undid the chain latch, opened it more widely, then bowed from the waist. "I am Marty Macintosh," he stammered, nervous. "Withrow Surrett is welcome in my home."

I let the corners of my mouth tug upwards just slightly and then held out a hand for Marty to shake. He stared at it before doing so. "Good to see you again, Marty. Still on the counting thing, huh?"

"Five fingers on the one hand, five on the other," Marty said, watching our hands shake each other way past the point of politeness or custom. "Together they form two hands of ten fingers, turn-the-table asymmetry. They're the same hand, opposed."

I clapped him on the shoulder and sighed. Maybe Marty wasn't doing so well after all.

Eventually, he got out of the way so I could walk inside. The place was dark but I could smell and see and taste thick dust everywhere. Marty wasn't going out much. The dim light in his bedroom had a blue-white glow that made me think it was a television set left on. It didn't flicker. Maybe he'd paused a tape or something. I had to wonder at Marty sitting around watching musicals with the volume down low but then I've read there are a lot of connections between mathematics and music theory. I couldn't harmonize my way out of a wet paper sack so it's all Greek to me. Marty is one of the counters. You might've heard the old legend, though it's fairly obscure these days: throw down rice or sesame seeds or kernels of corn or whatever in a vampire's path when he's chasing you and he'll have to stop to count them before he can continue his pursuit, giving you time to get away. Marty is one of those. Counters are actually just obsessed with numbers somehow; only a few of them are actually obsessed with counting. Sometimes it only takes them in spells, sometimes it's a specific kind of thing they can't resist counting, sometimes it's everything they see. I don't think it's anything special or supernatural. I think they're probably just people who had some latent obsessive-compulsive disorder or whatever and the trauma of getting turned made it come out or made it worse, or whatever. It brushed up against some switch in their mind and flipped it on. Of course, I'm no psychologist either, so maybe I'm full of horseshit. I don't claim to know.

Marty's place, as I said, was dusty and didn't smell like it'd been aired out recently, but we don't sweat or produce skin oils or the like, either, so it didn't smell like a human hovel. It just smelled like a house that's been shut up. There was dust caked on all the living room furniture except for one chair and it and the TV had been positioned to face one another. The rest of the furniture was just for show. Hell, maybe the rest of the furniture came with the place. I looked around, sniffed the air then pointed one thumb at the sliding glass door out onto the porch. "Smoke?"

"Sure," Marty said. He's a small white guy with dark hair, pale skin, an extremely thin build and great big eyes: what they call "black Irish" though I'm given to understand that's not an OK term to use anymore. He patted his pockets for a second. "Sorry the place is such a wreck. I didn't know you were coming."

"Just happened to be in town," I said easily, walking towards the door I'd indicated. "It's been a while, figured I'd say hello."

"Seven hundred thirty days, one hour, twelve minutes." Marty said it lightning fast, then closed his mouth and looked a little embarrassed. I raised both eyebrows and nodded.

"Like I said: a while." I opened the glass door, which wanted to stick halfway down its runner, so I gave it a hard yank and something made a bad noise and the door slid open. Marty looked slightly stricken and pointed at the far side of the door from the handle.

"My... that's my security bar."

I looked over my shoulder and saw what had made it stick – a length of solid steel that had been laid in the track to keep the door from opening more than an inch or two. Wow. He considered that security?

"Oops," I said with a more genuine smile than I'd had when I was still out front being looked at through the peephole. "Guess I hardly know my own strength."

Marty swallowed – goddamn, so young – and nodded. He even tried to laugh. It sounded strangled. I walked on out onto the porch, settled my hips into the corner of the deck and watched him. Marty followed me after a second and closed the door behind him, then tried to decide whether to sit or stand.

"Please," I said after a few moments, "Sit down if you want to sit down. This is just a friendly visit."

Marty nodded and perched on the edge of the resin chair, as anonymous as the apartment itself. He lit his cigarette with a hand that only shook slightly and pulled his arms tighter around himself, another very human sort of action but habit couldn't possibly make him feel cold. He was nervous. I decided to step lightly but with determination. I pointed at the twisted metal of the security bar and asked, "Much crime around here?"

"One hundred twenty seven police calls in the last five years," he said automatically. Numbers helped to soothe him a little bit, and he sat back, finally lighting his cigarette. "Forty three break-ins, thirty two automobile accidents, the rest pranks or mistaken calls."

I nodded. "A cat sets off the car alarm, that kind of thing?"

Marty nodded. "Seventeen times."

I smiled a little more. "So the bar is..."

"It makes me feel safe," Marty blurted out. "I get scared. I'm just..." He licked his lips, took a long drag, licked them again. "One."

I looked out across the back corner of the lot. There was a little creek back there that had run dry in the drought we'd experienced for the last, oh, decade. All the recent rain had washed clean away over ground so hard and dry it might as well have been a concrete culvert. Climate change, you know. It takes a certain length of perspective and attention span to notice it happening, but it's happening. My breath had misted a little when I talked, at first, but now I was starting to leak heat all over the place in the chill November air and my breath was misting less and less. "There was a murder down in Hardisonville the other night," I commented. "Is crime getting worse around Asheville in general?"

Marty licked his lips again. He was so incredibly pale, even by our standards. His lips were actually dry. He didn't feed enough, or at least hadn't recently. I wondered: if I opened his refrigerator would there be bags of blood or would there instead be a couple of bottles of ancient condiments? "There have been eighty three murders in the greater Asheville region in the last five years, up from an average of forty six every five from 1975 to 1995." Marty seemed to flinch a little when he said it.

"And were there any..." I paused and then went on. What the hell. "Any among anyone you know?"

Marty looked up briefly, nearly met my eyes, then didn't. "No."

I scratched my goatee briefly and wondered what about me had Marty so scared. He'd been like a nervous little rabbit the last time I'd been here, too, but not this bad. Might just be the passage of time, might be me. I guessed my physical size might intimidate him, but normally a fat guy like me doesn't scare anyone by making them think they'll get beat up; normally he scares them as an example of what might happen if they let that gym membership lapse. I decided to keep circling the crime—crimes in general—as long as that made him jumpy. The doctor asks you where it hurts and then pokes you until you yelp. I wasn't trying to torture Marty but I could tell I'd started waiting for him to say something and I didn't know whether that was because some instinct registered that he had something he wanted to say or instead that I felt like there was something he wanted *not* to say. "What kinds of murders?"

"Sixty four shootings," he said after running his fingers against one another for a moment. "Five stabbings. Three strangulations or smothering deaths, one poisoning."

"Ah, yes," I sighed. "Guns are so easy. Everyone watches too much TV." I chuckled. "Poisons are so much classier, and a knife?" I drew a breath and whistled. My own had stopped misting entirely. It felt downright comfortable out here and it was at most forty five degrees. "Well, a knife says you mean it. You've got to get in close with a knife. Nasty work."

Marty shuddered just slightly.

"Other kinds of crime? Assaults?"

"Concentrated in specific areas, they're the most common crimes reported in Western North Carolina as a whole. If you do the numbers," here Marty's voice got a little stronger. "There are more assaults per capita than any other crime when counted in a two-mile radius from the center of any city or town of more than fifteen thousand people." His eyes flickered over and he spoke even more easily. "Outside that radius they're domestic violence. Assault by a stranger happens where there are sidewalks, mostly."

"And in rural areas, they happen at the hands of someone the victim knows?"

"Oh, yes, definitely. Almost always." Marty licked his lips again. I could hear his tongue rasp against their parched surface. He was starving. He locked himself away in his house behind a steel bar that would keep people out, and watched movies and listened to music and read crime reports or statistics texts and slowly starved himself half to death. For right then, though, what I knew was that I'd started to crack open his shell and I thought I had just a whiff of the scent of what he wanted to say but couldn't.

"And what's the most interesting kind of crime?" It was a nice, open-ended question. *Let's see how he likes that,* I thought.

Marty's eyes cut to one side and then the other but his head didn't move. There was no sound except the burning of tobacco and occasional road noise from out on US 25, reflected and scattered by trees and distance. I didn't say anything else, waiting, watching him fight something inside.

"Disappearances," he finally said. It sounded like it hurt on its way out. He panted a little when he said it.

"How do you mean?"

"They usually end up falling under domestic violence," he half-whispered. "In the last few years, though, they've picked up. People just vanish."

"Thin air?"

"Yeah." Marty was licking his lips between every other breath now. "They don't show up to work or they miss a meal or they forget to call mom on her birthday and that's what it takes for someone to notice that they just aren't *here* anymore."

The missing. There are millions of them every year in America. They're one of my favorite advances of the modern era. I could go on about them for hours. In some ways, they're my numbers, my counting obsession. They're the rice thrown in my path, the mirror that casts no reflection. My brain gets hung up on them. "Where do those tend to happen?"

Marty struggled, staring at his own hand; took a drag; then stared at his hand again. "Oh, you know," he mumbled. "Around."

I arched an eyebrow. "Around where?"

"Specific places."

"Such as?" I could feel the thread of meaning. It was right there. It was being woven in front of me. I couldn't tell what it meant, but I could smell that a true answer to my question would be significant and Marty also knew his answer would be important. He was trying to tell me something he couldn't come right out and say.

"I could show you. I have maps. Online maps. Internet maps. The computer." Words came out of him like wobbling birds in a gale, clustered and uncertain.

"Show me," I said. He stubbed out his cigarette and got up and walked inside. I followed him. We walked down the "hallway," in scare quotes by virtue of its being three feet long, and into his bedroom. The blue-white glow was gone now, replaced by a red and green and yellow continuous fade-and-brighten cycle. It wasn't a TV with a paused movie; it was a computer monitor that had gone into screensaver mode. It was a *huge* computer monitor. There were stacks of printouts and file folders on the desk next to it, some in a big box made out of an upturned cardboard container lid labeled INCOMING and more in a matching homemade tray for OUTGOING. I flipped one open; it was a medical history.

"I do at-home records transcription," Marty said. I had no idea what that was other than being *this*. "Doesn't have a schedule, no office, but I get decent pay for what it requires. I've done forty seven records tonight."

"Already?" I had no idea if that was a lot, but it's always better to sound impressed than not when trying to crack open someone's shell.

"I type really fast."

I nodded. I bet he did type really fast. He pressed some keys in rapid succession and the screen cleared to a desktop image of the moon high over a mountain somewhere, the picture engineered to make the moon bigger than she really is. *Maybe it had been edited,* I thought. People can do that, I've seen some of the Photoshop competitions online but I don't understand how or what they exactly do. I don't even own a camera.

Roderick has seven of them, and a little laptop computer he named "Toto."

Marty pressed a few more keys, clicked something with his mouse, and a web browser opened. I do know what the internet is and I know there are web browsers and I have a computer at home in Raleigh that I can just barely get working enough to do some crosswords and some Sudoku puzzles and read my email. I even read a couple of blogs without ever commenting. Roderick says blogs are over and I should get on this Twitter thing but I don't want to say anything. I want to listen. I am a user and I know that and am OK with that. I will never be a producer of the things people look at online. We are consumers first and foremost. A vampire who remembers that will last longer than one who doesn't. The world can make more of itself all it wants. Our job is to skim off the top.

Anyway, his browser came up and I figured he would type in an address, what's called an Earl for some reason, but instead he opened a bookmark. He liked disappearances enough to have them mapped and bookmarked for quick reference. That was weird, even by our standards. On the other hand, maybe he had a bookmark for everything he'd ever looked at online.

The map loaded and centered on Arden. That put Asheville slightly off-center, to the north, with Hardisonville and Rutherfordton and Brevard and Cullowhee and all the other little towns and sleepy villages of the mountains scattered in an uneven circle around it. There were clusters of red dots and he started scrolling the map around and zooming in here or there. "This is a custom app," he said by way of more nonsense. "I wrote it myself. Whenever I open it, it queries the case databases of all the law enforcement agencies around here and maps any missing persons reports such that the dot represents the last reported sighting of the person who's being sought." I nodded as though I understood, but in truth I only mostly understood. What I for sure understood were two things: the "last reported sighting" part and that there was no way Marty was having trouble adjusting to life fifteen years after he'd died.

On the map itself, there were little starbursts of dots here and there – a few dots in Hardisonville, a larger bunch in Asheville, a couple in the middle of nowhere, off on hiking trails and the like where every year a person or three take the wrong turn before they're gone forever.

There was a relatively huge cluster south of Brevard, not that incredibly far from where Clyde had been found, not as many as in Asheville but more than was normal for a town that small. I leaned over Marty's shoulder and stared at the screen, then pointed at it. "Isn't that unusual?"

Marty sat in silence and said, "Want to watch a movie? I got some stuff off Bittorrent that's pretty good quality. There are these crazy guys in Sweden who have all kinds of bandwidth. You can get great speeds from them."

So Marty wanted me to see that starburst of dots south of Brevard and he didn't want to tell me why. A visit well worth having made, I told myself. "I'll take a rain check," I said. "Got some more folks to see. Listen, try to eat something, okay? You don't look so good."

Marty shuddered. "Yes, sir."

"Please," I sighed, "Call me Withrow." I hesitated. Probing further into his feeding habits would be offensive from anyone else, but I was the boss. He was technically my subject. There were places this sort of thing got asked in the open, in front of God and everybody, so I said screw it and asked. "Where do you get food, usually?"

Marty went blank. "I…" He worked his jaw.

"You can tell me," I said. "In fact, you have to tell me. I'm the boss. I have a right to ask and I swear I will keep it confidential." I put one hand up. "Scout's honor."

Marty blinked rapidly. His flesh was the color of onionskin paper. "I have someone. She's out of town. She travels for her work."

I nodded. "Then get someone else, someone on the side. You can't possibly live off the blood of one person. You'll try to take it easy on her, scared you'll take too much, and you'll slowly starve yourself to the point you're guaranteed to go nuts with hunger and kill her outright. Find two or three somebodies to be safe." Marty didn't like that unsolicited advice, but it was true. If he wanted to learn that for himself, fine, but I was right. I'd seen it happen a dozen times.

Chapter 5

I had Marty give me a printout of the map. It was small and fuzzy and the greater visual acuity afforded me by the biology of the undead didn't really help any. It just made it easier for me to spot the flaws, the tiny gaps where the printer had skipped a beat trying to spit out the highly detailed imagery. I'd sat in the Firebird and studied it for a few minutes, Smiles panting happily and bumping his forehead against my shoulder every now and then to remind me to pet him, then folded it neatly and tucked it into the inside pocket of my trench coat. I turned on the heat in the car as I drove through Tournament Landing and back out to 25, turning south towards Hardisonville itself. At the last minute I turned back onto the dark, disappearing lanes of 280 rather than keep going in my original direction. It was stupid of me but I was drawn to check out Clyde's house. He had a son, I knew, and I had to wonder what shape the kid was in.

Well, I say kid. He had to be pushing fifty by now. A little weird in most places that he'd still live at home but up there moving back in with mom and dad is a lot cheaper than paying for a rest home if they've gotten to need help. It's also a lot cheaper than having to get a real life. I'd heard a story on NPR one time years ago about this trend developing in Italy at the time. Mamasomething, they're called there: guys who never cut the apron strings, never let go, no matter how hard their mothers push them. From what Clyde had told me in the hours we'd spent together across the decades, that was Cliff.

The same happens to vampires sometimes, too. I'd reckon about half the time it's a maker who won't let go, but just as often it's a vampire who's too afraid to leave their maker's protection. Our relationships are as complicated as any between a parent and a child. Another thought of Roderick's lack of proper upbringing ran through my head and I called him on speakerphone.

"Cousin." He'd let it ring twice and answered with the smoothest voice in known history.

"I've got a question for you." I didn't bother with preamble, didn't bother with Marty's state of living. Roderick doesn't seem to require those niceties. He likes to ask pointed questions because they put people off balance and he doesn't have any obvious qualms about receiving them in kind. "What are your long-term plans? Where do you see yourself in ten years, or fifty?"

"Rich. Perhaps famous." Roderick didn't hesitate to answer. He'd thought about this before. "I'd like to have a few endorsement deals."

I drove in silence for a few moments, blinking rapidly to myself. Smiles was staring at the bright face of the magic box that sounded more or less like Roderick. "Endorsement deals?"

"Oh, absolutely." Roderick sounded pleased with himself. A Cheshire grin was in that voice. "I want to become so rich and so powerful and so respected that I can come out of the closet."

"The… the closet." I was blank and even.

"Naturally. Look at the world we live in, Withrow. We're creatures trying to hide in a surveillance society. Do you honestly believe no one knows we're here? The government? Credit card companies? Banks? They may not know what they know, but they know. Someone has figured out there's a small, relatively stable population of 'persons' who stick around forever and try to escape notice. They know we're not militia whackos because we're not running around some square state in secondhand fatigues. Eventually they will figure out exactly what we are and that…" He paused and chuckled. "Oh, that will answer so very many of their questions, won't it? They'll get answers to questions they don't even know they have. I plan to be on the bleeding edge of that, for sure. Once society figures out we exist, there will be some serious commercial possibilities."

"Commercial possibilities like honest to goddamn endorsement deals?" I had no idea if he was serious.

"Exactly. Not for any of the obvious stuff, though: you know, sunglasses and tanning lotion and the like. I mean, how tacky would that be? Jesus. Might as well show up jumping the shark, right? No, I will insist on endorsement deals that are at least a little ironic. Farm equipment, for instance. A vampire selling machines that make food for people who are the food of that vampire? I like that. It's a nice little cycle of life kind of idea, isn't it? I'm partial to MacDougal tractors. Their main color is purple and I've always liked purple."

"You mean every word of this, don't you?" I laughed abruptly.

"Absolutely, cousin. You should give this serious consideration. You ask me where I see myself in fifty years? I see myself living in the world of fifty years from now. Most vampires are busy trying to live in the world of fifty years in the past, not the future. Those are two very different worlds. It's how we become irrelevant. They're literally different centuries, and we choose in which to live."

We were both quiet as a quarter mile of highway flew underneath me.

"Does that answer your question?" He said it as mildly as he possibly could, like he was making sure I'd gotten down a telephone number he'd rattled off.

"I think it does, cousin."

"Cousin," he said, and the call ended.

I coasted back past the airport and into Kills River and off onto North Kills River to go back into the woods, off a paved road, further back. As I hit gravel, I passed between a pair of white brick signs that bore faded wooden letters: Independence Valley. There were a lot of ironies there. For one, the development wasn't in a valley; for another, no one with a homeowner's association lording itself over them could really claim independence. That's one I've learned the hard way. The neighborhood went up decades ago and the sign was a mark of its initial aspirations, quickly abandoned. It was built of bricks, painted white, but the bricks had been stripped of their luster by rain and snow, then picked at and knocked apart by a generation or two of bored teenagers with fuck-all to do in a place like Hardison County. Now they looked like broken teeth and they stood flanking a muddy rut of a road. So much for suburbia as a place to keep safe the dreams of a quiet, neatly mown future.

When I was a half-mile or so from Clyde's house, I stopped and pulled off onto the side where there was a gap in the trees and left the Firebird locked. Smiles clambered out the driver's side door behind me when I got out and I signaled him to stay quiet. Smiles isn't just a supernaturally powerful dog and he's not just well trained. There's some connection between us, from the blood I feed him, so that he understands what I mean. I still did have to train him, mind you, but it took way better than it would with anything short of a

Seeing Eye dog, maybe better. I still have the "in training" Seeing Eye dog vest I ordered for him off the Internet, but I only put it on him when we're going to the mall or something like that.

We walked a few dozen yards into the woods, away from the road, and then turned and made off up the hill before us. Even at three hundred fifty pounds or whatever I am, I can go through the woods without making a sound. I am a vampire, after all. These woods weren't exactly virgin forest, either. It might have been built a long time ago, and way out in the country, but a subdivision is a subdivision is a subdivision. Suburbs don't require *urbs* to exist.

Clyde's house was on the opposite face of the hill we were climbing, so that I'd come up to it from behind, through the trees, invisible to just about anybody and anything, including the other houses on his side of the street. These were built before everything had to be slammed down onto a postage stamp with six inches on either side, so there was some actual room between them, but I did want to remain aware of the other houses in the area. I wasn't concerned that Smiles would bark at a squirrel or the like because he's better behaved than that. I hadn't taken him in when I went to see Marty because people tend to react badly if they aren't used to him, and he gets really, really curious when he's in a strange place. I was gambling that tonight there wouldn't be any issues with that. I could keep him in check if I had to and I was half sure there wouldn't be anybody at the house anyway. His dad had just turned up dead. Cliff – Clyde's son – was at best staying somewhere with friends or family and at worst in police custody.

We crested the hill and I stopped Smiles with a fingertip held to the side in his field of vision. We both stood there and listened, me turning my head this way and that, him with his huge parabolic ears twitching back and forth, eyes scanning, nose down to snuffle from time to time. I'd turned off the heat in the car on he way here and in the twenty minutes I'd driven without it I'd given back off a lot of that body heat. I figured that thermal vision wouldn't show much and night goggles like those military guys have in the movies wouldn't show a damned thing with me all done up in black like I was. My skin is pale, but my bulk was hidden. Anyway, what were the odds anyone would have night vision goggles up here in the sticks? Paranoid, I know, but every vampire is a little paranoid. The movies get to us, too.

As the coast seemed to be clear, I moved us around to the left, away from the big-ass night light on the other side of the house – I'm sure the neighbors loved that – so that we were where the yard was drenched in the house's own shadow. There was only one light on and I'd have bet money it was a single lamp on a timer. There was a car in the carport on the lit side but it was a little station wagon that I figured to be Clyde's wife's car. I thought for a moment about Edith having dropped dead of a cardiac arrest like that and then shook it off. *Happens to everyone,* I thought. *Sooner or later.* Still, it was so difficult to think of her as being old enough for that to happen. The last time I'd seen her we were young and to my mind she always still would be.

Smiles and I crept forward through the yard and I peeked around the front corner to look at the road in front of Clyde's house. I didn't see anything at first but when I leaned back an inch, I caught a glint of light where I hadn't expected one. That damned security light in the yard contrasted with the shadows in which I stood, screwing with my eyes' ability to penetrate the darkness. I had to focus on letting my eyes adjust to the total darkness of the gravel road that ran below Clyde's front yard and on farther. With time I was able to make out the barest outline of the front driver's side quarter-panel of a car. There wasn't chrome or trim where I might have spotted it, which was weird, but enough time passed that I could see that it had been darkened or covered up somehow. *Really weird,* I thought. *Also: clever.* Someone was watching the house from a car they'd camouflaged for darkness. Probably the cops, I figured, and if they hadn't popped any sirens yet then they hadn't seen me. That meant either they didn't have any fancy goggles or they weren't watching the back of the house. They were being more thorough in some ways than I might have guessed – the camouflage and all – but not as thorough in others. I smelled a lot of study and not a lot of experience in that. Interesting.

Smiles was standing at attention with his butt pressed against the back of my legs, keeping an eye out behind us, but moved with me when I moved back around to the rear of the house and crept up to the door out of the kitchen and onto a patio. I was going to stand out like an ink stain on the Sunday tablecloth when I stepped up onto its pale gray concrete surface, but I had to see the place for myself for some reason. *No time like the present,* I told myself, and I swept right up to the back door and peeked in the window. Lamplight spilled in from the front of the house, but the kitchen was dark. There was a coffee cup out on the table, probably left there when Clyde was getting ready to come see me. I could see the world that very nearly was – the one in which he was still alive and this was still a normal visit – sitting right there around that coffee cup. The world's a funny old place and it only gets funnier the more of it you see.

I'd brought some cheap, thin gloves with me from the car – the kind that are supposed to be as warm as the thick ones but never are – and I put them on and very gently tried the knob on the back door. It wasn't locked. That's typical country living for you. The vampires have security bars on the sliding glass doors of their apartments and the mortals leave the doors unlocked.

I opened the door, slipped through with Smiles on my heels, and closed it after us in one smooth motion. Woods, back doors, sweeping motions: vampires are good at all that kind of stuff. It's what we do. With a gesture I directed Smiles towards the front hall where he sat down by the front door, head up, alert, and started sniffing the air. I turned down the hallway – a real hallway in this real house, as compared to Marty's abomination of neutral colors and cheap carpet – and slid past a guest bedroom, the master bedroom and towards a final door into what had been turned into an office at some point. There was a desk with no computer, a telephone extension, a big, green-glassed desk lamp of the old school sitting on it, a paper blotter and a peel-off day-by-day. There were no lights except what came in from outside – the yard light – but that was plenty for me. The calendar, I saw, featured pictures of puppies and inspirational Bible quotes; a product of Edith's influence on Clyde as they'd gotten older, I guessed.

I could hear a conversation outside but it was far away and it wasn't getting any closer: probably a nosy neighbor bugging the cops, and more power to 'em.

There was a small bookshelf covered in fairly clinical texts on police procedure and law and the like. There was a larger one that looked rough-made, unfinished, that had big ring binders on it with years on the spines. Clyde had kept around his case files, his notes, all the various tidbits about all the investigations he'd worked in forty years with the SBI. I clucked my tongue to myself and wondered how many vampires lurked unrecognized – or worse, recognized – on the pages in those binders. I had neither time for, nor interest in, thieving that night, though. There was something specific I was after, something I felt like would be the final nail in the coffin of whether Clyde's murder was tied to the one he'd investigated when we met the night of our high school reunion.

There were some big plastic boxes, some older boxes of cardboard: banker's boxes I think they're called. You've seen them before in the back of the closet of a parent or an uncle or aunt or grandparent who didn't buy a home safe and clung to all the paper detritus of a life lived in contractual debts. The boxes had been rifled through so haphazardly that I thought for a moment that the place must have been burgled. That didn't make any sense, though. The rest of the house hadn't been tossed around like these boxes had. Their contents were skewed or scattered hither and yon on the floor.

They were evidence boxes. Clyde kept a lot of things he shouldn't have. He'd said enough, when we were standing around in that field every year, for me to know that. Eventually we'd reached the age where it didn't take long to tell me how his life was going, and he'd stopped asking about mine; that was when he started telling stories. He kept evidence: mementos, little trinkets that served as memorabilia from a life spent tracking down people who'd done terrible and desperate and twisted things. He'd spent years putting them away for those things, and along the way he'd gathered up all the little bits of whatever they'd left in their wake and tucked them away in boxes at home.

There was one of those things, in particular, that I wanted to see for myself.

Many years after that first murder investigation, he'd told me he'd found and kept a little bracelet from the wrist of one of the victims. It had been on the wrist of the kid, the rich orphan who'd apparently played genital patty-cake with the wrong "song chaser" stranger. The bracelet was a rough leather band with little teeth—human baby teeth and the fangs from animals—alternating one after the other, in a ring down the center of the strip of leather. At either end of the string of teeth and once in the very middle there had been the head – just the head – of an old-fashioned, rough-hewn nail made of iron. It had a metal clasp to close it around the kid's wrist. It had been so weird, so out of place in that age of Detroit steel and scientific parenting and better living through electric appliances, that Clyde couldn't help taking a special interest in it. No fingerprints on it except for the kid's and the old woman's, the other victim. It was the "other thing" Clyde had said he'd found that, to his mind, pointed up the mountains to some hillbilly instead of to anything as modern as a complicated con job gone wrong. He had meant it when he said his theory wasn't popular in those parts back then. He'd kept it for himself when he couldn't get anyone to accept that maybe it had been a local instead of an outsider. He hadn't told me right after; he'd waited a few years until he'd been able to convince himself it would never matter one way or the other. It was the kind of thing they'd build the whole plot around in an episode of *Dr. Lawyer Cop* these days, I'm sure, but to him, back then, it was something to be tucked away rather than exposed.

When he held it out, I'd started to reach for it and dropped my hand at the last second. I didn't know what it was, but I didn't want to touch it. It was *wrong* somehow.

It seemed completely random to me at the time, but I had decided to just trust my instincts rather than try to over-think it. *Something* made me want to see if that bracelet was still there so here I was. I started to despair at the odds of ever finding it amongst the half-dozen or so crates of junk from his other investigations, especially since they'd already been rifled through. Then I started to worry that if I messed everything up I'd give away that someone else had been there, too. Then I said, well, screw it. I'm here, they're messed up, how much worse can I make it? So I dug in with both gloved hands and started panning for stones. Over the next hour or so – disturbed only by my own shuffling of papers and the sound of Smiles' claws on the hardwoods as he patrolled the inside of the house – I ended up sorting everything more or less back into chronological order. I didn't put it all away neatly in the boxes or anything, but I did organize it enough to be able to tell where in the mess his earliest cases should be.

There was no bracelet.

I couldn't know if anything else was missing, of course, as I'd never seen any of it before, but I knew for certain that the bracelet was gone. Clyde had not been wearing it the night he died, or at least not when I found his corpse; and yet, in the papers, I had found the note he'd shown me at the same time he showed me the bracelet. It had been taped up and pasted to the underside of the bracelet, he told me. He'd removed it to read it and never put it back. It was written on old notepaper, bright pink, as unnatural as anything in the world. The handwriting had been old-fashioned and scribbled, no punctuation, the capitals kind of skewed or just archaic.

> *When Sun is low and Moon is high*
> *Cold on you and danger nigh*
> *Drench in blood of what you fear*
> *Wear on wrist or keep it near*
> *It stops the danger keeps you whole*
> *It helps dear Jesus save your soul*

You don't get folk magic like that these days. That's some seriously old-fashioned shit right there.

So, the note was still here. Whoever took the bracelet hadn't known enough to know it was important, or they knew enough not to need the note to tell them the deal. I didn't really know anything other than the obvious, that this was some sort of charm bracelet against a specific danger. Clyde had pointed out to me what my eyes and nose had already told me: not a drop of blood on it. The kid had known he was in danger, or been convinced enough to wear it, but either hadn't had time or hadn't been sufficiently convinced to actually dip it in the blood of whatever he was afraid of.

Or what he feared was well enough specialized that he hadn't had any of its blood close to hand.

I clucked my tongue again and clicked my cheeks quietly. Smiles came into the room making less noise than his own shadow under a full moon and I held out the note. He sniffed it idly and then licked my hand. Nothing special or telltale that I'd failed to notice, I guessed. Nobody had disturbed us in the hour or so we'd been there and I'd managed to confirm that the bracelet was gone. All in all, I'd had a successful night so far. I got up off my hands and knees and we crept around to the back door, let ourselves out and disappeared into the woods without anyone the wiser.

PART II

Chapter 1

Roderick had spent a few productive minutes with a phone book and three different online maps, a satellite imagery site, and Withrow's backlog of newspapers and studied them all until he was confident he could find Clyde Wilfred's house with his eyes closed. As soon as the sun was down, he'd gone and found it and parked his car in the driveway of a house where a cheerful "Gone to Florida, back in six months!" had been taped to the side of the newspaper box by some idiotic, trusting retiree. Roderick had hidden his car there and found a perch twenty feet up an ancient oak fifty yards away and across the road from Clyde Wilfred's home within an hour of sunset.

Cousin Withrow hadn't wanted his help with this Last Gasp business, he could tell. That simply made giving it all the more fun. Last Gasp is not an easy time for a vampire. Roderick knew vampires who had gone mad when it finally happened. There were vampires who had tended their human kindred or friends or servants or slaves like a shepherd only to see them all taken in one disaster or another. He also knew vampires who had carefully tended the garden of their mortal relations so that they could bring the moment of their Last Gasp to fruition in their own time, in some personal way. He had known vampires who didn't even know they still had a human out there who remembered them as a person, someone who wondered idly in some rank and rumpled secondhand hospital bed whatever became of that handsome young professor who'd taught their astronomy lab all those decades of nights ago. Then they woke up one day with powers they had never imagined, never asked for, some useful and some utterly humiliating. A vampire who could fly all of a sudden was in for some very fun games of catch and no small amount of negative attention from their local power structure. A vampire who could make dandelions dance was a lot less fearsome but – for that very reason – ever so much safer from her own kind.

Roderick had watched with mild interest and then amusement as a small, black Cavalier with permanent plates, a government car of some sort, had pulled up the long gravel road, gone past the house, turned around in a driveway, killed its lights and then crept painfully slowly back to park a little ways up from Clyde Wilfred's home. The driver – an Asian woman, stocky build, hair slightly longer than shoulder length, dark pants and a dark coat and a dark cap and dark gloves and, most of all, a dark expression – had pulled out a pair of binoculars and begun getting comfortable. All the trim, the bits of plastic and cheap metal making a mockery of chrome, had been covered over in black electrician's tape to minimize the car's ability to be seen in the shadows.

Fascinating. Roderick had watched with the keen eyes of a predator and admired her ingenuity. It was that kind of creativity he so often found lacking in humanity. Its absence was one of the things that made them such boringly easy prey so much of the time.

The driver pulled out a dark blue blanket that looked grey in the starlight and put it over herself to stay warm. Roderick had worn a light jacket to blend in if he ran into anyone but he loved being cold. Cold was refreshing. The human world was one of light and warmth and he was a creature of frigid darkness. He had stayed extra still, up in the tree, so that all the unnecessary, cloying warmth could flow out and into the air and away, shed like a snake's skin. He hated that warmth when he was out at night on his own, watching, hunting. Warmth was for luring them, putting them at ease. Cold was much more comfortable and poetically appropriate to a vampire's work.

The woman had special binoculars – night vision, so interesting, more creativity!—and used them to watch the house for a while. Steam from her coffee made the windows want to fog up so she had to crack the windows every now and then and let it cool off again. It must be torturing her, he thought, a part of her so warm and a part of her so cold.

He settled against the tree trunk and watched her. He'd planned to watch the house in case anyone came sneaking around – in case Withrow came sneaking around is what he meant, of course – but she was here and so much more interesting than some empty old house in some empty old neighborhood on an empty old mountain between empty old towns. She was here with a purpose, which was more than he could say about anything else these mortals had done. That always got his interest. She would yawn, nod off for an average of two minutes at a time, wake with a start, jerk the binoculars up to her face, look intently at the house, then drink more coffee, then repeat. It was soothing to lose himself in her cycle of sleep and rushed, self-conscious activity. It was like watching a human day on fast forward.

His phone buzzed silently in his pocket so he turned around and had a quiet conversation with Withrow. He didn't even watch her to make sure she didn't hear him. She wouldn't, and if she did, he would just kill her.

She didn't. When they were done speaking, Roderick turned back around and went back to watching her. This human woman was like a television stuck on a really boring show and that, in itself, was interesting.

Eventually, he realized, he wouldn't be able to resist. He would have to go speak to her. He wished he had brought Doggie – his dog – to this place with him, but he hated making him fly. He was so very old now. He wasn't frail, but it didn't seem fair to make him fly. The dog would have been a great excuse to be out, though. Oh well, it's not against the law to take a walk after dark. He would just be out for a walk. Yes, humans did that. They walked all the time. They loved to take little walks. *It's good for their heart,* Roderick thought, and he smiled. If he thought about it hard enough, he could make his heart beat. He'd gotten very good at that kind of thing. He could even remember to breathe for ten minutes straight if he focused.

Slipping around to the far side of the tree from the fascinating police person in the fascinating car, he climbed down in darkness and made his way through the trees to way back up the road, far from the car, far behind it. He zipped up his jacket and rubbed his hands together to make them warm again. He reached up and ran his fingers through his long, blond hair, stringy and greasy no matter how he washed it or how much product he used. He rubbed his sunken eyes and slapped his own jutting cheekbones, his hollow cheeks, to try to make them look a little more lived in. Then, whistling a happy tune, he set off at a leisurely pace down the middle of the road towards the so very interesting little car with the irresistible little woman in it.

H'Diane had a warrant to search the house and had gone through and done so—very carefully—so she wasn't sure why she was staking the place out. Oh, there were reasons enough. The victim's son was nowhere to be found. There were cops with pictures of him up in their break rooms and all over their email, statewide. The newspaper had run a picture of him. There weren't many places he could hide. If it was a slow weekend for news then MSNBC or somebody might turn up asking questions. H'Diane shook her head, shook herself more awake. There was a theory professed publicly that such attention was a good thing in an investigation. Spread the word as far as possible and you make it that much more likely someone who knows something will call it in to the people who need to hear. Truth was, cops hated it when reporters turned up and made the latest Missing White Woman story a media event. Spectators seemed to suck all the oxygen out of the real investigation. Lots and lots of volunteers would turn up to help search the woods for missing campers but they weren't trained and they didn't know what to look for. They'd just trample the undergrowth for a few square miles, call it a tragedy and that would be that.

Detective H'Diane Bing realized abruptly that she'd started to doze again. She hadn't gotten any sleep worth a damn the night before. She was nodding off in the car and completely screwing up the surveillance. She might as well go home. She could park a deputy out here if she wanted. She had no good reason to do it herself. The son hadn't turned up at work for two days, hadn't been spotted anywhere else. She would get paged in a heartbeat if they found him somewhere.

That all made sense, except that she cared so very much about getting this right herself. It was her first case as a detective. She had all these entrenched deputies with their local culture; there was LaVonde, with all her years writing and now editing the political beat in Asheville; and H'Diane felt like everyone knew what to do but she herself didn't. She had walked out of a career as a competent beat cop when she took down the chief in her last job. Oh well. She'd sworn to uphold the law, no matter who broke it. It wasn't her fault he'd been a murderer. In lots of departments that would never have been held against her; in some towns the local media would have turned her into a temporarily untouchable hero. In some, it was a black mark that would never wash away. She could hear her father now: *I didn't bring you to this country so that you could throw away a good future,* he'd said. What had kept her in police work at all was the next thing he said, *But I didn't bring you here so that you throw away your principles, either.* That was all it took. She'd applied for detective training the next day and started night classes at UNC-Asheville in Criminal Justice.

Damn. Nodded off again. She poured more coffee out of the thermos and into the cup, drank some, set it haphazardly on the dashboard of the car, fished around in her lunchbox for a protein bar. She nearly dropped it when she heard gravel crunch behind the car. Glancing in the mirror she saw a stringy-haired white kid in a black leather coat, hands in the pockets, walking this way. Too young to be Cliff, she knew right away. He met her eyes in the mirror and then smiled a little and began to whistle a tune.

LaVonde stayed late at the office that night. She'd dug out those first few articles about the killing Clyde Wilfred had investigated, the one that happened where his own body had been found, but they had just scratched the surface. There were people who still talked about it online to this day, she'd learned. Most of them were conspiracy nuts, the usual assortment of John Birch Society types who think the commies killed a rich kid as an example to capitalists everywhere, the ones who were convinced it was Bigfoot and said the tears at their throats had proven it. Hell, she'd even read one very clinical and, well, "rational" wasn't the right word for it, but it was certainly written in the moderate tones of someone merely discussing the evidence with an open mind; anyway, some guy named Marty had posted a theory in a local discussion board in which he proposed that it was a vampire. What she was looking for, though, she kept seeming to circle without exactly finding. There was no one around anymore, no one at all, who was related to the victims or had known them when they were alive. Every now and then she'd find a story—a blog post, a discussion board entry, whatever—where someone explained that they were third cousins to the guy whose daughter babysat for the sister of one of them, sure, but never anything closer than that.

That was odd, she had to admit. People were usually eager to associate themselves with tragedy, no matter how tenuous the bond. She'd have expected someone to have *something* a little closer than that, surely? Someone who was a cousin of the victim? Something? Anything?

Nothing.

Roderick walked around the car staying no less than ten feet from the driver's door. The woman inside, the policewoman, watched him with an expression of relief. He'd startled her. Tsk. He had not wanted to frighten her. He wanted to *talk*. This was not a good beginning. He smiled politely, she smiled back, he kept walking. Ten feet past the car, he stopped and turned in a precise circle on his heels, as though his feet were attached to a pole that had been driven into the ground and he could just turn in an even circle like that.

"Do you need anything?" He perked up his eyebrows, his eyes, kept the polite smile. He was addressing her in the helpful, alert, friendly manner of waiters in nice restaurants. He remembered restaurants. They smelled bad now.

The woman wrinkled her eyebrows. She hadn't understood him. He'd spoken too quietly. Roderick drew a slow breath to refill his lungs and then said, more loudly, "I'm sorry, but do you need anything? Is your car broken down?"

H'Diane opened her mouth, held it that way for a moment and then laughed suddenly. "No, I'm fine. Thanks."

Roderick positively beamed at her. She was a vision of joy. Look, she *talked*. To *him*. He hadn't been so excited in at least five minutes. "Just enjoying the evening?"

The woman held her mouth open again then looked around and past him at the house before looking back to Roderick. "Yes. Out for a walk?"

Roderick lifted his elbows away from his sides as though to hold his arms out but didn't remove his hands from his pockets. "Apparently!" He chuckled. She chuckled. "A little chilly, but I prefer it that way."

"Yes," the woman said in agreement. She held up the mug of steaming coffee and gestured with it, took another drink. "It's going to stay that way for a few days, they say."

Roderick heard the sweep of heavy fabrics in the back yard of the house she was watching and then the latch of a door being released. He stepped forward, back towards the car, blocking the view. "Indeed? And which 'they?'"

The woman blinked at him. "The... weather 'they.'"

Roderick did take his hands out of his packets then and clap them together. "Oh, yes, of course," he replied. "I meant..." He paused. "Well, whatever." Without a moment's hesitation he turned halfway and looked back at Clyde's house, over his right shoulder. "Pity about that, isn't it?" His eyes stayed there, like he was looking for something.

H'Diane coughed and cleared her throat. "Yes, it's tragic. Did you know him?"

Roderick looked back finally and then took two more steps towards her. He was thin as a knife but H'Diane found her view off the house entirely blocked. "Heavens no," he finally said. "I'm visiting some relatives." He closed his mouth, then opened it again. "I'm in from out of town."

"Ah," H'Diane said. "I did notice that the accent is different, but with all the retirees around now, you never know."

"As is yours," Roderick said. "The accent." She could only see his silhouette but his cheeks were pointed in a way that made her assume he was smiling.

"I didn't grow up here," she said. "Well, I mostly did. Parents didn't, though. I never really picked it up. It was hard enough knowing two languages: English and Vietnamese. I didn't need to add mountain drawl to the mix." She chuckled at him and so he laughed in return.

"So do you know who did it?" His voice was like a laser, somehow.

H'Diane sighed heavily, very suddenly, like something had escaped from under pressure and come blowing out of her lungs in its escape. "No comment," she said. "And no reporters in general." She scowled now, and reached for the ignition as though to leave.

"Oh, no, no," Roderick quickly said, and in a step he closed the gap so that he was leaning on the front fender of her car where it met the seal of the door. Her eyes jumped to where his hips touched that metal joint and then back up. "I'm no reporter," he added. "Just a concerned citizen." He smiled again. Standing sideways as he was, H'Diane could see the right half of his face, more or less, by the security light from the victim's yard. *Funny how a big old night light like that turns everything blue*, she thought. He smelled strongly of soap and shampoo and cigarettes and absolutely nothing else. Something about it made the hair on her neck stand up. "So is this where you wait for him to return to the scene of the crime?" The half-expression on his half-face might have been mockery or amusement or simple salacious voyeurism.

H'Diane sighed so quietly that only Roderick could possibly have ever heard her. "No. Besides, this isn't the scene of the crime."

Roderick arched one eyebrow at her—well, at least one, she couldn't see both—and then smiled. "I read in the paper that you don't know where it happened."

H'Diane closed her mouth and said nothing. She'd had about enough of all this. Just taking a walk her *ass*. She should cuff him right now just to see what he coughed up down at the station. She started to say something to him, started to reach for the car door, when he produced another winner.

"Let's say you never find whoever did it." His voice had dropped half an octave and he'd cut the volume by a lot. It was distressingly intimate to hear him like that. He drummed the tips of four fingers and a thumb on the roof of her car, idly, and looked back at the house. "How long until the case is closed? Like, how long do you look before you just say, oh well, we'll never know? I ask because I read that the man who was killed had a case like that as one of his very first and I can't help wondering what that must be like." He sighed quietly. "That would really, really stink."

H'Diane started to tense just a little and thought about starting to slide a hand towards her pepper spray, but then the guy just shrugged it all off. "Oh well. You'll find him. Or her. It could always be he had a woman on the side." His voice was just as bright as it had been at first, his body no longer some close, cloying presence right against the door of her county car. He was once again just some skinny blond guy in a biker jacket. Sort of. It was to biker jackets what those new Beetles are to a Super Bug: a yuppie impersonation to one person's eye, a stylish update to another's. "Anyway, you should probably go back to doing what you were doing and I should stop interrupting." He leaned down a little, waved with the fingers of one hand, then stepped off neatly and went whistling back the direction he'd come from originally. Two minutes later, H'Diane stopped gripping the wheel and allowed herself to look in the mirror.

He was gone. *Must be a bend in the road back there*, she thought to herself. *There simply must be.*

She sat in perfect silence for three or four more minutes, eyes rotating between the rear view and side mirrors and the road in front of her. The house could take care of itself for a little bit. Finally she convinced herself that the freak in the jacket was well and truly gone. Ten minutes later she'd fallen asleep in the driver's seat and wouldn't wake up for nearly two hours. She would hate herself for the lapse in discipline but her body would be incredibly grateful. She never once heard Roderick Surrett climb back in his tree and start humming old lullabies to himself.

CHAPTER 2

I was careful and quiet going out of Clyde's place—out the back door, straight through the yard, into the trees, over the hill and back down to my car. I drove out of where I'd stashed it and went on back down to North Kills River, then over and back onto 280 and south towards Hardisonville. A few hundred yards ahead I had to decide. 280 forked so that 191 went south to Hardisonville proper between farms and little patches of aspirational housing developments whereas 280 turned west in the direction of Brevard, a sleepy destination at the other end of a long tunnel of night and nothing. I thought of Marty Macintosh and his map of disappearances around Brevard and I kept going on NC 280.

The newspaper said Cliff worked in Brevard. He was a security guard at some old film plant that had shut down a few years back. Not much of it left, I imagined, but they paid someone to keep an eye on it all the same. The cops hadn't been able to find him but I still wanted to see it for myself. I wanted to go there and see if I could tell when he'd been there. If he was dead, too, this was something weird and tragic but not really anything *scary*. Mass murderers, serial killers, revenge killing: all that stuff is pretty low-rent in my world. Vampires are not murderers by habit. We have a culture of secrecy, of stealth, and attracting the attention of the local law every time we eat dinner is about as far from stealthy as one can get. That doesn't mean killing never happens, though, or that we are particularly horrified when humans turn their various powers against one another in some final and drastic way. I figured Cliff was probably dead. If he was still alive, though, I had some questions for him. First among them would be, where's the bracelet?

I shook my head and let my mind wander while I drove the four-lane highway around twists and curves and up and down gentle hills. The only place the road really got interesting was at the border of Transylvania County—I'm not making that up, it's really named that—when it climbed hard up a high mountain and then swept fast down the other side into Pisgah Forest. At the bottom of that steep descent, it ran through a little neighborhood that had grown up around the highway when it was two lanes and as quiet as could be. When the road had been widened they had just cut it into people's yards. Front porches and mailboxes were perched just feet—sometimes it looked more like inches—from the slow lane on either side. Someone in the past had put houses here to take advantage of the only straight shot to Asheville and the road had nearly knocked their houses over in thanks.

Transylvania County was named for a business, supposedly, not that region of Romania it so closely resembles: high peaks, deep crags and hundreds of waterfalls along rivers of every imaginable size. Either way, the name is derived from Latin: *trans sylvan*, meaning "through forests". That definitely describes Transylvania County, which is basically a few thousand people standing sideways on a bunch of woods-covered cliffs. It's home to some tremendously gifted musicians and artists and to some of the most backwards, inbred redneck freakjobs you can imagine. I love it for its quiet woods, so silent at night, and its many miles of trails and streams. It's a good place for a body to get lost for a while. It's also a good place to help another do the same.

I swung a left onto 64, still two lanes here, past the fish camp and a barbecue joint and then very abruptly I was back in the middle of nowhere. More turns, more two-lane roads, and I had arrived at an intersection in the middle of nowhere. An old country garage was on one corner of it and a sign pointed to the right that read, "Clarke Industries." I pulled into the dark gravel lot of the garage to look over that printout Marty had given me. I was in the very thick of the disappearances Marty had noted over the last five years. They didn't all happen here, to be sure, and they hadn't happened all at once, but they were clustered here more densely than anywhere else other than the middle of downtown Asheville.

I turned back onto the road in the direction of the old plant and immediately had to start climbing. The car dropped into a lower gear and I put my foot to the floor and listened to it work. Gravity and the steep grade were not my friends on this one and I'd dropped to thirty-five, then to thirty, before I'd made it around the first couple of curves. The engine roared and I juiced it into passing gear to try to get some licks in of my own against them both. Eventually the grade got a little kinder and I was able to build some speed and relax a little.

Here and there a house dotted the side of the road but never less than a mile from one another and never very far from the road. This was the middle of nowhere; Clarke Industries had once owned what's now an enormous land preserve owned by the state. In the very center of that was their film operation. I wondered at first why anyone would huddle their house so close to the road and then wondered again why anyone would come this far out to build a home in the first place, with all these trees and mountains and yards at thirty degree slopes to make them feel alone and uncertain, always slightly angled, waiting to tumble away down the hill the first time something gave way.

It was a lousy place to live unless you were a person who hated other people. It wouldn't make a bad place for a vampire, though.

I kept going and going, around sharp curves and up one steep hill after another, and wondered if the mountain would ever stop or if I would eventually just burst through the clouds and find myself driving all the way to the moon. At last I rounded another curve and saw another sign for Clarke Industries with "Ahead 1/2 Mile" at the bottom. Thinking back, Clarke had always been up here. They're one of those big international conglomerates that make stuff that never has their name on it: they make the chemicals that go into things rather than the things themselves, or they make highly specialized components, that kind of stuff. This plant, they'd made film. It was one of their few commercial products. Of course, business had dried up in the age of digital cameras—computer-aided imaging, they'd called it in a newspaper story when the plant closed down—and so this place had been boarded up.

A minute later, I saw the sign sitting at the mouth of an innocuous little road that turned left and disappeared into trees. There were the rusted, overgrown remains of a softball pitch in a field opposite the road, skeletal remains of an earlier time when families attached to the plant would come here for field days and vacations. After I turned into the drive of Clarke Industries I noticed that one side of the drive was solid woods but the other was an enormous muddy expanse. I slowed a little, the moonlight reflecting weirdly on the landscape, and when I paid more attention I could see that it wasn't a dirty field: it was a drained lake. A couple of small docks and a pier made of planks jutted up out of the filthy dried pit like jagged teeth in a beggar's mouth. I had a ways to go on this driveway and by the time I'd gotten to the plant I'd passed the moldering remains of a Clarke Industries Employee Credit Union and some tennis courts and what looked like carved wooden signs for an exercise trail back into the thick woods on the left and off gods know where. I'd read one time that the whole property covered 35,000 acres. Amazing, in this day and age.

There were cars in the parking lot: half a dozen old pickup trucks and a couple of shitty little subcompacts. I pulled up across a couple of spaces right at the gatehouse and rolled down my windows. I sniffed the air and at first I didn't smell anything much. I started to think driving this far out of my way was kind of a stupid idea, wasting time when I could be talking to vampires I knew existed, but then I caught it.

The whiff of predator: the telltale scent of a fellow hunter. Smiles could smell it, too, and he made a noise like a chainsaw starting.

I sat very still and breathed deep and even. The night was clear, the moon approaching full but not there yet. There were lights on in the parking lot but only a couple and right where I was. *That wasn't very smart,* I thought to myself. I should have parked in one of the darker corners.

A vampire rarely forgets a scent. It was very faint, very far away, but I could smell it and I'd smelled it before. It was the scent of the predator who'd been at that crime scene Clyde had investigated decades before. I was certain that place and this were connected by a vampire who'd been to both and that vampire wasn't me. Well, no time like the present to make an introduction.

I climbed out of the car, left it unlocked behind me and crossed to the door of the gatehouse. A high chain-link fence with barbed wire looped in complicated non-patterns at the top surrounded the plant itself. It was rusted but a glance in either direction told me it seemed to be whole. There was no light on in the gatehouse but I figured it was worth checking to see if it was locked before I bothered climbing over and winding up with a torn coat. The gatehouse was a small, square, brick building with a flat roof and large windows overlooking the parking lot and the drive into the plant. The plant itself was a series of connected, dark-faced and multi-storeyed monoliths perched like a Mayan ziggurat complex on the hill that rose behind it. The paint was peeling on the ones that were painted and the brick facing of the others had started to crumble here and there. Loose bricks littered a scraggly, weed-covered lawn untended for so long the grass had all died from drought and now there was hardly anything anyone could consider alive at all. I took it all in for a few moments – nobody had taken any shots at me on the way in or while I sat in the car sniffing the air so I figured I needn't skitter and hide – and out of curiosity pulled out my phone and checked for signal. Much to my surprise I had three bars. Progress marches forward, even in these old hills.

Finally, I steeled myself and pulled on the handle of the door into the gatehouse. I couldn't tell whether or not I was surprised when it opened with a tug. Smiles preceded me through the door then I stepped inside and listened. I heard nothing, saw nothing. We kept walking through a little waiting room. The magazines were ten years out of date, dust was everywhere a guest would have sat and nowhere a guard would be stationed. Smiles snuffled here and there and sneezed a time or two. We kept going and pushed open the door directly opposite the entrance. That left us on a once-manicured lawn that stretched up a slight incline between the gatehouse and the plant itself. I stepped quietly but easily up the hill on broken sidewalks while Smiles turned and watched behind me. At the top, I found three entrances, one to either side and one farther back. A rusted metal sign indicated CLERICAL to the left, CHEMICAL to the right, PRODUCTION straight ahead.

If I were going to hide out in a plant, I thought to myself, I sure wouldn't pick the secretarial wing and I wouldn't want to be around a bunch of chemicals I didn't understand. A big, cavernous factory floor, as I imagined the production floors would be, seemed the best choice. So on I went, straight ahead. The double doors into the production facility had cracked glass on the left side and were unlocked. Bingo.

The building itself seemed to be mostly hallways in rectangles defining the inner perimeter of the building. Offices, storage closets and the like were littered around the outside. The inside was utilitarian and sparse, gray- and green-painted walls of cement blocks, hard tile that would have rung like a gong when anyone else walked on it. My preternatural abilities allowed me to stay mostly quiet but I had to move quick and light as I went and I could certainly hear myself move. Smiles padded along in silence, his nails occasionally scraping but only very rarely. He is almost as good at sneaking as I am, but never quite as good what with all those claws and rabies tags on a thick leather collar. We glided along together, with me noting doors for dressing rooms – they'd made the workers wear uniforms when the plant was in production – and signs for a cafeteria. I listened at the door for the men's locker room and didn't hear anything. Locker rooms and bathrooms and the like are a popular place for our kind because they so rarely feature windows. Sunlight is bad. Sleeping in a locker room is almost always good. I'd heard tell of a couple of vampires who lived in a locker in a high school gymnasium and kept just enough staff in their thrall to keep doing so for the long term. I kept going, up some stairs, following signs, more or less wandering. My nose eventually picked up something and with concentration I could nail it down as ham.

It was definitely ham. I could also smell vampire, but it hadn't gotten any stronger. Luncheon meat seemed to be my best lead. The cafeteria, then.

I kept going, slowing down and creeping so that I didn't make a sound, even on the tile floor. The signs for the cafeteria and the scent I'd picked up led me to a pair of double doors with small windows of shatter-proof, reinforced glass set in them. I was mostly in shadow, out in the hall, and the cafeteria was mostly lit, so I risked a peek through the bottom corner of one of them and if I hadn't seen with my own eyes the corpse of Clyde lying dead in a field then I'd swear he'd gained fifty pounds and was sitting inside. The man in the cafeteria was eating gas station gourmet: a cheap ham sandwich and a bag of chips. It was Cliff. He was sitting there chewing slowly, staring at his food, eyes a little glassy. Sweat stood out all over his forehead. He was tall, like Clyde had been, but he was carrying around a bunch of weight his daddy never put on. It had the effect of giving him something of a baby face, but he had to be pushing sixty by now. The bags under his eyes were fighting the youthful illusion created by the absence of wrinkles. A lot of times a really fat person keeps looking young way past their time as their skin never quite has room to sag or crease or otherwise collapse under the weight of too many years. Cliff had that going and his blond hair had started to turn gray but it was stringy and dull to begin with and the gray just didn't have a lot to contrast against.

Now, I had a fairly simple decision before me: waltz in and do the nonchalant conversationalist thing, bust in like hellfire, or keep walking. I was standing there trying to judge the best approach from his expression—a little stony, a little nervous, a little like an injured person going into shock, a little of the deer in headlights thing, a little woeful resignation—when I caught that scent again. The way I figured it, the vampire was either stalking Cliff or protecting him. This would be some delicate work, and I am absolute shit at delicate work. So, I stood up, adjusted my coat, straightened my shirt a little, grabbed the door handle, ripped the door off its hinges and threw it straight across the hall, against the wall. It shattered one of the cement blocks and splintered to pieces, the reinforced glass spraying in eighteen hundred directions on narrow vectors of noise.

I barged through the door, arms pumping at my sides, the rubber of my boots clomping against the tile floor. Smiles' massive bulk clattered evenly and rhythmically by my side. Cliff jerked his head up, mouth open, and stared as we strode into the cafeteria, threw a table out of my way one-handed and walked right up to stand across his own from him.

"Hi," I said. "Let's get straight to the important part. Are you being protected?"

Cliff blinked his eyes at me, very slowly. His jaw hung there like a detached sole as though it didn't at all work. I leaned down and snapped my fingers in his face. He jerked back a couple of inches but otherwise just kept staring.

"I asked a question," I growled. "Let's hear an answer."

"Guh..."

I reached out and gripped Cliff's jaw in my hand. You know that scene in *Better Off Dead* when Ricky's mom grabs the French girl by the jaw and says, "Frieeeeeeeeeeeeends?" I was holding his jaw just like that and I worked it up and down a couple of times. "C'mon, kid. I know who you are. I know why nobody's seen you around. Well, I sort of know. I imagine you're in here hiding from the cops. Stashed the car somewhere and you just chill in here and wait for it to blow over, whatever 'it' is. Thing is, you left the gatehouse unlocked. We just strolled right on in. Been in town all of two or three nights and I just find you like *that*." I snapped my fingers again. "So my guess is you're being protected. I mean, you could always be just as dumb as a sack of rocks, I reckon, but you're Clyde's kid and he was always a smart cookie so I'm guessing you've got some brains, too. So where is he? The one who's protecting you?"

Cliff was still slack-jawed. I looked around, sniffed the air, then leaned close and sniffed Cliff. I snuffled and snorted like a happy terrier, right up in his face and around his neck. I could smell the other vampire in the air but I couldn't tell if I smelled him *on* Junior here. Smiles was standing with his back to me, watching behind me. Finally I let go of Cliff's face, reared back and slapped him across the left cheek just as hard as I could with the flat of my right hand. The blow sounded like a cap gun going off, bouncing off all that concrete and tile and metal chairs and metal tables and Formica counters and fluorescent lighting. Finally Junior's chair came out from under him and he took three quick steps around it and back to hold it in front of him on the floor, like that would stop me. At least it was a reaction.

"Alright," I sighed. I reached into my pockets and pulled out my phone nonchalantly to check the time. "So where is he?"

"Who the hell are you?" I was surprised to hear that come out of this old man-child who was carrying a big beer gut and had puffy cheeks and burlap bags under his eyes with a nose that spoke of years of drinking the cheap stuff. I noticed now that his stringy hair was also neatly combed and matted in place with hair oil. Hair oil, in this day and age. I laughed a little, an abrupt chuckle, and he didn't at all know what to think of that but he clearly knew I found something just a little funny and at his expense.

"Withrow Surrett," I answered him, voice quiet. "Your daddy ever mention me?"

Cliff flinched. He didn't blink, he didn't look away, he *flinched*, like I'd taken a swipe at him with a knife. Now, at what had he flinched?

"I asked you another question," I said. "Now that makes one I've been asked and in turn answered but two you've seen fit to ignore. That's not very polite."

"How did you know my father?" His voice shook a little but no other part of him moved.

"I went to high school with him," I said. I shrugged. Easy answer. That made two, though. I'd take it out of his hide to settle the score at this point.

"But you're..." He looked at me, up and down. "But you're half my age."

I waved the back of my hand at him like so much lint to get rid of before seeing someone important. "OK, so you're not being protected, in which case

I shouldn't be here and neither should you. Let's make this easy; just look me in the eye and I'll make it all better." I started to gather up the will to work a little hoodoo and, for starters, wipe his mind of any memory I'd ever been here. I figured next I'd send Cliff on a nice little trip down to the police station. Vampires won't screw around with the cops if they've got any brains at all. I figured that was the safest place in the world for him.

"Who are you? You didn't know my father." Apparently he was still stuck back at the beginning of the conversation. I shoved the table aside with two fingertips and started towards him to grab his jaw again and do this the hard way.

"Could've saved us both a lot of time when I got here if you'd just told me you're an idiot." I sighed and had my hand two inches from his face when Smiles let out a whine and a scent washed over me like a massive wave: the predator I'd smelled when I first got there, and several others. I withdrew from Clyde about three steps and chanced a look over my shoulder. A textbook Bubba was standing there in old coveralls and a flannel shirt, chewing a cigar with his hands in his pockets and one eye squinting at me. Crow's feet crowded his eyes and his hair was a thin and greasy jet black. He leaned against the door jam where I'd ripped it out of the wall. He was small, mostly spherical in the middle. He had a salt of the Earth look that probably made people's eyes glide right over him if he ever went out in public. He looked like everyone's embarrassing redneck cousin, the one with a Confederate flag license plate on their truck. He was flanked by six guys in varying shades of redneck who were all trying to look tough. A couple of them were still alive but the rest were vampires so new they were practically still in the packaging.

"Alright," he drawled, "That's about enough of that."

I turned around and looked the new guy up and down for long moments, then inhaled deep. I pointedly did not look at his color guard. I could see his own nostrils flair a little as I did so, which I took to be him smelling me out rather than being offended. I didn't much care one way or the other, though. This guy wasn't on Bob's old list. That meant he wasn't someone in the establishment. That meant I didn't give a good goddamn what he thought of me.

"And you are?"

The guy chomped his cigar for a moment and then stood up straight and put his hands at his side, bowed very slightly, mostly from the neck. "They call me The Transylvanian."

I snorted. No diplomacy or conscious insult, just a gut reaction. The Transylvanian. *Classy.* Transylvania County, after all. What I said, though, was a little nicer. "Withrow Surrett. I'm the boss in North Carolina. Came up the mountain to make some calls on people, see how they're doing. You're not on my list."

The Transylvanian smiled for just a moment and then nodded. "I've never cared much for the formalities, but good to meet you." He tucked one hand into the pocket of his coveralls: a dingy beige worker bee set that had the Clarke Industries logo stitched over the heart. None of his baggage handlers relaxed.

Scavenger, I thought.

He didn't offer the other hand, just reached up and took the cigar out of his mouth then ashed it with a dismissive wave I could choose to interpret as mimicking what I'd done a couple minutes earlier when I dismissed Cliff as ignorant of his circumstance.

Speaking of Junior, Cliff was still standing there just as quiet as a church on Saturday night. Something about the eight of them standing there like I was a turd on their lawn nearly made my blood boil but I kept my features composed. I took a slow, narrow breath and then made myself smile a little. "So. Why *weren't* you on Bob's list?"

The Transylvanian took two steps into the room and reached down to get a chair off the floor, then sat in it with one work boot propped on the opposite leg's knee, casual as could be. "Couldn't stand Bob. Surprised he lasted this long, to be honest. Always been the kind to keep to myself anyway." He shrugged half-heartedly. "So what brings you here if you didn't know I existed?"

I picked up a chair of my own and straddled it, my back to Cliff. This was a conversation for grown-ups, not him. I chucked a thumb at him over my shoulder. "None of his business, is it? Just ours." I didn't bother to include the other guys in the supposition.

"Cliff," The Transylvanian drawled after a moment's consideration, "'Bout time for your rounds, ain't it?"

Junior tried to say something immediately, got strangled, cleared his throat, waited a beat and cleared it again. "Sure. Hit me on the radio if you need anything." I could just see a little plastic-coated wire sticking out of one of the side pockets on the coveralls. The two of them were right at home, weren't they? Cliff gathered up his lunch, tossed it in the trash and walked out the doors on the far side of the cafeteria without looking back. Smiles didn't like what was going on at all. He sat up straight beside me with his eyes on The Transylvanian's goons and his ears pinned back.

I glanced sideways to watch Cliff go before I looked back at The Transylvanian. "Which Bob did you hate? There were three of them that I know of."

He arched an eyebrow at that and smacked his lips. "All of 'em, then, most likely. The one I met was back in, oh..." He thought, counted on his fingers, then looked at a wall calendar that was out of date. "1911, I reckon. However long that's been."

Alright, so he was old. Not ancient by any stretch, but older than me assuming he was at all telling the truth. I smiled a little and settled my gut against the back of the chair I'd straddled. "Well I put an end to the last one myself. Got tired of being told how to live. Figured I'd do a better job of keeping the peace but staying out of people's personal business." I shrugged. "I'll leave the details to the imagination but the plan worked and here I am." I reached out to give Smiles a scritch behind the ears. He didn't react, keeping his eyes nailed to the other guys, moving from one to the other in practiced, measured succession. "'We', rather."

To be honest, I wanted to tell this yahoo how I'd killed Bob. It had been ugly and brutal and a part of me was very, very proud. I'd left a psychotic leech named Sarah in charge in Greensboro after that in return for her helping me. We'd ambushed his car, killed his men, nailed him down with suppressing fire, and burned him and his Lincoln Mark III to the ground at a deserted exit on Interstate 40. The last time I'd looked at Bob, he was a pile of bubbling fat and a skeleton that was dissolving into ash in the bottom of a ditch. Sarah had looked me right in the eye after that, shaken my hand, smiled a pretty smile and started barking orders at her people. She's like that: she'll kill a man with you and then flounce out the door and ride her motorbike away into the night with a wink and no helmet. I admire many of her mental qualities but Sarah is pretty seriously messed up.

All that passed through my mind in a flash of memories and then I took another breath to speak again. "So what's your story?"

"I keep to myself," he said simply. Another shrug. "I don't bother nobody and nobody bothers me. Nice and easy."

I pointed around for a moment. "This place is going to get torn down sooner or later. How long have you been here?"

"Long time." The Transylvanian looked around the room, too, then back at me. "They won't tear it down as long as my boys are here."

I smiled at that. So he needed to mention them since I hadn't acted impressed. Interesting. "I figured they were the wrecking crew."

"They certainly know how to make a mess when one needs making," The Transylvanian grumbled. I ignored it. He was just puffing up his chest feathers.

"What drew you to the place?"

He smiled a little, relit his cigar – it had gone out somewhere along the way – with a cheap lighter from a gas station. "It was a film plant. Do the math."

I shrugged back at him. "Pretend I'm bad at math."

"We're on the third floor," he said after he had the cigar going good. "Eight floors are above us. Those are where the choppers, the rollers and the rest of the lines are. Clarke Industries kept all the heavy equipment up there with film running through them out in the open: total darkness, twenty-four seven. They ran this plant in pitch black for decades. Otherwise, the film gets exposed." He smiled again. "Easy to hide, easy to sleep, easy to wake up, easy not to be seen or remembered or otherwise noticed at all."

I gestured at his crew with one thumb. "And now you've got a few guys to keep an eye on the place at night and in the day. Clever. Must keep you nice and cozy."

He nodded at me in a friendly way. "I haven't been outside since they built the place in the '40s."

I looked mildly surprised. "So what the fuck were you doing out and about on Green River Road in the 1950's?"

He blinked.

I smiled. It was a good smile, with teeth in it.

The Transylvanian worked up a grim little twist at the corners of his mouth and took a drag. I watched him closely. I could see, hear and smell the gears turning in his head. Whether they were gears of memory or gears of lies, I couldn't tell.

"One of my brief forays into the world," he finally said. "There was a new vampire in town. He was hunting for the rest of us. He wasn't Bob; I knew that. There wasn't hardly anybody around in those days. This whole region was a lot less populated than it is now and there were fewer of us around to match. I went out looking, didn't find him. He knew someone was onto him, though. I think he cut his losses and ran or went to ground for the long haul." The Transylvanian shrugged lazily. "Never heard from him since."

I chewed my cheek for a minute. "So you're saying the 'outsider' the locals fingered for a murder out that way – this song chaser guy – was a vamp looking to move into the area, found out he wasn't alone and decided to kill off his moneybag and the rest of the help and high-tail it elsewhere?"

He nodded. "That's how I figure it."

I took a long breath. "How'd he find out you were looking for him?"

"Never knew," The Transylvanian said simply. He lifted both hands as he said it, palms up, flat. "I was a lot younger then, barely eighty. It's easy to make mistakes at that age."

"And if you spend all your time up here in a film plant, why'd you care that he was around? How'd you find out about him in the first place?"

He smiled a little again and said, "He was living out in the world, among people. He attracted attention. People gossiped. Talk is dangerous. That isn't how we work. My maker raised me up right: keep your head down, stay out of people's way, don't let yourself get tied up in their affairs. There are back roads that run from here to there, short cut, over the hills and down into Hardison County. People who worked here heard the stories going around about that kid and his houseguest. It wasn't that hard to figure it out from my perspective. The way I saw it, if he was out carrying on, living in a place where people are, he's asking for trouble. If he'd been under someone's thumb, had a maker to keep an eye on him, something, maybe that would be different. But we can't just let ourselves go out in the world and live there like there's nothing different about us." He smacked his lips a little, taking a puff from the nasty, cheap cigar. It smelled like it had been soaked in fuel from the same gas station where he'd gotten the lighter. "By making people talk he endangered me. He endangered all of us. There's a simple solution to that: get rid of him. Scare him off, talk him down, whatever it takes. I don't know what it would have come to had I caught up to him, but that was my goal: take the bull by the horns and give him a talking to, one vampire to another. I figured he'd be more likely to listen to one of his own than anyone else. It was a vampire problem so a vampire had to take care of it."

"But you didn't take care of it," I said quietly.

"Well, I did, sort of." He shrugged again. "He left, two people turned up dead in a tragic but *never solved* murder. I figure he was probably just going to tap the kid for his cash and bail out anyway, eventually, or something worse."

"Worse?"

The Transylvanian looked at me like a child who'd asked the meaning of a curse word. "Turn the kid, make a vampire out of someone too well-known and try to keep them around. Everybody knows rich people's business. That's why they noticed the kid's new friend in the first place, isn't it?" He laughed a hollow chuckle. "No, him killing off a couple bleeders and getting out of Dodge because the pond wasn't big enough was the best possible outcome."

I nodded noncommittally and then sat in silence for a few moments. "So why protect Cliff?" I gestured vaguely out into the factory somewhere. "What's the angle there?"

The Transylvanian sighed slightly. "If his daddy turned up dead in the same spot, I can only guess that vampire is back. If he's back, he's trying to send a signal: he won't be chased off this time. He's going to eliminate everyone who reminds him of that embarrassing incident from his past, and Cliff deserves better than that. I had an insight into what had happened and told him if he came here and stayed a while he'd be safe. Least I could do. He didn't have any ties to that vampire."

I glanced in the direction Cliff had walked, nodding with my head. "Unfortunately, as long as he's alive he's a suspect in the eyes of the mortal authorities. It doesn't really help us to keep him around, does it?"

Something flickered in the old man's eyes and his smile was gone. I filled the vacuum with a little grin of my own. "Not that we should kill him. I'm just thinking out loud." With that, I stood. "I appreciate your time and your explanation. I've got a lot of rounds to make, though. This area may have been absent any vampires the last time you were out and about but times have changed and I've got a lot of social calls to make in very little time."

The Transylvanian didn't get up or offer to see me out. He just watched me, waiting to see if he could sense the gears in my own head. I didn't say goodbye or good night or good luck, I just walked with Smiles towards the gaping doorway I'd destroyed. The six guys standing there didn't get out of my way until the very last second, and when they did, I smelled that same human scent I'd picked up in Clyde's car the night he was murdered. I didn't flinch, didn't do a thing to show it had registered. I simply grinned real big at all of them – him especially, some young guy wearing a Redskins jersey under a black hooded sweatshirt – and trod heavily down the hall, down the stairs, out across that once-manicured front lawn, back through the gatehouse, out to my car and climbed in. Smiles slid into the back seat, impossibly lithe, and I drove away at a leisurely pace. The whole time all I could think was how much I hated being lied to by anyone, much less a country bumpkin like this Transylvanian pipsqueak, and how I was going to find out why that guy had killed my best friend so that I could explain to him what was going on before I murdered him.

CHAPTER 3

LaVonde had spent two extremely unproductive days at work. A couple of stories had slipped through that would probably generate snippy letters from readers upset at the eternally slipping standards of copy-editing and et cetera, et cetera. She didn't much give a damn. Well, OK, she did give a damn. That's why she'd given people assignments everywhere but Hardison and Transylvania Counties; she wanted that territory to herself for a few days. It wouldn't do, if she was going to look into a story related to yet another story in which she already had a conflict of interest – and there were no two ways about that, she knew that conflict existed and simply could not deny it – to run into one of her own reporters at a gas station in the middle of nowhere, a long way from the office.

The thing that had gotten her so interested was this thing that H'Diane had barely even commented on when she'd prodded her a little over dinner the night before: this mysterious outsider from the case fifty-five years before. She went over the details again: shows up in town, claims to be a song chaser, hooks up with a rich orphan and a completely out-of-place old lady from the next county over, goes out into the woods and the locals turn up dead. The outsider is never seen again. Something about that stuck between her teeth and she'd worried it for hours that night as she remoted into the *Citizen-Times* archives and sat reading story after story, rehash after rehash. She'd spent a while on a geneaology website with the old woman's obituary, sketchy though it had been, open in another tab. Vital records were a closed matter in North Carolina so she couldn't just go look up for herself whether she had any family left. If LaVonde were to locate anyone with a connection to that old woman then it was up to her own research skills and the obsessive-compulsive habits of family historians everywhere. Ah, well; this was why they called it *investigative* journalism, she told herself.

Eventually she'd turned up the existence – at the time of the old woman's death – of a cousin who lived in Asheville. From there she'd gotten that the cousin had a daughter who was getting on into late middle-age but seemed to still be alive. There was an entry in the Google telephone lookup for her, and a street address out in Flat Rock, and tax records for a car in that name. She'd sat there with the phone in her hand the next morning, looking at the number, trying to decide what to do when finally she decided it was now or never. LaVonde just had to hope that this cousin, a Jesse Beth Harvey *nee* Ramsey, would be willing to talk.

East Flat Rock was, once upon a time, farm land and tiny communities of interrelated families. It had morphed over the 20th century into prime retirement real estate. New housing developments went up all over the mountains. The *Citizen-Times* had done a story on water use and erosion and all the other impacts of heavy, sudden development that had managed to piss a lot of people off. She wasn't involved, but she remembered the mix of people the story described: long-time families who saw the land as theirs and viewed themselves as victims of an invasion, versus transplanted retirees who saw the locals as bumpkin mouth-breathers with no objective but a pastoral history that didn't exist.

LaVonde drove through all that, admiring the old forests, the old homes, the bed and breakfast places, the trailer parks, the signs proclaiming the availability of homes *STARTING IN THE LOW $300'S* according to their over-sized text. She clucked her tongue. White people with white houses on a white patch of clear-cut earth. She would never, ever understand.

Five miles past the Carl Sandburg Estate she turned left onto a gravel track with a state sign – bent, rusting metal once painted green – that read MERRY LANE. *I doubt it,* she couldn't help thinking. LaVonde slid her Subaru past a few brick box houses and past a clearing and then at the very end she found an old, white clapboard house in more or less good repair with an ancient screen on the door. There was a newish station wagon of domestic make, fairly small and fairly fuel-efficient, sitting in the driveway. Fresh gravel marked a second place for a car. LaVonde pulled into it, checked her face and hair in the mirror behind the visor, got out and walked up onto the porch.

Jesse Beth Harvey was standing behind the screen, wrapped in an old bathrobe. "Come on in, girl," she said heavily. "Too cold to leave the door hanging wide."

She made their way in and Jesse Beth shut the door behind her. LaVonde noted a house that had clearly been home to generations of one side or another of this family. There were knick-knacks in every corner, immaculately clean, and portraits of Jesse Beth and a dark-skinned, smiling man LaVonde took to be the husband. Jesse Beth had warned LaVonde they would have to talk while he was in town at a job site. They'd have an hour, maybe two. LaVonde would have to leave by three in the afternoon. *He don't know that side of my family*, Jesse Beth had said. Whether that meant they weren't acquainted or that he didn't know something about them, LaVonde had been left wondering. She guessed the latter.

They sat in the kitchen. LaVonde remarked on the spotlessness of it. Jesse Beth eschewed any compliments, saying it was the best she could do, no more, certainly no less. They chatted for a few minutes about LaVonde's work. She showed Jesse Beth the badge she wore to get into the building every morning. Eventually Jesse Beth seemed to relax a little. The instant coffee did something to wake up LaVonde's curiosity and finally she got right down to brass tacks:

"So, it was your aunt who was murdered fifty-five years ago?"

Jesse Beth fell silent, looked at her hands, at the coffee cup in them, then back at LaVonde. "Actually she was my cousin," Jesse Beth drawled. "But my sisters, they were older, they called her 'Aunt Ginny.' She was named Virginia."

"Virginia Ramsey," LaVonde said, and she reached for her notebook.

"I'd rather you didn't write this down," Jesse Beth said softly.

LaVonde had heard that a million times, so she nodded and smiled a little. She didn't need to take notes, her memory was top-notch and she didn't plan on quoting anything Jesse Beth said in any story; she was here purely on her own recognizance. It had merely been a test, and now she knew that it had been the latter before – there was something about her cousin/aunt that Jesse Beth's husband didn't know and Jesse Beth would just as soon keep secret.

"Do you know what she was doing out there?"

Jesse Beth pursed her lips and shook her head. "None of us ever knew. She was a real secretive person. She never told much about what was going on in her own life."

"Do you know if she knew the other victim?" LaVonde started to say the name, then made a little show of checking her notebook for a moment. "Phillip English?"

Jesse Beth shook her head a little and sighed. "I doubt Aunt Ginny knew him. She didn't have much occasion to be around rich people like him."

"What did she do for a living?"

Jesse Beth sought around for a moment. "This and that. Took care of babies. Birthed them for some folks who liked..." Jesse Beth cleared her throat. "People who wanted something more traditional."

"Mid-wifing?"

Jesse Beth nodded and the ghost of a smile appeared at her mouth.

"And you? Do you do any mid-wifing?"

Jesse Beth turned a shade paler, and LaVonde smiled back. "Is it a tradition in your family?"

Jesse Beth looked away. "Kind of."

LaVonde nodded, cleared her throat, sat there in silence for a few moments, then *really* opened with both barrels. "Was Aunt Ginny a witch-woman?"

Jesse Beth arched one eyebrow in stark... something. LaVonde started to classify it as disapproval and after two seconds decided it was more like defense: the startled surprise of a certain kind of Southern lady caught with her hand in the cookie jar. "What makes you ask that?"

LaVonde laced her fingers together in her lap. "Phillip English had been seen in the weeks prior to his death in the company of a guy from out of town, said he was a professor from a college up north somewhere and that he was here as a song-chaser. Are you familiar with them?"

Jesse Beth produced a tiny, guarded smile and nodded. "I had some kin who were recorded, way back, 1930's. Part of the New Deal, they said. They got paid to sing the old songs, some spirituals, that kind of thing." Her nostrils flared briefly. "The reason it was talked about in my family is, see, the fellow recording them wanted them to sing old slave songs and..." She laughed abruptly. "They told him no. Told him no so loud he left town." She smiled again, that same smile she'd had about mid-wifing.

LaVonde smiled back and nodded at her. "Well, here's what that makes me think: if he were legit, he'd have to have someone local to show him around, take him to the sorts of people and places where he could hear those old songs.

By the 1950's, most of them were already faded around here. If he'd gone up to, say, Swain County? Sure, he could stumble around and find some shape-note singers and study them and get a real warm welcome as long as he behaved himself, but here? This far down the mountain you'd need someone who knew the place already. If your Aunt Ginny was a mid-wife or..." LaVonde ran her tongue across her teeth under her lip, smiled again, "What they called a witch-woman, she'd have that knowledge. Lots of people back then still kept a lot of older folk traditions. A woman who could deliver babies, take care of them, maybe..." LaVonde waved a hand vaguely. "Maybe cure warts, an illness here or there, set a bone and rehabilitate them when it knitted?" She pointed the end of the sentence up as a question, trailing off.

"A lot of people still keep those folk ways, Ms. Burke."

LaVonde stopped herself from looking surprised. She just smoothed her features over and said, quite neutrally, "I've heard that, but never had the privilege of meeting any of them myself."

"Privilege?" Jesse Beth looked wary again: defensive in some way.

"Well," and LaVonde paused to let the gears spin. "Those arts are considered long-lost in most places. Seeing someone who still practiced them would be like getting to see a..." She took a sip of coffee. "A rare and beautiful antique that's still going strong."

Jesse Beth sat back a little. "What, like Larry's furrow?"

LaVonde wrinkled her brow. "Furrow?"

Jesse Beth chuckled a little, nodded her head in the direction of the back yard. "Larry's got a garden patch out back. We grow our own corn, beans, tomatoes, potatoes, all the vegetables the store will rob you for. We grew bell peppers one year when they were a dollar a piece at the store. That's good money." LaVonde smiled, still not really following and Jesse Beth chuckled. "Anyway, Larry's got this furrow – it's a big, old, iron furrow, like a little plow. You use it to run a shallow trench through plowed ground. It's good for corn, beans, lots of kinds of plants that go in a straight line from one another. A man can push it by himself. See, once upon a time we were told we'd get a mule, a plow and forty acres. Now, people around here weren't as bad as they could be in other places – this county voted 9 to 1 against secession, you know, and slavery was just about unheard of and there were a few free blacks living out here, in the country places, where no one had to see them and no one could much be bothered to hurt them – so Larry's great-grandad eventually got the furrow but neither the mule nor the forty acres. Larry still uses that same furrow. Parts of the big wheel on it are about worn down to paper, but it still works and he still uses it. You mean like that?"

LaVonde still had a curious expression on her face but nodded. "Yeah. Like that. People kept the folk ways to make the fields produce, to keep the cows healthy, to make the children strong. Seeing that – like Larry's furrow – would be a privilege."

Jesse Beth smiled quietly and then sat all the way back in her chair, drained the last of her coffee. "Witch-women did all that, sure," she said. "But that ain't all. What do you think people did before, say, Roe versus Wade?" Jesse Beth smiled a little less. "What do you think they did when a baby was born the wrong color? What do you think they did when a baby was born the wrong sex?" Jesse Beth clucked her tongue. "A witch-woman didn't just make things grow. Sometimes she made things go away. A lot of time that was real nice work – finding a baby a good home when the mother knew the father would be liable to kill it and her, helping a difficult labor get through, explaining things to a girl who'd just her first time of the month. It wasn't all pretty or wholesome, though, Ms. Burke. Sometimes it was ugly."

"Are you saying your Aunt Ginny was..." LaVonde had no idea how to finish the sentence.

"She fixed problems. That's what witch-women do. If a community is too stubborn or backwards or narrow-minded or full of itself to admit it's got problems, someone has to fix those problems when they happen anyway. You make a lot of friends doing that kind of work."

"Not *all* friends, I'd guess."

"No, not all friends." Jesse Beth smacked her lips, stood up to make another cup of coffee. LaVonde sat in silence as Jesse Beth spooned more Folgers into her cup, took the still-hot kettle and poured water in, stirred, added a little milk from a paper carton.

"Is that soy milk?" LaVonde was more than slightly surprised to see what she thought of as a sure mark of yuppiedom in Jesse Beth's personal Kitchen of the Ages.

Jesse Beth turned around, stirring with the spoon she'd used before, then put the spoon back on its saucer by the stove. "It's good for women of a certain age," she replied demurely. "Keeps us... active."

LaVonde fought back the chortle, cleared her throat, smiled. "Okay. So, back to Aunt Ginny. Would Phillip English have hired her to fix a problem?"

Jesse Beth shrugged a little. "Maybe. But if it was a problem big enough to make him drive all the way out to Pisgah Forest, where nobody would know him, and hire an old black witch-woman who could barely see the end of her own arm anymore, well..." Jesse Beth took a sip of coffee, smiled. "It was a very bad problem."

"Gotten the wrong girl pregnant?"

Jesse Beth made a *pffft* noise of dismissal. "Rich people never lacked for doctors to do their abortions, Ms. Burke."

"So what was it?" LaVonde tried not to sound exasperated, but she was. Jesse Beth was dancing around something, flirting with it, in a way that annoyed LaVonde still even though she'd had a thousand interviews go the same way. That this wasn't for her, she realized abruptly, that it was for H'Diane, is what annoyed her. She wanted to solve this problem. She didn't want the woman she loved wandering around in the dark in the middle of a murder investigation.

"Something old, to go to such an old woman. Something no one saw anymore, or talked about, anyway. Something dangerous. Something that scared him so bad he couldn't tell anyone else but an old woman no one would ever believe." Jesse Beth was staring at the coffee intently. LaVonde glanced over at it and couldn't see anything so special. It was like Jesse Beth was staring at herself in the mirror, or something she'd never noticed until she caught it out of the corner of her eye as she walked by. She seemed to sink into a quiet reverie, and finally, "Yes. Something old and dark. I've thought about that a lot, Ms. Burke, and every time I think on it, that's where I end up. He was scared of something old and terrible and he went to a witch-woman because he thought only a little magic could save him."

LaVonde knew the approaching end of an interview when she heard it. Without any preamble she stood up and started gathering her things together. "I'd better go," she said, clumsy as she gathered her things. "It's been a while. Larry might be back soon."

Jesse Beth looked at the clock – nothing even a little like an hour had passed, they both knew. She stood up, though, cup in her hand, and walked LaVonde to the door.

"Thanks for letting me talk to you about your aunt," LaVonde said from the porch. "Like I said, it's not for a story, it's just for me. Still, I appreciate it."

"You got a personal problem that needs solving, huh?" Jesse Beth smiled kindly. "I know that look when I see it."

"Not me," LaVonde blurted out. "My..." She hesitated. "Partner."

Jesse Beth nodded, took a pull from the mug, smacked her lips again. "It's an old story," Jesse Beth sighed. LaVonde thought she meant the story of the lover in trouble, but Jesse Beth added, "But maybe it'll help you some. Feel free to come by again sometime if you need something. Just make sure to call first."

LaVonde stood there for a moment, nodded, and left. It was that simple. Nothing leapt out at her. Jesse Beth didn't watch ominously from the front door of her home. Nothing. She just drove back out of Flat Rock and through town and then on back to her home, leaving Jesse Beth and her homespun witchcraft in the shadows of an alien hollow curled against the base of an unknown mountain in the opposite end of Creation out of sight of some husband or another. The whole way, she wondered how on earth she could manage to work this information about the old woman murdered so long ago into a conversation with H'Diane.

H'Diane was standing in the field where Clyde's body had been found, staring at the trampled ground, shivering in the wind. The sunlight here was weaker and the winter harder somehow. All the dead, trampled grass had a sharper edge to it and the clouds looked worse. The middle of her murder investigation was not a great time for the drought to lift, to be honest, but everything was a mess already anyway. Her mystery 911 caller had probably been the one who mucked everything up out here and now she had a request from a local paranormal group to "investigate" at the crime scene. She had zero desire to give them access to her crime scene, but she had wanted to spend some time out here just soaking in the details, waiting for inspiration or insight to arrive, and, for reasons she expected would remain opaque to her, the Sheriff had personally asked her to do these "investigators" the favor of granting them a meeting at the scene itself. They probably included the kid of a campaign contributor or something. Sheriffs are usually cops, sure, but they're politicians, too. H'Diane had been warned by LaVonde, when she took this job, never to forget that particular background detail.

She heard a heavy vehicle pull up the drive and then several doors open and close. Great, the whole gang showed up. They probably thought they were going to get to set up shop right here and now. H'Diane took a little pleasure in knowing she would get to burst their bubble.

Four women were eventually visible emerging from the brush and woods that ringed the clearing. Most of them were dressed for a winter stroll but one was dressed in something closer to adventuring gear: beige cargo pants with loaded pockets, work gloves and a puffy parka in high-visibility yellow. She had dark hair and the outfit managed to blend the notions of desert fatigues and utility worker. She carried herself with a confidence one step above the others and then some. While the others fanned out, she directly approached. The woman had a card in her hand before she reached H'Diane and held it out, her driver's license in the other. "Detective Bing?"

"Yes." H'Diane took the card and read it: North Carolina Para-Science. *Gobbledygook.* "I'm the lead investigator on this case. I understand you'd like access to the crime scene. I'm afraid I can't allow that. I appreciate your desire to see the case resolved," and here she looked back up to meet the woman's eyes before giving a very faint smile. "I'm sure that's your interest, and not something more... sensational." She smacked her lips with distaste after saying it. "Still, I can't allow disruption of this location. This is still an active investigation. I'm afraid I can't permit you to have access to it."

The woman looked around. "And yet, here we are."

H'Diane smirked a little. "I was asked to meet you here. I see it as extending the courtesy of showing you there's nothing screwy going on and to demonstrate that a large portion of the field has been roped off with police tape. I wanted you to see for yourself that we aren't allowing anyone in; that this isn't just about you."

The woman nodded and shrugged a little. "Fair enough," she said. "What about when the investigation is over? This won't be a crime scene forever."

H'Diane nodded. "True. After we're gone it's up to the property owner. Any deal you work out with them is just that: between you and them."

"I'm not trying to rush you by asking, but do you know when you'll be through here? A general time frame, or whether it will be days or weeks, anything like that?"

"Days," H'Diane said. By this point, the trail was cold. She'd be lucky if they ever found another piece of evidence in the course of her career and that sat hard with her. She had not been ready to lose her first real case but it had slipped through her fingers before she'd even known it was happening: that call to 911, the mucked up footprints, the house in a tiny neighborhood in the middle of nowhere. "I'd expect us to be done in a few days."

The woman nodded. "Thanks. I – " She stopped and sighed and her features softened a little. "You're right. We just want to help in our own way. I don't want to get in the way of the cops. You're doing your job and you're the professional here, but on the chance our methods might turn up anything of use to you, anything at all, I want to make sure we get a chance to try."

"What exactly are those methods?" H'Diane tried to sound exactly and merely polite when she asked. No reason to insult a friend of the Sheriff but no reason to encourage them, either.

"Well, Janine over there is a sensitive." The woman made air quotes as she said it and H'Diane knew the look of disbelief when she saw it. "Marilyn does dowsing and talks to the media because she's older and looks like everyone's grandmother." The woman shrugged at H'Diane and smiled. H'Diane was surprised by the honesty. "Sue handles our finances and general gofering and I do tech."

"And your name is?"

"Jennifer McCordy."

CHAPTER 4

Two nights later, Roderick and I sat out on my back porch around 3:00 AM. After my run-in with The Transylvanian, I'd mostly needed to think, so I just drove around for the night. I stopped in little country gas stations where, in the age of credit card readers, they can all go home at a reasonable hour and leave the pumps on to keep skimming off the night owls. The next evening, I sat around playing Solitaire and failing to watch some show on television about hot criminals. I find it amusing to watch television throw a little tea party about sanitized deprivation. A show about actual vampires would get cancelled halfway through the first episode because it would be too gruesome and too dull for them to stomach: far more so than their "reality" television. People are too accustomed to everything being filtered and screened and edited, even the "real" things. Everything gets dressed up to look good for the cameras. They want to see some under-educated schlubs screw around and then talk shit behind each other's backs, not literal backstabbings. Humanity likes to flirt with the darkness but it doesn't want to put out.

Roderick pulled up around midnight. He was dressed in flannel and an old pair of cargo pants and hiking boots. I asked him where he'd been hiking and he smiled. "Asheville is full of backpacking types. I'm just blending in, cousin." His long, pale hair was a little less stringy and a little better kempt and I wondered if maybe this trip was doing him some good. He snickered at the television show in a way I recognized from my own private reactions to it. I clicked off the set and we went out on the back porch. He sat an old wicker chair and I told him all about the outsider, The Transylvanian, his little brood of helpers, Cliff, all that. He listened with that weird little half-smile he has and then we sat in silence for an hour or so.

That's something vampires get very good at: just letting time pass, doing nothing much.

The back yard was in bad need of a mow. The guy I'd been sending PayPal to every month hadn't been out in October, figuring it would be so cold and so dry that it wouldn't need much. Weeds, though, don't pay much attention to the weather. I'd have to send him an email and ask him to get over here sometime after I left. There wasn't much of a yard: mostly trees and woods and then forest. I could see the lights of a couple other houses, off through the trees, way off, but I doubted they noticed me. I tend to keep the place fairly dark when I'm around. I sat and listened to a little critter of some sort rustle around in the grass and the leaves. Might have been a squirrel, might have been a chipmunk, might have been a mouse. There was an owl in a tree somewhere about fifty yards off. It hooted every now and then and I wondered when it would make its way over for its meal.

Finally Roderick said, very softly, "It seems to me like there's one very obvious explanation."

I turned towards him, surprised my neck didn't creak like an old door hinge when I did it. I nodded, watching him light a cigarette. His eyes were kind of glassy, kind of dreamy. He was staring at absolutely nothing and it amused him somehow.

"The Transylvanian is going to turn Cliff. Soon, I would imagine. Otherwise, why kill off the family?" Roderick shrugged. "He sounds like the old-fashioned type, anyway and he's obviously fond of having a brood of loyal followers around. But that doesn't explain the deal with the English and Ramsey murders. I can come up with some way in which he sees killing Clyde and taking the son as his own to be tying up the loose ends of that killing but it doesn't explain why he killed them in the first place or why he particularly cared that Clyde investigated that murder for the FBI."

"SBI," I corrected quietly. "State."

Roderick fluttered a few fingers, still staring at that amusing nothing. "Whatever. So why does The Transylvanian – wicked name – why does he care so much?"

I shrugged and continued to sit back in my big, round, padded papasan chair.

"And what about that charm?" Roderick's voice was so low it was nearly a whisper and his eyes widened a little at the mention of it. "What a fascinating little detail. I wonder if Cliff took it?"

"He wasn't wearing it when I saw him." I tried to figure out what Roderick was staring at, maybe something I'd missed, maybe a seam in the screen mesh that enveloped the porch on its three exterior sides. I couldn't find anything to look at, myself.

"Maybe under his shirt?"

I shook my head. "Maybe so. I don't know."

He smiled at me without looking at me, a wicked little twist of his mouth. "I would love," he finally said, "To meet the other vampires in the area."

I snorted at him. "Why's that?"

"Well, Bob didn't have The Transylvanian in his notes, right?"

I nodded. Roderick still wasn't looking at me but he seemed to notice it, as he responded after:

"So the Bobs Regime didn't know about him but The Transylvanian did know about the Bobs, right? He said he knew this outsider wasn't Bob. So he knew a vampire who was known to the Bobs, or some chain of vampires to connect them, but Bob never found him *and none of them told Bob about The Transylvanian.*"

I blinked, and reached up to scratch my scraggly goatee and stubble. I hadn't shaved tonight, just stayed in and looked scruffy. Vampires get locked in whatever state we were in when we were turned. Forever. I have to shave every night if I want to look decent because I didn't shave *that* night: the night I was turned. There were all kinds of things Agatha had told me to do and that I didn't, but she had told me explicitly to have some stubble. That way, if beards took over as the style, I could say I was just regrowing mine and, if being clean-shaven became expected instead, I could shave in a minute every night and fit right in. Agatha's smart. She's been at this for a while. That says a lot about her, not much of it good. For his part, Roderick wakes up every night with a split nose and bruises on his wrists from a pair of police handcuffs. He heals fast – we're talking seconds here – but he has them again the next night, like clockwork. It makes me grateful all I have to do is shave. No electric shaver can take down a vampire's beard, I have to use an old blade and put some weight behind it, but if that's as bad as it'll ever get then that's just fine by me.

"You know," I said, "You've got a point there."

Roderick went on. "So he's being hidden by others in the area. There's no way the brood he showed off at the film plant are all the cards he's holding. He probably has some all over the area. If he wants lookouts at the plant, that's one thing. If he's finding out about what goes on out in the world, too, why wouldn't he plant a few eyes and ears there, too? It just stands to reason. But he didn't bring them up or brag about them, so those are the ones he wants to keep hidden from you. He wants to intimidate you and keep you in the dark. Doesn't exactly sound like he's just minding his own business."

I struggled with several emotions, none of them good. I'd been so focused on Clyde and Cliff and The Transylvanian's connection to them that I hadn't stopped to think through the implications of what he'd shown me when I was there: this pack of humans and vampires he's got running up and down the place on command. "And that's another good point."

He finally turned and looked at me. One eye was slightly more dilated than the other, something I've seen him do when he's about to become unpredictable. "Does that mean I get to go?"

"No," I said, too fast. He started to twist up the corners of his mouth again in that wicked smile and I followed quickly on my own heels. "This is the first time I've been back since I came around to introduce myself right after I took Bob down. If I show up with a bunch of muscle, it'll look like I'm already in need of protection, already on the ropes. I want to finish cementing a sense of authority and control."

The truth was that I didn't fully trust Roderick with information about who all the other vampires were in the area. He wouldn't have scared a twelve year old with that bird chest and those spindly arms, but I was hoping to flatter him. Really I wanted to put him off treating this as a game. Roderick tends to break a few pieces when he plays a game. This – The Transylvanian, the mountains, all this Last Gasp bullshit – was not a game. It was my life. My unlife. Whatever. I had one hand up in a placating gesture, palm flat, facing towards him, fingers together and pointing up. Roderick smiled slightly more widely in a way that made the vampire core get twisted up in a reaction I didn't wholly understand. I grimaced a little. "Seriously, no. This is my turf. Do me the favor of respecting my wishes."

"Your... *authority?*" Roderick's smile turned into a full, slow grin.

I frowned at him and huffed. "Don't be ridiculous. I'm not going to play that sort of stupid game with my own kin."

Roderick laughed sharp and high and fast. "I'm kidding, Cousin Withrow." He put both hands up. "I promise not to do anything you wouldn't do."

I frowned again. "No cryptic half-meanings," I growled.

He laughed again, clapped his hands together twice in sheer delight. "OK! OK." He laughed more. "I promise not to take anything upon myself that disrespects your..." He licked his lips, opened his mouth as if to start with a vowel, namely *au*, then closed his mouth for a moment, breathed again and said, "Wishes."

I hrmphed at him.

He held out one finger. "Pinky swear."

Sometimes you just have to go with the flow, meet someone where they are rather than where you want them to be. Reluctantly I held out my own hand and our little fingers clasped one another, cool as marble in the night air. "Pinky swear," I said. He smiled at me, batted his absurdly long eyelashes and then started staring at his pinky finger in silence.

We were silent for a long time, undisturbed even by the sound of breathing except for Smiles' heavy, dozing snores, then I looked away from the little electronic Sudoku thing I'd bought out of a gas station's dollar bin. It wasn't backlit but I could, of course, read it in the dark. Roderick was still staring at his pinky finger, still holding it crooked exactly as before, with the dead butt of a cigarette in the corner of his mouth. I drew a breath that sounded like sandpaper. "Any new ideas for your product endorsements?"

The lights went back on in Roderick's eyes, like a golem whose magic word has been inscribed for the first time. "Waverly home appliances," he said without hesitation. "Preferably the washer and dryers. Did you know they make an all-in-one? It's a front-loading washer that then becomes a dryer when it finishes a load." A long, slow smile spread out across his lips and the cigarette butt tumbled unnoticed to the floor of the deck. He was still looking at something I couldn't see, but at least now I could see him looking.

"You've seriously spent time thinking about this, haven't you?" I smiled at him. "What's your selling point for the washer-dryer business? Why vampires as spokespersons?"

He scoffed, brow knit, eyes wide. "Really, cousin? Blood, obviously. 'When I need an alibi, I say Waverly Wash & Dry!'" He sang it like a '60s advertising jingle, voice high. "It has a ring to it, right? Who could resist their brat screaming that at them in the White Goods aisle of a Sears & Roebuck?"

I chuckled a little, but that was a relic of the time when I thought he was just joking. "I don't know how to break it to you," I said, "But Pedro Almodovar already had your idea. It's in *Women on the Verge of a Nervous Breakdown*. Late '80s, early '90s? Sometime in there. I watched it on tape."

Roderick's face fell a little and he said, "Damn, you've seen that, too? How many people have seen that? Has everyone seen that?"

I could see a pout coming on so I waved it off. "I'm sure no one else remembers." He smiled and I laughed again, but only half-hearted. "You're, um, you're not thinking about trying to go, you know… " I cleared my throat. "…Public."

Roderick turned now to look at me again – finally. "Of course not, don't be absurd. The world that will accept us is a very different one from this." He waved a hand at life in general, out there somewhere, vague and all-encompassing. I didn't dare to suppose what he meant, but he let me know on his own. "This world is way too at odds with its own inherent injustices. It thinks it can solve its problems by people being nicer to one another. It hasn't yet realized that one day the nice people will simply have to make the not-nice ones stop." He paused. "It will be a world that's okay with us outing ourselves as manipulators and attackers and killers because it has made peace with that part of its own human nature. They're going to have to accept all the humans they don't like before they can accept all the people like us who simply used to be. They'll have to be ready to accept that we aren't just monsters in opera capes. We're humans who've been given fangs."

Another hour passed in total silence. Smiles would move around in his sleep or paddle his feet a little while he chased something in his dreams. He moved from Roderick's side to mine and back again while owls hunted in the silence around us. Occasionally I would hear a heat pump kick on at some house nearby, fighting back against the insistence of a November night in the mountains. Roderick continued to stare off into nothing, smoking a long chain of cigarettes, sometimes lighting the new one off the dying embers of the last. I fiddled with the puzzles from time to time but mostly we waited for the other to say something in particular. I marveled at the experience, to be honest. Humans are always eager to have something to prattle about no matter how stupid it makes them sound. Vampires usually don't like to be around one another for long. We have something like a community, sure, with a set of semi-official rules of behavior and some social niceties we at least try to look like we observe, but we don't exactly throw a lot of bat mitzvahs. We mostly do enough socializing to figure out who's the local boss and how to stay off their radar and then we go back to living our own lives while paperwork piles up for the fake ones.

My visit to Roderick in Seattle had been a shock to the system. It turned out vampires don't work that way in the Pacific Northwest. They aren't quite the Brady Bunch but there is a strong social element to their iteration of the culture of attempted immortality. It's a long story, but my visit occurred during something of a crisis they were having Roderick was involved, and I had the opportunity to meet a lot of vampires by my standards: half a dozen or more in just a couple of weeks. They weren't all friends or even polite but their boss – Emily – she seemed to take a genuine interest in their affairs. I don't know if I would say she was concerned with their wellbeing – what's wellbeing to one of us? – but she gave a damn. She promised she'd keep an eye on Roderick for me. I hadn't even known he was a vampire until then. Agatha told me I should go out there and kill him, but I've already covered how she feels about having a mortal relative become an undead colleague. I considered it, to be honest, but seeing how they operated changed a lot of how I viewed my place in the world. I had just killed off Bob Three to liberate myself, to make myself the local boss so people would stop fucking bothering me, and there I was with a whole new passel of binding complications. I'm not always thrilled about that, but I turned out to resent having a cousin around a lot less than I'd thought I would. Now here we were, silent, together, on the same side. I still didn't completely understand why he had picked now, and here in Asheville rather than home in Raleigh, to visit me: not like it was so unbelievable that he would repay the compliment of a visit but rather because my gut just told me there was something going on. My gut is always telling me that, though. In some ways, opting to enjoy Roderick's company rather than overanalyze his motives was me choosing to try – just once – telling that suspicious little voice in the back of my head to go fuck itself in hell.

"What did she tell you to make you say yes?" Roderick's voice was soft and a little dreamy but his eyes seemed to be focused off in the yard. I supposed he'd spotted the owl. It sounded like it was nearby. One of the bits of vampire folklore that gets passed around is the notion that birds of prey are drawn to us because they can sense the presence of a successful predator who isn't direct competition. Places where we are, the reasoning goes, must be places where it's safe for a creature to hunt.

I took my time responding. I knew exactly what he meant and I knew the answer but I didn't know if it would sound stupid. I didn't know why he wanted to know, either, though I supposed it was simple curiosity. A man with no legs wonders what it would be like to walk again; an orphan vampire who claims never to have known his maker – not able even to remember or describe them – wonders what it would be like to have a choice. "It wasn't just one thing," I finally murmured. My voice was tight. I'd never talked about this with anyone. No vampire had ever offered me her own reasons, either. I didn't even know whether having been offered a choice by Agatha was unusual or was standard operating procedure. I wondered if Roderick's question meant most of us do get that choice. I wondered if that's how it worked in Seattle. I wondered if he simply assumed that everyone else gets a choice but he didn't because he knew he was a weirdo. "She asked me if I wanted all the time I could want to practice my art. That was the thing that got my interest at first."

"That's a pretty good carrot," Roderick said. He smiled a little, but it wavered. This question was important to him. He couldn't cover over it with the spackle of careless flippancy.

I smirked back at him when his deep green pupils shot over at me in the corners of his eyes. "Yeah, you could say that," I said. "But the other thing she said was that it would make being alone forever into a virtue." My voice stopped all of a sudden. I couldn't imagine myself saying that to any vampire in Raleigh. Seth – this sullen "kid" with a build like a running back who looked like an

'80s punk band and talked about as much as two mimes – was my second in command there, the closest thing a boss gets to have to a work buddy. I certainly trusted him to keep an eye on things downtown and tell me about any new vampires who rolled into his particular view, but I was never going to have a sleepover rap session with him. I gulped hard. I didn't have the capacity to get out more words all of a sudden. I don't even know what I would have said, anyway.

"That's an even better one." Roderick didn't smile. He didn't look over. He kept gazing out at the owl or the woods in general or maybe simply the night itself. I read a thing on the Internet one time, a blog post in which a vampire talked about the night as being like a great work of art: no matter how long or often we study it, we find something new waiting for us there. That's one thing about the modern era: young vampires use the Internet like crazy. We're going to have a whole different culture in fifty years and ones like Agatha are going to have a hell of a time understanding it. Maybe Roderick was right. Maybe one day we'd be getting endorsement deals; or maybe the old ones like Agatha – like The Transylvanian – would swoop down from their mountaintop castles, their ruined estates, their penthouse suites rented under another name and kill all the Rodericks and the Marty Macintoshes. I wondered if Roderick would drag me kicking and screaming into that future with any success – so far he had – and I hoped so because I wanted to be on their side if I had to be on any side at all. "What was the stick?"

"The stick?" My voice gurgled up through a crack in my reverie. "There wasn't one." I laughed, a single chuckle. It made me think of Mary Lou Reinhart and her short, sharp bark of a laugh when she mocked one fool notion or another. "She didn't need one. I was interested in having eternity to paint, sure. I love painting. I love making something and wondering if this is the one that'll be truly eternal. I love to think something of mine could wind up on the wall of the Met or the Louvre or, I don't know, anywhere could be pretty cool: the wall of a good coffee shop, the side of a rental truck, a postage stamp. The walls of rich people's houses pay pretty well, sure, but to put brush to canvas and create something completely new and have someone else want that idea in their lives? That was fantastic."

"But it wasn't enough." Roderick had slung his legs over the arm of his chair and now he twisted around in it to look at me.

"No," I said. I couldn't look back at him. I couldn't meet those orphan eyes. "So she went for the gut shot. She got me with the promise I could be by myself, too, and be praised for it. That was something new. That was something different. Lots of people become famous or respected or successful painters. Not a lot of them do it in their own lifetimes, sure, but it happens. I felt like I could just gamble on being one of them if I really had to. Back then, though, there was so much…" I flexed my fingers and closed my hand on nothing. "Social pressure. The war was over and Our Boys were home and I hadn't been one of them – thank Christ – and there was all this rah-rah home team bullshit in the air. I don't mean about the war, I'm as glad as anybody we beat the Nazis, sure, but I mean about everything else. Everyone just wanted life to go back to normal, emphasis on "normal". Square pegs didn't get a lot of love. Tribal identity was big. Conformity was big. We were ramping up for the Red Scare. It was the era that gave us McCarthy, you know. I'd hear talk about San Francisco and New York and San Diego and anywhere else lots of soldiers had settled when they got back from the war: of gay bars and handsome sailors dancing in the half-light, all scared to death someone had seen them walk in and twice as scared someone would see them walk out together. I knew I wouldn't strike gold with some G.I. Joe in polished shoes and a jaw that could cut cold butter, though. There I was, fat and gay and angry at a world that valued baseball over Art degrees, estranged from my family, living in an apartment over an appliance store, waiting for the world to change. Along comes someone who listens and pats me on the shoulder and doesn't use a Bible to do so, and she tells me there's a community where I'll fit right in because I don't have to talk to anybody if I don't want to? She was describing a life I didn't know was possible. She changed the world for me, just like I'd been waiting to happen. I said yes, then. She made me think about it for a while, an insanely long six months, and she rode my ass to lose some weight or get a haircut or something but I didn't care about any of that. I just wanted her to open that door into whatever secret world she offered me so I could disappear from this one." I put a hand over my mouth for a moment to make myself stop talking.

Roderick watched me the whole time, unblinking, and when I was done and enough time had passed for him to be sure I was all talked out, he twisted back around into his lounging slacker position. "Thank you, cousin." That's all he said before we were silent again for a long time.

I went back to my Sudoku and slotted numbers into their places, working my way up in complexity until Roderick left two hours later. I didn't see him out, I just nodded and he went out the screen door on the porch. Smiles licked his hand and swept past him to come lay down next to me; he'd been napping by Roderick for a while, something I genuinely took as a sign of Roderick being okay in the end. I heard Roderick's rental rocket start up with a high whine and drive away. I went to bed early and lay there for forty five minutes waiting for the sun to come up. Vampires don't sleep, not real sleep. The day sleep isn't like nodding off; it's death. It's turning into a corpse while the sun lights the sky. That's mighty mystic, if you ask me, but there's no two ways about it and there's no pseudoscience in the world to explain it away. The sun came up, my eyes slammed shut and when I opened them again it was the next night, shortly before six in the evening.

The newspaper said the cops were still looking for Cliff. One deputy had said he might be armed and dangerous but the detective working the case, some asian lady with a funny little H' in her name that I knew meant she was of Hmong descent – they'd supported the US during the Vietnam War, and a ton of them were settled in North Carolina after – she'd said he was simply a person of interest and that if he was seen by anyone they should call 911. "He might be wounded, sick or in danger," she said. "We want to help him however we can." She was certain she would never see him again, or not alive, anyway. I could tell that from the way she spoke about him. "He might need our help, but that's our job. Certainly no one should try to be a vigilante or a hero." She knew these people pretty well to say that. She knew there would be people out there who would shoot first and ask questions later.

I folded up the newspaper, watched Smiles finish his bowl of chow and then clicked my cheeks to get his attention so I could load him into the car and go pay some calls.

CHAPTER 5

The funny thing is, in all of Western North Carolina – everywhere west of Hickory, to be honest – I had two vampires left on my list. Bob had known of three vampires in this entire third of the state. Well, not a third. More like a quarter. Down East is pretty big territory. Still, this wasn't exactly one neighborhood or one city and all I had were a vampire in Black Mountain and a vampire in Waynesville. I couldn't believe there weren't any vampires in Asheville itself. It's a city with a population in six figures. That basically begs for at least one vampire in it, maybe a couple of vampires and their well-trained spawn still learning the ropes. It was just big enough for the occasional slip-up without attracting much attention. I simply refused to believe there weren't any vampires there. If the vampires here were hiding The Transylvanian from Bob, it occurred to me, from whom might Bob Three have hidden vampires *he* knew about, but no one else? For that matter, given he'd come from a long line of Bobs, maybe his maker had hidden one from *him*. Or farther back that that, maybe. Maybe there was some ancient old vampire in the middle of town who was so good at hiding and so terrified of the modern world that no one knew he existed at all. Hell, he could live in the sewers if he needed to. Plenty of rats and other things down there to feed on when push comes to shove.

I shuddered a little and Smiles picked up on the apprehension in my thoughts when I did so, whining briefly and then sticking his head up against the glass of the window on his side, watching out the side of the car.

Waynesville was slightly closer and so that's where I went first. The vampire on my list was one I hadn't managed to track down last time, no more than to leave her a message on her answering machine and, when I got back to Raleigh later, find one from her on mine in return. So, she'd been alive as of then. Just not very talkative. That's fine, I don't want them as friends, I want them to know I'm in charge. This time I'd done a little more leg-work ahead of time, though, and I had tracked down from Bob's other diaries that she worked in a rest home in Waynesville.

A rest home. How perfect. Tons of people laying around waiting to die and they get replaced all the time. She probably pulled down just enough money working the night shift, with a shift differential, to get by in almost total anonymity. I shuddered again. If someone had walked up and described that to me and asked my opinion I'd chuckle and say she sounded like the perfect vampire – quiet, unobtrusive, surrounded by no one who would remember her – but arriving there on my own somehow made it horrible. It was impossible to avoid imagining myself in the same life and that made me think one more sunrise might sound like a good idea.

I pulled off the highway and drove through Waynesville – a one-horse town to beat the band, just a small Main Street strip and some houses perched on the sides of steep slopes and back roads – and eventually found the improbably named Shady Spot Assisted Living Estate. That was an ambitious and corny name, all at once, and I shook my head. Sometimes, I think, the universe needs a better editor. The place itself was an aging brick building, one story, tiny windows spaced evenly down its side with individual air conditioning units in each one to crowd out any light that might manage to get in. The yard was neatly kept and there were some benches and an abandoned croquet set outside. It looked weathered and forgotten. I doubted seriously that anyone in a joint like this was up for a game of croquet of an afternoon.

It was the tail end of visiting hours by now – nearly half past eight when I got there and the sign said *Guests Welcome From 8:00 A.M. To 9:00 P.M.* I didn't hurry, though. A place like this, some hole in the wall where people are sent when their families are too exhausted or strapped for cash, wasn't going to have a lot of staff or a lot of give-a-damn left.

I opened the white, wooden, heavy door in silence, stepped inside and stood there sniffing the air for a few seconds. I wrinkled my nose up hard; I could smell death, slow death, agonizing death. Some of them had started to decay around the edges and they weren't all the way dead yet. How she managed to work here was a question I couldn't imagine answering on my own. Maybe she got used to it. Maybe she thought it smelled good. I cringed. I'd left Smiles in the car and all of a sudden I wished I'd brought him inside.

A great big Doberman might stand out in someone's memory, though, even one of the ones here, but now that I was inside I felt confident none of them would have a clue what was going on. I walked back outside, half-jogged across the parking lot and opened the passenger door. Smiles slid out and onto the pavement, sniffed the air and didn't like it.

Together we went back inside and he growled once, deep and low and long, before I shushed him. I steeled myself and sifted the smells until I caught that scent of vampire – clean, coppery smell, sharp as a knife – and I followed it down to a room at the end of the hall. There was a small sign on the wall with an arrow pointing that way that read QUIET WARD so I kept going at half-pace. As we passed each room, every door half-open, I saw people in what were clearly their last weeks, maybe days, maybe hours. Finally my nose led me to one room in particular and I stood in the opening, hands in my pockets. Smiles seemed to know there was nothing in this place as dangerous as the vampire he could also smell. He didn't turn to watch my back; he pushed aside to stand guard in front of me.

Carla Van Buren looked to be fifty-ish. She had hair that was mostly gray but I could also see some of the thick, dark brown it had been at some point in the past. She was tall and dumpy and looked very Nordic in terms of her frame. I figured she'd come by the name honestly. For all I knew, she was an original immigrant. I didn't have any idea how old she was.

She was folding sheets in one corner of this particular patient's room. The woman was as pale as one of those sheets and Carla was watching her with the intent gaze of a predator sizing up the prey. I wondered whether she'd fed from this woman and left her looking like that or whether she was mulling over feeding from her and finishing her off. I didn't see a lot in her harsh expression that made room for anything else. She had to have seen us, had probably smelled me before I'd gotten there, but she didn't look over. She just kept folding until the sheet was sharp enough to slice through a two by four plank and then set it aside.

"She isn't going to make it through the night," she sighed. Her voice was very soft, out of place in a body that big. It sounded like a much nicer person was being held prisoner inside. "I've called her family. I don't think they give a damn. She owns about two hundred acres a few miles that way." Carla pointed with a thumb to one side. "One of the day nurses, she told me the other night when I came in for my shift that the family had a team of surveyors out there last month. They can't wait to see her go." Carla nodded at the old woman. "They just want to sell to a developer and forget she existed."

I looked around. The room was tiny, neat but crumbling, like it seemed everything here had gotten to be in the last fifty years. "They must need the money."

Carla smirked at me and started folding another sheet. "So, I take it you're Withrow?"

I nodded at her, leaned my frame against the door jam. "I got your message last year. Thought I'd pay a visit while I'm in town."

"Thought you'd make sure I'm not shacked up with the mayor and the chief of police with a finger in every pie, you mean."

I shrugged at her, nonchalant. "Maybe," I said.

"Don't worry," she finally said with another heavy sigh. "I keep to myself."

I nodded at her, looked down at the floor, kicked the heel of one boot against the toe of the other. "That's all I need to know," I replied. "Just want to make sure everyone knows I keep an eye out and an ear to the ground even though I'm in Raleigh. If you have trouble, I'll help if I can. If you make trouble, I'll end it."

She fluttered her lips in a half laugh, half scoff sort of way. "Big bad city vampire come to tell me what to do?" She looked me up and down. "You couldn't find me in these parts if I didn't want you to. I don't need to be talked to like a kid, neither. I bet you were knee-high when I was tits-deep my Last Gasp."

I smiled a little, shrugged again, inspected a fingernail. "Maybe, maybe not."

"Maybe not," she said, and her eyes narrowed a little. "So how long are you going to be around?"

"A few days," I said casually. "Just got a couple more calls to make on folks, figured I'd spend a few days re-familiarizing myself with the area, then head back to Raleigh." I snapped my fingers – Smiles neither jumped nor spun nor looked away from Carla – and dug in my pocket, pulling out a little notebook. I flipped to a shopping list. I mimed reading the words there, or consulting them. The page read: light bulbs, fabric softener, dark fabric detergent, vacuum cleaner bags, rawhide treats. What I said was, "By the way, there's one vampire around whose number I couldn't find in Bob's stuff after I killed him, and for that matter I couldn't find a name, either. Somebody down in Asheville? Sounded old from Bob's notes but that's about all I've got."

Her eyes stayed narrow. "Could be anybody," she said.

I chuckled and scratched my right cheek. "Could be. Didn't get a chance to ask Bob himself, what with his being a puddle by the time I was done taking over. He might have had more notes but I torched his place in a fit of pique." I smiled benignly. "Anything you can tell me would of course be appreciated."

Carla went back to folding her sheet more intently, snapped it into place with quick hands, picked up another, stared at the dying woman in the bed. "Charles. Chucky, they call him. I hear he likes the bars in Asheville." She sneered a little. "City vampires."

I smiled politely. "Of course. I should've thought of that myself. What's he look like?"

She laughed. "I don't know. Haven't seen him. He could be anybody."

I raised both eyebrows. "Not much of one for social calls, eh?"

She snapped that sheet together and into place, too, and put her fists in her armpits, arms crossed. "No," she said. "That's not how I think we ought to work. We live our lives in isolation. We don't make trouble. We pick a people and we stick with them, blend into them. Is that against the rules now?"

I laughed quietly and put up both hands. "No," I said. "Not at all. I think exactly the same way. I also don't like to tell people what to do. I like to be left alone and I like to leave others alone. That's why Bob Three isn't here and I am."

A quiet buzzing came from somewhere in Carla's pockets and she pulled out a little pager thing and looked at the tiny screen. She pressed a button so that it went silent. "Mr. Wilson in 203 needs something."

I nodded and started to step out of the doorway to let her through but she moved to the old woman in the bed rather than towards the door. Smiles hadn't followed with me: he'd read her body language before I did. I arched an eyebrow and she looked cross. "A little privacy?"

I made a small O with my mouth and turned my back. Smiles was less polite but she didn't seem to care. I could hear, just at the edge of even my ears, the slicing of skin, suckling, then silence. I could hear the old woman die in her sleep. To be honest, it was a pretty peaceful way to go. It doesn't feel good to have someone bite open your neck and drain your blood, but if they do it on your right side you don't live long enough to feel much of anything: the brain starts to starve almost immediately. A vampire who wants his prey to live has to bite on their left so the brain keeps getting blood while the victims gasp and flail and bleed.

I could hear Carla lick the wound closed – the only reason any of us are still a secret at all is that our saliva makes it heal quick – and stand up and straighten her dress. When I turned back around she was using the old lady's mirror to check that there wasn't blood anywhere on her uniform. She looked back at me and I could smell... something. It smelled like lightning.

I had never seen a vampire use their Last Gasp abilities. I'd heard crazy bragging stories but the rarity of fact mixed in with all the self-aggrandizing, bullshit fiction made it impossible to know if I'd ever seen it really happen. I wasn't even sure I believed the stories. I'd made it just fine without anything other than the hoodoo and the way the blood made my body supremely more able than that of any mortal man, no matter how fit and regardless of how I looked. The stories, though, said that when we drain the life out of a creature, actually take their life from them by drinking, we consume something special. I can't say if it's the soul, exactly, or an essence or what: some metaphysical whatsit left over from the person's living blood leaving their living body to sustain us. I don't know any of that shit. I don't think about it much. The point is, supposedly when we've had our Last Gasp and we do kill someone by draining them – and the smart ones among us don't do that very often at all – we can do something unquestionably supernatural. It's different for all of us. If a vampire is very carefully raised up, so that they never kill, they never find out what that is. Their makers, if they're real careful, don't tell them it exists because then the kids would just want to do it as soon as possible to find out their super-secret power. Sometimes it's something useless; sometimes it's the ability to read minds; sometimes it's downright scary and magical. Like I said, unique for every one of us and no way to tell until we try it and see what manifests itself in our personal arsenal of abilities. I imagine there are vampires out there whose power is so obscure or useless or whatever that they never do find out what it is, no matter how many people they kill, because they don't have any reason to *try* boiling a kettle of water with their mind or turning everything in sight bright blue on command. Others, of course, milk it for everything it's worth. Agatha can live, complete with heartbeat and a need to breathe and an appetite for real food, until the next sunrise. I only know that because she did it once to fool a doctor for a life insurance exam when she was getting ready to dispose of one of her paper identities and she wanted it to turn a profit. She's embarrassed by it. She's ashamed that it's even possible for her to live as a human again. On the other hand, lots of us learn to manipulate our bodies in interesting ways. I'd wondered plenty of times if she was just yanking my chain to gain some upper hand psychologically: to say, look what I can do that you can't. After all, she's the one who taught me how to eat again and there was nothing special about that but all the practice it had taken.

Until Clyde's death, I'd never had the possibility of learning what mine would be, assuming I had one. I'd wondered, plenty of times. Maybe I would be able to turn everything real dark, just drown all the light in a place so that it's pitch black and I'm the only thing that can see. That could be plenty cool, and I'd always seemed to see the lights flicker when I felt my emotions pulse in some way; on the other hand, it's so obviously unnatural that I don't see it would be much of an advantage when it comes to hunting and such. If it turned out I could turn invisible then I'd have use for it, of course, but that would mean killing people and I can't quite bring myself to think it's OK to murder someone just to take a joy ride.

Carla was starting to sell me on the idea this Secret Vampire Power stuff was for real, though. She'd just taken that woman's life and the air all around her smelled like lightning fixing to strike. I blinked at her and she looked back at me in the mirror and smiled a little, mysterious, secretive. Her pocket buzzed again and she mashed whatever button made the pager go silent without even taking it out of her pocket. "Don't worry, Mr. Wilson," she said to the air, "I'm coming, I'm coming." She swept past Smiles and down the hall towards the other end of the building. We followed her. I was too curious to contain myself or act polite anymore and she hadn't bothered asking me not to follow anyway. I could hear Carla's pocket buzzing again and this time she didn't bother to turn it off, she just picked up the pace to a sort of half-trot. I took longer steps to keep up, walking heavily, boots ricocheting on the cheap old tile. It felt a lot like the inside of that dead factory where The Transylvanian lived, for just a moment, and I pushed those thoughts aside and half-ran myself to see which room was 203. She got there two steps ahead of me and shot through the door. I stopped in the doorway, a hand on either side of it, leaning forward a little. She walked in and the room brightened with her presence. I mean it. Light was coming from her, from somewhere I couldn't see, in some way I couldn't see. The room was dark until she walked in and then it glowed a little with something pure and sparkling.

Mr. Wilson was a desperately old husk of a man with whispy white hairs on his head and a clean-shaven face twisted in agony. Both hands were on the buzzer and he had a death-grip on the call button. Carla's pocket was going crazy buzzing and I could see from the way his eyes bulged that Mr. Wilson was about to asphyxiate in the middle of a cardiac arrest. Carla had her back to me, then looked over her shoulder, smiled again and stepped around the bed so that it was between us and I could see. She had gone from propriety to exhibitionism in the span of one dead woman.

Carla put one hand on Mr. Wilson's throat then placed the other on his chest. Light spilled out from between her fingers. Mr. Wilson let go of the buzzer all of a sudden, as his face went slack and he started breathing again in fast, shallow, ragged gasps. His eyelids fluttered and closed, and his whole body relaxed so that he was finally slack and sleeping with the call button laying askew on his hip. Light shone in crazy patterns on the ceiling, shifting even though the man was completely still and Carla's hand was pressed firmly to his chest. Smiles barked once, sharp and frightened. There was a hum in the air like the white noise of a TV screen turned up a thousand times. The light glowed so bright I thought it might hurt my eyes and I'd started to raise one arm when the light flickered, flashed red all of a sudden, guttered like a candle and died. The room was plunged into darkness and Carla lifted her hand away at long last to feel the guy's pulse.

"You can heal people?" My voice was hoarse from surprise.

Carla didn't say anything right away. She checked a couple of beeping machines next to Mr. Wilson, then walked back over to the door so that both Smiles and I got out of her way and she closed it behind her. "Tomorrow Mr. Wilson will call his lawyer," she whispered. "He'll change his will so that I get seven percent instead of six." She smiled softly but distantly, somewhere between a matron and *Mommy Dearest*. "He owns the development company that woman's family wants to sell to." Her smile stayed nailed in place. "I'm giving him until I'm up to ten percent. Any longer than that and his family will start to wonder how the hell he's hung on so long. They didn't bring him to this shit hill because they couldn't afford better or nothing: they brought him here to be ignored until he died." She smacked her lips suddenly and turned to me. "Thanks for stopping by, Withrow. It's good to put a face with the name."

I said a polite goodbye and left as quickly as decorum would allow.

Chapter 6

"So she's a nurse who heals for money and profits?" Roderick's tone was casual but his eyes were wider than normal and the way he licked one corner of his lips over and over gave the lie to all that nonchalance. "Big deal, right? Welcome to the for-profit medical industry. It's kind of what private insurance companies do all the time."

I had to smile a little. He had a point, sort of. "I still don't like it," I grumbled. "It's a little... I don't know, a little squicky."

"Squicky?"

I'd met up with him outside one of Asheville's low-rent nightclubs for college kids. If I'd had to guess, I'd say he'd been hunting. He likes the young ones. Emily tells me he very rarely does them any serious damage, so whatever. As long as he kept his nose clean, I didn't care. We all have to eat sometime. From there we'd walked most of the way back to his hotel in the middle of downtown.

"Squicky." I shrugged a little. Roderick finished a cigarette and tossed the butt onto the sidewalk as we neared the doors to his hotel. "It's a word, isn't it?"

"It's a *web* word," Roderick said with a smile. "You've been going online, haven't you?"

I shrugged again, trying to look like I didn't understand. "I've been using the email account you set me up with, yeah."

Roderick shrugged in mimicry of me and grinned. "Look at me," he said in a silly, high-pitched voice. "My name is Withrow and I'm a big mean vampire who doesn't like anybody and I think computers are for pussies."

"I use PayPal!" I blurted out, then I fluttered my lips and laughed. "I don't think computers are for pussies. I just, I don't know, I get self-conscious about all this stuff. I'm worried someone will expect me to understand it – like really *get* it the way guys stand around and talk about intake manifolds and *get it* – and I won't and they'll think I'm some old fuddy-duddy."

Roderick's eyes softened for a fraction of a second. "Oh, Cousin," he sighed. "Guys don't stand around talking about intake manifolds anymore, and nobody gives a shit how the Internet works."

We were silent for a few seconds while he toyed with lighting another cigarette. I supposed he was right on both counts. A little piece of the way I'd had of understanding the world – a segment of the overlap between the world of my life and the world of my unlife – fell away and I had the impression we were both watching it tumble away into space. I broke the silence. "Hey, you didn't happen to notice anyone... else in that bar, did you?"

Roderick wrinkled his brow at me and shook his head. "No. Anyone special?"

I sighed and waved a hand at nothing. "Maybe? Carla claimed there's one of us around who likes the bars, nightclubs, that kind of thing. Wasn't on Bob's list. I suggested to her that I'd heard about a vampire not being on the list. I figured it was a good way to maybe unearth one of The Transylvanian's extended brood, like the six -" I caught myself, counted again in my head and corrected it. "Like the *five* he was showing off back at the plant. She said there was one downtown who likes nightclubs but that's all I've got."

Roderick looked around theatrically, hand to his brow as though scanning a distant coast. "Last time I checked, Cousin Withrow, this was Asheville, North Carolina. There aren't a lot of nightclubs. He can't be that hard to find."

I frowned at him. "Maybe not by Seattle standards, but by North Carolina's it's doing reasonably well."

He smirked but didn't let it distract us.

"Would you like me to... look for him?" Roderick waggled his eyebrows a little, excited at the thought of being let off the leash of guest-hood for a while.

I opened my mouth for a moment, closed it, then said, "No, leave it to me. It's not that you aren't capable, it's that I need to be the one to find him. It's my state. I still can't afford to have anything but a personal contact. I want to establish myself in their minds first."

Roderick shrugged at me, that same mimicry, and smiled. "Your call, Cousin. Your call."

We'd made it to the hotel lobby and were passing the reception desk – I was just going to see him up to his room and then go on to the last one on my list of known vampires – when he said that and the night clerk jerked her head up straight and said, "Oh, Mr. Surrett? Mr. Surrett?"

We both spun on a heel, but she was looking at Roderick. He smiled sweetly for her, as sweetly as he could with that hollow face and the unflattering fluorescent lights. "Yes?"

"I heard you say 'call,'" she explained, digging through some papers and finally producing a hot pink sticky-note. "It made me remember. You had a message earlier, while you were out."

Roderick crossed the distance to the desk in two long strides – she flinched slightly, it always freaks them out when we approach suddenly, even though they've long forgotten we exist – and took the note in one smooth movement. He looked at it, then crumpled it and stuffed it into a jacket pocket. "Thank you, dearest." His voice was sweet and smooth. She blushed profusely, then stammered and finally, after long seconds of Roderick staring at her from across the counter, put her head back down to look at some paperwork.

Roderick turned and stepped back over to me, smiling oddly, winking.

"Who called?" It wasn't my business but I asked anyway. I tried to sound casual.

"Emily," Roderick sighed with a flutter of eyelashes. "She's probably afraid that I hurt someone and I'll be in trouble with you. Tsk."

I hrmphed and then he laughed, so I laughed, and we climbed into the elevator. It wasn't funny, but in its own way it was good to hear him acknowledge that Emily worried about him.

"Who's next on the list, Cousin Withrow?"

I sighed and rubbed the back of my neck with one fat hand. "Guy by the name of Blaine. Drives a tow truck. It shouldn't be a big deal. I like the guy, good manners, keeps to himself. We've met plenty of times, this is mainly just a social call, make sure there's nothing he needs."

Roderick and I stepped out of the elevator and walked around the corner to the door of his room. "Well, do let me know if anything interesting comes up," he said, and we shook hands and I left. I had five hours until sunrise and a lot of driving ahead of me.

Blaine Simmons was young, but not as young as Marty Macintosh. He'd been turned in the '70s, best I could guess. He drove a tow-truck at night for money. It was weird to me, the way the vampires up here didn't have money of their own when they were turned. Usually we turn folks who can take care of themselves, people who can disappear from the land of W-2's and become just another name on a piece of paper or in a database somewhere at the IRS without earning another paycheck the rest of their days. Roderick is luckier than I am in that regard but, like I said, my family did have money and it wasn't long after I'd been taken that I got every penny they had. In the mountains, though, they were all working stiffs, to use the vernacular. That's a pun of which we're very conscious. We use it anyway.

Anyway, Blaine and I had met up briefly at a truck stop the far side of Old Fort Mountain the last time I'd been here. Our conversation had been quick, but he'd been cooperative. He didn't care when I took over and was cordial every time I came through. It didn't much matter to him who was in charge down in Raleigh, he said, he'd keep his nose clean and let the politics sort themselves out. That's an attitude I can respect. I may have taken an active hand – a *very* active hand – in vampire politics in the last fifteen years, but before then I'd seen myself as part of Agatha's extended operation and the Bobs that ran the state – one after another in a line of vampires who were all aspirational idiots in golf pants, fucking *golf* – could go to hell. I guess I really did believe that, come to think of it, since I personally sent the last one there.

Blaine and I were set to meet at the same truck stop and I'd gotten there twenty minutes early just because that's how things worked out. Given it was Blaine, I tried not to tell myself it was because I wanted to surprise him in case it was a trap, even though counting on a timely arrival in a specific spot was precisely how I'd gotten Bob. Old habits die hard and vampires are creatures of habit.

I leaned on the hood of the Firebird for a while with Smiles poking around here and there a few feet away, checked my voicemail – service out here, I couldn't believe it – thought about calling Agatha and decided against it. Things up here were unusual, and Carla Van Buren had certainly thrown me for a loop with her little display of abilities, but I didn't need to go running straight to mama the first time I saw something I didn't expect. I paused and wondered whether Agatha was thinking of calling me, instead; sometimes it happens like that between maker and made, that sort of synchronicity about little things. Ah well. She'd call or she wouldn't.

Five minutes after he was supposed to be there, Blaine pulled in with his beat-up old tow truck. He cranked the window down and looked, as one might expect, exactly as he had before. "Got a call to go on," he said over the engine's loud rumble. "You'll have to ride with me."

"It'll be a crowded cab up there, with me and you and them and Smiles, won't it?"

"Nah," he said, waving a hand and spitting tobacco juice onto the pavement. Drugs don't effect us, but like I said, creatures of habit. "Just a fix-a-flat gig. Triple A." I nodded, patted my pockets, checked that I'd locked the Firebird and then walked around to the passenger door. Smiles hopped up and I climbed – eventually – after him.

"You get a lot of the late night stuff?" I buckled my seatbelt – we're immortal, not impervious – and adjusted the strap and settled in. Smiles sat on his haunches on the seat between us.

"Enough," he said, and then he nodded. "Enough to keep me going."

"The Triple A stuff must pay well, I reckon."

He shrugged, waggled a hand up and down. "Good for what it is, usually, but it ain't as much as you'd think."

"Or as you'd want," I said, smiling a little. Blaine was a real down-to-earth vampire, real easy-going. It was easy to relax around him. Less money or more boredom and I could have wound up with a job like this. Of course, Agatha wouldn't have turned me if I had. Whatever. "Right?"

He smiled and half-shrugged at me, steering by the enormous wheel those old trucks have. I could hear, deep down below us, the movements of an old-fashioned manual steering system, the thrumming of the gears as he shifted them, the mechanics of forward motion. "I figure out how to make ends meet," he said.

That stuck, for some reason, and I didn't know what to do with it. It just barely snagged at the edges of perception. It was a perfectly conversational comment, but I still had Carla Van Buren on the brain and somehow the tone he used suggested something hidden, something secretive. I didn't know what to do about that just yet, so I went with the suggestion of secrecy and said, "Say, I hear there's a guy in town not on Bob's old list. Likes the nightclubs."

"Nightclubs?"

"Asheville," I said. "Not Old Fort, but up in Asheville."

He thought about it, turning it over; I could see from his face that he was thinking about it, and then he shook his head. "News to me. I don't get up there much. Most of my calls are interstate calls or backroads around here."

I nodded; made enough sense, it wasn't like there weren't plenty of tow trucks in Asheville. Out here was where he'd have less competition, people so grateful they wouldn't think twice about a pale guy who smelled of gasoline – and only gasoline – showing up in the middle of the night to get them out of a fix. "Carla confirmed him for me but said she'd never met him, either."

Blaine blinked, slowly. "You talked to Carla?"

I shrugged a little. "Sure, gotta talk to everybody. That's what making rounds is all about."

He nodded, reached for a red plastic cup with a bunch of tissues stuffed inside and spit tobacco juice into it with a loud squelch. "Well, she may get into town more than I do."

I nodded, shrugged again. "Whatever, just curious. I'm sure I can turn him up. Not a lot of places around for him to hide, you know?"

Blaine smiled and laughed quietly. "True, true. Still, I'd be surprised if he gives a damn what you've got to say." He hurriedly glanced over. "No offense, of course, but it's a big state. Raleigh's a long way away. Lots of people up here would just as soon let Raleigh go to hell as be told what to do."

I thought about that and rubbed my goatee at him. "Fair enough," I said, "But somebody who screws around up here threatens all of us, everywhere, much less in Raleigh." I looked over and Blaine made a vague head bobble of possible agreement. "Besides, you know how it is. There's always someone in charge. Anywhere there's a heap, no matter how much shit is in it, some rat's going to scramble to the top. Might as well be somebody who respects your independence. I doubt Bob was all friendly-chatty when he came around."

Blaine smiled a little. "I never met Bob."

I arched one eyebrow. "Never met him? You were on his list, though."

"Oh, he knew of me, sure, but I never quite managed to meet with him." Blaine shrugged. "I was a lot busier back then."

I smiled a little, then frowned a little, then asked as I looked out the window on my side. "Business bad lately?"

"Naw," Blaine said. I could see him grinning in his reflection in the window. "I just didn't have anybody working for me then. These days, I go out pretty rarely. Special occasions, a shift every now and then to keep my hand in, but truth told, I've got six guys working for me."

I turned around halfway and blinked at him in silence. "Six guys work for you?"

He grinned wider. "I know, pretty good, eh? Easy money. Two guys on each weekend shift and one on each shift during the week. I just fill in on nights when somebody's sick." He coughed, quietly. "Not that they get sick often, if you catch my meaning."

I blinked again, this time very slowly, and worked very hard not to tighten my grip on the handle of the door. "You're... feeding them?" It's something we can do. It makes them strong. It's what I do to Smiles. We can do it to people, sure, but it makes them, well, different. It makes them all crazy in the long run: dangerously crazy. It isn't encouraged.

"I'm careful, I'm careful," Blaine said with a dismissive wave of his hand and another squelch of tobacco juice. "Feel free to smoke in here, by the way." I told him I didn't anymore but I rolled down the window a little anyway, grateful for the blast of cold air that ran through my hair when I did. This wasn't like Blaine. Blaine kept his head down. Blaine stayed out of the way and people stayed out of his until they had a flat tire. He drove a beat up old truck from the '70s and ran solitary. Blaine wasn't the sort of guy to have someone around he had to take care of, much less six of them.

"I know what you're thinking," he finally said. "That ain't Blaine, you're thinking. Well, times change. We have to change with them. I can't spend the rest of eternity out here on the highway, can I, all on my own? I had to start building up my base, setting myself up to disappear from the mortal world." He shrugged, as though all this simple eloquence were his natural way. "It's what we all have to do, especially these days. Facial recognition? Retina scans on driver's licenses? What if the government puts out a national ID card? Hard enough getting by on a Social Security number that's fifty years old as it is." He squelched into his cup again. "Just figured, you know, time to stop pretending I'm one of them." He waved his hand vaguely at the world outside the cabin of the truck. "I had to start being what I *am*."

We finally slowed, coming around a curve, and the conversation died abruptly. Blaine was scanning the side of the road, glancing at the odometer on his truck, then we saw him – a little Latino kid, maybe seventeen, standing by a hatchback with the car halfway off the road, emergency flashers on. Blaine pulled up behind the car, put his own flashers on and then got down out of the truck. "Just be a minute," he called. Smiles whined when he left but I patted his neck and looked over the car: early '80s Datsun, from before they became Nissans. I was surprised the car had made it this far. The kid was struggling with English, I could just barely hear him speaking to Blaine and Blaine's feeble attempts to respond in Spanish. I actually speak it, so I thought about getting out to help, but really, how many ways are there to tell someone, *See that flat tire?* The kid and Blaine walked around to the front passenger's side, Blaine came back for a big jack he had in the back, then he lifted the car up with it and started changing the tire with the speed of a very practiced hand. The kid got bored of watching him, turned his back and folded his arms over his chest to try and get warm in the cold night air while Blaine finished up the tire.

Eventually I got bored of watching, too, and started staring off into space, turning over in my head what Blaine had said about it being time for him to recede from mortal affairs and mortal attention. Getting a cut off of six different guys? Owning his own business? Not the Blaine I'd expected at all; not the Blaine of just a year ago, even. He was growing up, growing into his own as a vampire. I had to admire him. I have plenty of money, to be honest, but I still paint. There's a sense of satisfaction from finishing a work and a validation from selling it that can't be had another way. I can undo as many lives as I feel like, and I have undone many of them, but that doesn't feel half as good as having someone appreciate something I've produced that reflects my own.

It was out of the corner of my eye that I saw Blaine move once he'd released all the hydraulic pressure on the jack and let the car sink back down softly. He simply turned, grabbed the kid around the chest and upper arms, from behind, and sank his fangs right into the kid's neck on the right side.

I sat up straight in my seat. That was twice in one night someone had let me watch them feed and normally we are, without going into too many details, solitary hunters. I stared, mouth open. Blaine drank and drank. Going in on the right like that, I knew he was going to kill the kid but it still made my guts squirm to watch it happen. Finally he pulled his head back and, I assume, licked the wound closed. The kid spun as he fell so that I could see his eyelids flutter and his eyes roll back. Blaine wiped his mouth on an oily rag he pulled from his back pocket, then walked over to the truck, opened the door and grinned at me. "Pardon the midnight snack but, y'know." Midnight snack? That was enough blood to keep a vampire going for two weeks. He rummaged around behind his seat and came out with a little airplane bottle of liquor, checked the label, nodded to himself, then went back over to the kid. I saw him twist the top off and splash a little of the hooch over the kid's shirt and face, then pour the rest into his mouth and tilt his head back so it would go down his throat, then stood back up and chucked the little bottle out into the woods off the side of the road. I watched it fly in a lazy arc and disappear into the trees.

Blaine walked back, climbed into the truck and belched noisily. "Pardon me," he said.

I grimaced into my fist, not sure what the hell to say, and then said, as he put it in gear and started to back away from the car, "You know, I *don't* know."

"Know what?" Blaine belched again. It smelled... well, it smelled good. I had gone out the night before to kind of top off at a biker bar outside of town so I wasn't exactly hungry but, y'know, food's food. Sometimes you want the cookie even though you just ate. Smiles made a noise somewhere between begging and revulsion at the smell.

"You said, 'Pardon the midnight snack, but you know.' Know what?" I looked over at him with what I hoped to be a completely blank expression.

Blaine wrinkled up his nose and mouth and waved a hand in the direction of the kid and his car. "You know. *Them.* Can't stand 'em in my territory."

"Them?" I knew what he meant and though it disgusted me it didn't particularly surprise me. Still, I was going to make him say it.

"Mexicans," he said, face still scrunched like the kid had tasted of crabapples.

"There's a Puerto Rican flag sticker on his car," I said, casual.

Blaine snorted at me. "Whatever. I don't like 'em on my turf."

I stopped myself from raising both eyebrows, so instead simply said, "Turf?"

"Well..." Blaine chuckled a little and tried to look sheepish but failed miserably. "It's all really your turf, I know, but still." He chuckled again, a little eheh-heh-heh, as fake as an aluminum Christmas tree. I was suddenly reminded of Franklin Not Frank Reinholdt from the neighborhood association back home. "I'm the one who actually lives here."

I sat in silence, debating whether to reach over and tear Blaine's heart out of his chest to make the point that, actually, it really is *my state* or to simply let it slide on the grounds that he's harmless. I couldn't decide, so I didn't produce any reaction, one way or the other. I just sat in silence for a couple of minutes. Blaine was headed back towards the truck stop – my little visit was over and he was showing me to the door – which started to infuriate me. I couldn't really express why in any conscious way at the time, though obviously I have some, well, let's just say I have some issues about territory and being in charge. I waited until we got back to my car. Blaine pulled into the parking lot of the truck stop, I undid my seatbelt, the truck came to a halt – for a moment I wondered if he expected me to just jump out as we went by and roll the rest of the way to the Firebird – and Blaine held out a hand to shake before I got out after Smiles hopped past me and out the door.

I reached over, took his hand, shook it politely and then ground the bones into dust between my fingers. Blaine started to scream but it came out strangled, his mouth open, his eyes bulging. His other hand started to go for the gun on the dash but I reached out and twisted it like a pipe cleaner. I was so furious that my fangs were out, my eyes dark. The lights in the parking lot flickered for a moment. I was really, incredibly, unbelievably angry.

His turf? This racist pipsqueak reject from the Dipshit School of Tow Truck Driving?

I pulled him towards me by useless hands, which made the veins pop out on his neck. He wasn't looking at me, he was looking away, marshalling the pain into something more useful. I'd pulled a fast one by waiting until we were somewhere sort of almost public. He couldn't do a lot to fight back, not without attracting some serious attention.

"Whose territory is this?" I hissed it, very softly, an inch from his eyes.

He made a little noise in his throat and his arms twitched like he was going to try to fight me. I could feel bones start to mend between my fingers. I waited a second until there'd be something to break again, then did so. That produced a grunt and a long, high-pitched whine.

"I said," I whispered, "Whose territory is this?"

Outside, in the parking lot, Smiles produced one quiet growl.

Blaine mimicked it by simply grunting at me again. He could have spoken if he wanted to. He could have assuaged my ego by saying that it was mine and I'd have gotten out and he could have spent a few minutes mending those bones all over again and gone about his merry way, but he didn't.

"I intend," I said, voice still very soft, mouth – teeth – just an inch from his left eye, "To find that out. I intend to find each and every one of you, and I am going to make certain that everyone – you, Carla, The Transylvanian and his four punks – that each of you understands that this is *my* territory." I cleared my throat, drew a long, heavy breath. "I'm going to say that again," I whispered. "This is *my* territory. If it's inside North Carolina on the goddamn map, it is *mine*. Do you understand that?"

He started growling and the bones in his wrists were knitting faster this time, so I broke them yet again with the simple pressure of my thumb and index finger on the little bones where the hand meets the arm. I moved my thumb and forefinger just a little farther up his arm, very slowly, making sure to keep pressure on the breaks, and then snapped the larger bones that run from wrist to elbow in three different places on his left arm. He was pale and shaking and I'd swear that I could smell blood, probably blood-tears pooling in his eyes.

"Good night, Blaine." I said that in a normal voice and he spasmed in surprise at the sudden volume. "Do feel free to call if you need anything." I let go of his arms, climbed down to the asphalt and shut the door behind me. When I got into the Firebird, backed it up and drove away, Blaine was still sitting in the truck, still shivering a little, teeth gritted, his hands out of sight.

The way I figured it, one of us would kill the other the next time we met.

Chapter 7

Roderick licked his lips, dry from the winter breeze that blew continually on his balcony overlooking downtown Asheville. There wasn't a lot of downtown to be seen. Seattle was so much bigger, so much more. Asheville was a tiny little bowl of light surrounded by dark mountains. He'd seen photographs in the day that explained why they were called the Blue Ridge but at night, those peaks in silhouette were the color of an old bruise. He could walk from one end of downtown to the other in less than an hour. It was all so insignificant, a dot of organized effort on a vast, rolling mass of slanted chaos. Asheville seemed so alone.

It needed a friend who could really appreciate it.

Roderick smiled and licked his lips again, stringy hair blowing over his face and into his eyes so that he reached up with one skeletal, pale hand and pulled it away. "Hello, Asheville," he said to that bowl of light. "Would you like to play a game?"

The town didn't say anything in return, of course. A part of him was sad that it didn't. If he'd been in the right frame of mind, they might have had a whole conversation. It was a happy little thought. He liked those sorts of thoughts.

His phone rang, ruining the moment. He sighed, licked his lips one last time and pulled the phone out of his jeans pocket. It was Agatha. Poor dear. She did worry so.

"Good *eeeeeeeeeeeeevening*," Roderick purred into it when he opened it.

"Hello, Roderick." She always sounded so officious and slightly offended, like a bank manager about to tell someone the loan application had been rejected.

"What occasions this pleasant surprise?" He turned around and leaned his back against the railing on the balcony so he could stare at his own reflection framed by that of Asheville in the dark glass of the sliding door.

"Just checking in," Agatha tried to sound friendly and casual but she wasn't a great actor. "You didn't return my call."

"I was having a bit of a rest first," Roderick said. He liked his reflection. He liked it a great deal. "I apologize if I worried you at all."

Agatha was quiet for a moment and the cadence of her voice was very precise when she spoke. "Not at all. I do want you to understand, however, that any member of my family simply must return my calls in a timely manner. I don't call without reason. That goes for adoptions, as well."

"Does my cousin promptly return your calls?"

Agatha chuckled lightly, as casual as morning dew. "Now, now. No prying."

Roderick smiled but said nothing. He just let the silence hang there until it made her uncomfortable and finally Agatha got down to business.

"Now," she eventually said, "What has Withrow uncovered?"

"Well, he might not be telling me everything." Roderick was unabashedly coy, curling up around the suggestion of half-truths lurking in some shadowy corners. "But, he seems to think The Transylvanian is hiding vampires from him. The guy showed off some babies and Withrow figures that means there are more around. I suspect he's going to start looking for those hidden vampires very soon."

"And you haven't given him any... help? Any little nudges in the right direction? How many did The Transylvanian display for Withrow's benefit?" Agatha's voice was a little apprehensive and Roderick had to smile again at his own reflection when he heard it.

"Just three. I've given him no help at all. He's bounced some ideas off me, we've brainstormed a little, but I haven't given him a moment's assistance. Should I?"

Agatha was quiet, then finally, "If he tasks you with something specific, yes, by all means. Still, I want to see how this plays out without direct intervention."

"Of course. You're the boss."

"Please, just call me Agatha."

"What does Cousin Withrow call you?"

Agatha was quiet again, then hung up. Roderick held the phone open until it went to sleep and he was in the dark again with his own reflection. The city's lights shimmered around his shoulders like a mantle, like a great cloak of stars.

He hoped very much that Withrow would call him again soon; otherwise, this was going to get tiresome. Roderick would have to start getting creative if he was left to his own devices.

H'Diane and LaVonde were sitting on the couch of their living room. Music was playing on the stereo, piped in from LaVonde's computer in the bedroom. They each had a pile of papers around them and on them and in their hands. H'Diane was doing some reading on old cases, ones that had never been closed. She'd been desperate to get her head out of the Clyde Wilfred killing for five minutes. They'd watched the house, they'd put out bulletins, they'd run his picture on the news, they'd gone up there to that damned factory a million times, watched the road in and out, everything, and they hadn't turned up a thing. Cliff was nowhere to be found. That first forty eight hours of the investigation were long gone. The trail was cold. Hell, there wasn't a trail to have go cold in the first place. There was nothing. They didn't have a murder weapon, a motive, a suspect. Of course they were listing Cliff as a "person of interest," which translated roughly as "the closest thing to a suspect we have at this time," but they didn't have anything like enough to press charges.

H'Diane had heard a couple of the deputies talking it over in the break room the other day and one of them had said what she'd already caught herself thinking: *that kid is dead in the woods somewhere, just like the rest of them, and we'll never know.* It wasn't going to look good for H'Diane if her first case as a detective went unsolved. Nobody had hated Clyde Wilfred for letting his own biggest case go unsolved, but that's because he'd already closed a few by the time that happened. H'Diane shook her head and tried to focus her thoughts on the old case files she'd brought home to get all this out of her head in the first place. She sipped her coffee, set one folder aside, opened a fresh one and started to read.

LaVonde, very casually, piped up from her side of the couch. "You know, I talked to the cousin of the woman in that old murder the other day."

H'Diane didn't really hear her, or at least didn't process it, at first. "Who's that?" Then she blinked and looked away from the papers in her hand and looked over. "Wait, what?"

"Virginia Ramsey. The old woman who was found out there off Green River Road back in the '50s." LaVonde barely even looked up, so thoroughly engrossed was she in the old clippings and printed microfiche articles she was reading.

H'Diane blinked again, then set the papers in her hand off to the side in a haphazard pile on the coffee table. "Why?"

LaVonde shrugged. "I just got curious. Looked her up."

H'Diane looked incredulous. "Curious? With your copious free time at the paper?"

LaVonde blushed slightly. "She says her aunt—they're cousins, but they called her an aunt—anyway, she says her Aunt Ginny was..." LaVonde suddenly stopped and looked around for her own coffee cup.

"Was a..." LaVonde made a little forward-motion gesture with her hand.

LaVonde grimaced a little and looked away, then took a sip of coffee. "A witch-woman. She solved, um, problems. For people. When they couldn't go to the doctor, for instance."

H'Diane sat with an even expression for two seconds and then said, "She was an abortionist?"

LaVonde kind of waddled her head back and forth on her neck and then sighed. "Among other things. She cured sicknesses, sat with people, did births, sometimes arranged quiet adoptions. I get the impression it was a little of everything."

H'Diane sat and drummed her fingers on her knees for a moment, watching LaVonde very studiously *not* look back at her and finally said, "Why?"

"I said," LaVonde tried to smile, "I got curious."

"No, no, fine." H'Diane waved a hand around and dismissed that whole line of inquiry. "Not that. Why tell me?"

"Well..." LaVonde laughed finally, and shook her head. "It's probably nothing. It's ridiculous."

"No, no, no: you don't get away that easy." H'Diane smiled. She couldn't help it when LaVonde was acting uncharacteristically shy. "Out with it."

LaVonde looked away again, rubbing her thumb against the eraser tip of a pencil, concentrating hard, and finally she set her jaw and turned back. "Her cousin told me she thought Ramsey and English—the kid—that they were in danger from something…" H'Diane started to interrupt and her expression suggested it might be with something of the *no shit* variety so LaVonde kept pressing and cut her off. "Something old and dark. She made it sound… ancient." LaVonde actually shuddered a little. Jesse Beth's words had stuck in her brain for two days now: *Something no one saw anymore, or talked about, anyway. Something dangerous. Something that scared him so bad he couldn't tell anyone else but an old woman no one would ever believe.* "She made it sound really scary and bad. Like, horror movie scary."

H'Diane arched both eyebrows and set her coffee mug down, leaning forward a little, sitting cross-legged with her back against the arm of the couch. "What do you mean?"

LaVonde shrugged it off and shook her head. "I don't know," she sighed. "Just… Jesse Beth, the cousin, the way she said it. It gave me the creeps. Like something awful could be out there, lurking out of sight, something old that nobody remembers anymore or talks about."

"What, the old man with the hook for a hand? The phantom hitchhiker? What kind of campfire story did she tell you?"

LaVonde snorted.

H'Diane reached over and put her hand on LaVonde's knee. "No, I'm sorry. I shouldn't have made fun of you. You… well, it seems to have really scared you. But I doubt I'd get very far if I walked into the station tomorrow and told the sheriff I was going to charge an ancient and horrifying presence in the forests of Western North Carolina with two murders. It would be awfully convenient, though, to wrap up both at once."

"Still," LaVonde said with a smile, "Promise me you'll be careful. OK?"

H'Diane met her eyes and smiled. "I promise."

They sat back and both started to go back to their reading when, finally, H'Diane set her papers down again. "OK, I have something to tell you."

LaVonde set her own aside rather quickly and this time she was the one who leaned forward. "What's wrong, baby?"

"Nothing's wrong," H'Diane smiled, "But it's weird that you would tell me that. See…" She cleared her throat. "I went through the case files at the station from that murder, the Ramsey/English murder. Clyde Wilfred kept something from the crime scene. It was this little leather bracelet that he found on English. He told one of the deputies at the time that it was a talisman. He didn't know what it was supposed to protect against, but he was very clear that it was supposed to be a... charm."

"Do you think Ginny Ramsey made it for him?"

H'Diane shrugged. "I wouldn't have said that ten minutes ago, but now? Maybe so."

The next morning, LaVonde called Jesse Beth. She answered on the third ring with a heavy, already-tired sort of hello.

"Jesse Beth," she began, "This is LaVonde? We met the other day?"

"I knew you'd call again," the woman said. "I could see it on you when you left."

LaVonde just let that go. She had something to ask for. "Do you ever do... talismans?"

Jesse Beth didn't answer for a moment and then said, "No love magic and no divorce magic."

So it was that easy: like an ad in the yellow pages or calling up to order a pizza. "It's not that," LaVonde said. "I was wondering: you said you thought your aunt was trying to help him with something evil and frightening from the past. Something old that people wouldn't talk or think about anymore at the time."

"I don't know whether she made any talismans for him, Ms. Burke. I wouldn't know how to make the exact same thing."

"No, I understand," LaVonde said, "But could you make something that would... warn someone? Or something? Something that would protect against that sort of thing if it tried to show up, or if you got too close to it or something?"

After a long few seconds of thought in which LaVonde was certain that Jesse Beth had hung up every time the line popped, she spoke. "I could do something sort of like that. Maybe. By when?"

"As soon as possible," LaVonde said, too quickly.

"A hundred bucks," Jesse Beth said, "And you can pick it up tomorrow."

Janine was walking in a circle around the field, ten feet from the yellow police tape, with one hand on her own forehead and the other held out in front of her. She'd been doing so for five minutes. Jennifer was pretty sure that was bullshit but everything was reopened for consideration after she'd killed a dozen zombies and met a vampire.

Marilyn had been dowsing up and down the field for a bit but now she was helping Jennifer. The property owner had told them they could fiddle around out there as long as they liked in return for five hundred bucks of Christmas money Sue had slipped them in an envelope. It helped to know a rich lady once in a while. Jennifer knew the sheriff's department wouldn't bust any chops as long as they stayed out of the actual crime tape. More of Sue's monetary magic at work and Jennifer was grateful for it.

"So what are these we're hanging up?" Marilyn was smart, efficient, and took orders well. Jennifer liked her for it. Marilyn could also give orders, an even more rare talent. Without her around, Jennifer was pretty sure this paranormal investigator bullshit would have worn her out a long time ago. It was yet another of the ironies of her life as she saw it: she hated all the junk science that got bandied around on those television shows about people looking for ghosts in old tourist traps, but those same shows had made it somewhat slightly more socially acceptable to go knocking around someone else's property looking for bogeymen than it had been before. Jennifer had seen the world crack open for just a couple of nights in her life and she was determined to find the truths that were out there. She had promised a vampire named Withrow that she would never go looking for him, never try to seek him out, and she had meant that, but she had made no promises about any others. It hadn't taken long to sit down and come up with a set of circumstances she could consider possible markers of a vampire attack. Bloodless corpses were the most obvious. Newspapers didn't often play that angle up because it was just over the border of being *too* freaky for the people who subscribe to get sale papers and advice columns. Jennifer had learned in time that cryptozoology message boards always caught those cases, though: to them, they were evidence of chupacabra.

Jennifer smiled. How many times had ignorance and blind faith enabled real learning? How many monks had believed bloodletting cured the common cold? All that wrongness, but maybe without them we wouldn't have blood donations. Ah well. In the end, it all came back to blood after all. Maybe zombies and vampires were the only things out there. They were the only things she had seen herself, directly, so they were all she would allow herself to believe possible. She remembered abruptly that Marilyn had asked a question. "Oh, these? They're game cameras. If anything comes back here and trips the motion sensor it takes a picture with a low-light lens. Grainy, but better than nothing."

Marilyn nodded. "Something like a bear or a catamount?"

"Yes," Jennifer lied. "Something like that."

PART III

Chapter 1

"The way I figure it," I said to Roderick as we rode down the elevator from his room, two nights later, "They've probably called a powwow by this point."

"Which 'they?'" He was dressed like it was '80s night at a goth club he didn't like very much: white pleather jacket, white parachute pants, a white shirt. It should have made him look less pale but instead it just made him look washed out, more pale than ever. His hair was loose rather than in a pony tail. I was dressed in my standard-issue black jeans, black boots, black trench coat, a black t-shirt for a band I'd never gone to see: *SQUIRREL NUT ZIPPERS*. I'd figured it was for the candy, at first, before someone had explained.

"The local vampires and whoever all they're hiding," I said with a shrug. It seemed so obvious to me. There was clearly a parallel organization up here, some gang of vampires who thought they'd escaped notice. The part that bothered me most about them was that they were right. They had escaped my notice for years upon years, and they would have kept doing so if one of the people protecting them hadn't murdered my last mortal friend, and if Marty Macintosh hadn't sweat bullets to tell me without telling me that something bad was going down.

"And whom do they hide?" Roderick dug a bent cigarette out of a soft pack on the inside of his jacket. From the look of the package, the cigarettes were at least twenty years old. We don't have much call to care about stale smokes, though.

"I don't know for sure, but I have a theory," I sighed. I crossed my arms over my chest as Roderick stuck the cigarette in one corner of his mouth, palmed his lighter, began flipping it end over end between his thumb and index finger, impatient to light it but unwilling to draw a lot of attention to himself in the hotel were he slept during the day. I watched him flip the lighter back and forth a few times and then opened my mouth again. "This may be crazy, but I think there's a bunch of them. Not just the two The Transylvanian paraded around in front of the other night and the one Carla confirmed might or might not exist."

"Why?"

"I dunno," I said. I reached up and rubbed the back of my neck again. "Just a hunch. And now here I am, reminding people I'm the boss and asking a bunch of questions and suggesting that I know a little – but not a lot – about at least one of them. If anything is going to get them to respond, surely it's that. You know, Carla and Blaine both fed in front of me."

Roderick grimaced in disgust, the cigarette bobbling between his clenched lips. "Gross," he muttered.

"I know. Weird behavior. I suspect there's a whole parallel society here: some sort of social scene to which neither of us are privy. It's strange to think of because there are so few of us we don't normally have trouble keeping tabs on each other. I mean, I thought I honestly knew the name, at least, of every vampire in anything like a city in this whole state." I crossed my arms again. "I think if we find them, we find out the big secret."

"And what if we walk into a bar full of super-secret vampires?" Roderick nearly lit the cigarette, then caught himself. The elevator was taking about ten years getting to the lobby, I had to admit.

"Easy," I said, stifling a yawn. It was still early. "We kill all of them but one and make that one talk."

"And then?"

"Kill him, too, of course."

Roderick finally got to light his cigarette outside the front doors of the hotel. He was staying in a nice place right smack in the middle of town. There were four night clubs, three open-late coffee shops and two performance venues in Asheville proper. There was also the country and western place out at an old Holiday Inn by the airport, but that was where I'd go if we couldn't turn up anyone at any of the places downtown. For some reason, downtown just seemed like a better place to start. We tend to be urban creatures; always have been, according to tradition. You always hear stories that somewhere or other—New York, Los Angeles, Paris, wherever—there's a vampire who was a Roman Senator or a Greek philosopher or an ancient Chinese Mandarin, though I've never met any of them. All the history I've heard was oral tradition. Vampires are all mouth, anyway: teeth and tongue and talking. We don't write much down. I guess the kids with blogs and Twitters are changing that now.

Roderick and I agreed to split up to make it easier. If I went one way, I'd be able to check out the juke joint and the goth bar, one of the performance venues and two coffee shops. Roderick could check the rest by going the opposite direction. If either of us spotted anything worth investigating we'd text the other with the letter T, easy to get to, easy to find, easy to type in a hurry. Roderick gave me a little salute and a mean smile and turned right to head off into the night. I watched him go for a second, thought about asking if we could go together, then shook it off and went my way.

We had a lot of ground to cover.

The coffee shops were a bust. There were a bunch of high school kids and a few college students who'd ventured away from campus. I could smell a pot deal going down in the bathroom. So typical. Nothing ever changed. I ordered a small coffee, black, and had a taste of it before dumping it into the trash on my way out. My maker had taught me to keep food down but I'd never been much for coffee.

The performance venue was this club right there on Pack Plaza, downtown in Asheville. There was some big-name band playing there and some protesters outside. I'd read about this in the paper: the club sold tickets online and a bunch of people from out of town had bought them all up. Hardly any locals could get in. They were pissed; there were letters to the editor. I figured if that was their biggest problem, Asheville was probably in pretty good shape.

I crossed the square, past the Vance Monument, the front steps and big glass doors of the BB&T building, the closest thing Asheville had to a skyscraper. The county jail and city police station were down the hill, across a long expanse of green lawn. In the summer, during Bele Chere, this would be packed with bands and crafts vendors and crowds and funnel cakes. I wasn't there, of course – we give "sunburn" a whole new meaning—but I'd come down once after dark and watched some of the very last acts one of the nights. It had been fun but not really my scene. Too many people walking around laughing and drunk and having fun. Too much life for one of the walking dead to really enjoy himself. The last thing on my list was the little goth bar, this place catty-corner on the square from the rock club with the protesters. It was actually the likeliest place to find them but I wanted to eliminate the easy targets first. The night was cold and crisp and very clear and the moon was rising in the east like a big eye in the sky.

I could smell vampires before I got to the door. I stopped, looked around, sniffed the air. A kid in a fishnet shirt and a heavy winter coat came out the door of the little goth place and I felt the smell hit me like a weight pressing against the inside of my lungs. It was oppressive. It was like gagging on the reek of a corpse.

I flipped open my phone and texted Roderick. Fifteen seconds later I got this back: OMW.

Whatever that means, I thought to myself.

"On my way, of course." I'd asked Roderick what it meant when he got there and he'd laughed like I was a kid asking what a cuss word meant. "What else could it mean?"

I shrugged it off and pointed at the bar. I was sitting on the edge of the reflecting pool in Pak Plaza, facing the door. I hadn't seen or smelled anyone come or go, but every time the heavy door opened and closed again I got another dose of heavy vampiric presence. "In there. Lots of 'em, by the way it reeks."

Roderick settled in beside me, occasionally looking at his phone to tell the time. That was another thing he'd successfully scavenged from humanity: he never much wore watches anymore. It was nearly midnight—I'd taken a long time walking and checking out the places on my list—and the moon was very high, over halfway across the sky already. Finally, at midnight, a little girl in a sort of Funereal Cheerleader look bopped out of the door and down the street and when the smell hit me I saw Roderick physically recoil—at first—and then lean forward, eyes closed, nose up, right into the smell.

"I think this is going to be so fun," he said. He smiled like it was Christmas morning.

I wasn't carrying any guns, of course, and neither was Roderick. You don't just go walking around town packing a bunch of heat. We wouldn't need it, anyway. I wanted destruction. I wanted to reach out and end their lives with my bare hands, and a gun doesn't give you that sense of satisfaction. All the Freudian fantasies of all the second amendment fruitcakes in the world are no substitute for seeing the life go out of another's eyes while your fingers are still wrapped around their neck. I wanted that immediacy of experience. I wanted to feel it happen. I wanted to express and assert myself in a very direct, tactile way that a gun would never allow.

"Are you much for fighting?" I tried to ask it with as much sensitivity as I could.

"Cousin. Tsk tsk tsk." Roderick smiled with only one corner of his mouth. "I enjoy a broad array of interests and murder is definitely one of them."

Roderick and I stood up at the same time. I cracked my knuckles back and forth against the palms of each opposing hand, a loud and lengthy process that sounded like treading on a box of lighted firecrackers. Roderick simply took his hands out of his pocket and zipped his pleather jacket up to the neck. I looked at him slightly oddly, I guess, because he smiled again and said, "I like this shirt too much to get a bunch of blood on it."

I laughed—I had to, I couldn't pretend I was any better than he was—and we walked in step to the front door of the club. I opened it, gestured for him to enter, he demurred theatrically, insisted that I go first. I did so, finally, and the guy checking IDs at the door looked us up and down. I don't know what he was going to say—it could have been a get the hell out as easily as a word of hello—but I put my fist straight through the glass window he sat behind and into his face so that he went down in a heap.

Roderick pulled the door shut behind him, wrapped one hand around the old-fashioned handle and twisted it so that the door would be stuck then yanked the neon OPEN sign's cord out of the wall. I opened the door into the club proper, where no one had heard the thing with the window and the greeter because of the music. It was thumping, bass-heavy stuff with a gravelly voice going on about some damn thing or another. Roderick stepped up beside me and closed his eyes to sniff the air again. A few kids turned to look at us but

I didn't pay them any attention. There was a back room somewhere, I could tell that, because the aroma was still thick in here but it trailed off past the expansive wooden bar and around a corner somewhere. I figured maybe half a dozen vampires, I couldn't be sure. Roderick was savoring their aroma way too much for my personal liking, so I walked over to the bartender—tall, skinny, long hair, very good looks, early thirties, with a Van Dyke going just the right amount of gray to invite closer inspection. I bet he got a lot of action with a face like that in a joint like this. There was a time when I would have come here just to flirt and leave embarrassingly oversized tips. I chucked a thumb in the general direction of the back room and leaned forward. "Blaine come in?"

The bartender looked me up and down and sweat formed on his upper lip. He wasn't clueless; he knew enough to be scared, anyway. "Maybe," he said. "Lots of people come in."

"Not so many they can't all get out in a hurry, though, right?" I reached into the inner corners of his mind, my own will crunching his to tiny fragments. Anger helps the hoodoo sometimes. "I think maybe you're closing up early tonight."

All the color drained out of his face as he gazed around and past me. "I think maybe we're closing early tonight," he droned in response.

"Everyone needs to go out the emergency exit." I said that slowly and distinctly, close to his ear as he leaned farther in. "There's something wrong with the sprinkler system and they need to go right now. The pipes in the back are making a funny noise."

He leaned back, swallowed air once and with glassy eyes walked over to the DJ booth, climbed into it, turned down the music gradually and leaned into a microphone. "Everyone, I hate to do this but we need to close up early. I think there's something wrong with the sprinkler system, there's a funny noise in the pipes in back, so I need everyone to go out the side entrance over here." He gestured with one hand and everyone looked at him, looked back at one another, looked back at him. "Seriously, folks, I hate to do this but it's a safety hazard. We'll be open again tomorrow night." Sullen kids started to pull jackets and some backpacks and various things together and leave. I waited one minute, then two, and the twenty or thirty people there were all gone. The bartender came back with the same glassy expression and looked at me. "And now you and the DJ," I said as I heard something wooden splinter nearby.

The bartender walked over to the DJ, grabbed him by the arm and dragged him, protesting, out into the street. The side door swung shut just as Blaine came around the corner from wherever the back room was. I guess he was going to ask what the hell was going on. He saw me and froze in place, mid-step.

Roderick had hidden in a shadow in a corner. He stepped out of it and drove a chair leg—that was the splintering sound—right through Blaine's chest so that it stuck out covered in blood. Blaine gasped and wheezed and pawed at his own chest.

I smiled, walked over and took him by the neck with both hands. "Blaine," I said, very calmly, "I felt like maybe you didn't get the point the other night. It's a shame; I kind of liked you." Then I slammed his head down on the corner of a table so hard the table flipped up and over onto him. I grabbed it by the stem in the center with both hands, raised it, positioned the edge of the table over his neck and lifted it over my head to swing.

"Very creative," I heard Roderick say, then I brought the edge of the table down so hard on Blaine's throat that his head came off with a wet snap and a wrenching sound. I half-turned to watch it as it flew away across the tile floor, bounced once and then dissolved into ash in the span of a second. I turned back and his body had done the same. He was a pile of clothes and wasted potential.

I dropped the table on its side and dusted my hands with a little more drama than I'd originally intended. "That's one," I said.

Roderick grinned and clapped his hands a little. "Cousin," he breathed, voice high and shallow, "I think I love you more than I've ever loved anyone in our whole family."

I grunted. "Come on: less talk, more kill."

We both set off for the back room where we could smell more vampires and hear nothing; they'd probably heard us dispatching Blaine. These wouldn't be surprised. We were going to have a fight on our hands.

The back room was small with walls painted a cheap black that had flaked and chipped so dots of the white innards of cement blocks were visible here and there. It had a pool table in the middle with a red felt cloth on it and a couple of pillars of chalk in the corner and not a lot else: a few posters for bands that performed in a different time and place, a bunch of high wooden chairs, a couple of coat racks. What surprised me was how many vampires were in there. Half a dozen, easily. Luckily for us, they were all young. Roderick still had that white pleather jacket zipped up to his neck. I would have found it constricting to say the least, but he's such a skinny little thing I'm not sure he noticed he was wearing it. He dropped into a crouch for about a quarter of a second before springing straight through the air and landing on the first one with his knees wrapped around the fellow's chest and his thumbs in his eyes.

The vampire in question was some Latino guy, so the second surprise was that Blaine couldn't handle a Puerto Rican with a flat tire, but he was fine with a hispanic vampire? That was one of those little factoids that snagged in my brain as I went about other business: namely, I had a pool cue down off the wall and was busy shoving it between the ribs on a skinny black kid whose fangs were out and whose eyes were bloodshot. I wondered idly if that was the guy Carla had meant – Charles, AKA Chucky—but I didn't have a lot of time to think about it. A scan of the room in my peripheral vision let me know Carla wasn't there, which I found interesting. I hit home with the cue, felt lukewarm blood spray out around where the stick was protruding from the guy's heart, and I let his weight help me snap it off at the wound so I could spin it with one hand and ram it through the mouth and up, into the brain pan of one that came flailing towards me the moment we walked through the doors.

Three down, three to go. Nope, make that four. Roderick stood up from the one whose skull he'd just torn open with bits of gore and brain dripping from his hands and there were four still standing on the opposite end of the pool table. Our entrance and those three killings had taken something in the neighborhood of four seconds. Ashes were still floating in the air from the first ones we'd killed.

Those remaining stared at us, two with their mouths open, one with her mouth closed, one with his fangs out and this ridiculous tongue-waggle like the lead singer for KISS. I made a little *pfffffut* noise of amusement.

"It isn't fair if you get more than I do, Cousin Withrow." Roderick was staring at the four of them, eyes flickering back and forth between them so fast a human wouldn't have been able to keep track.

"Actually, given this is my state and it's my autho-" I paused, and edited. "My *wishes* we're acting on, it's totally fair."

Roderick made a little tsk noise and then the four of them came at us. One—a big fat white bubba of a guy—leapt onto the table and sprinted forward, but I put my head down and one knee on the edge of the table so that I simply rammed him in the crotch with my forehead when he got to me. He went over my back, head first, hands grasping but finding nothing there; I rolled forward, spun around and leapt back over the edge of the pool table to plant both knees in his belly and punch him so hard in the chest that his sternum cracked and splintered ribs made little point marks at the outside of his *Boot-Scootin' Boogie* t-shirt. It looked like he was smuggling a giant spider under there.

Two seconds.

That was about as long as I should spend on any one target at any one time so I bounced off him and up into the air—more splintering noises from his chest cavity—and twirled with all the grace of a ballerina.

That's what told me they were all young, no more than twenty years a vampire, if that. They were slow and graceless and they moved like mortals. A vampire is outside the laws of physics in a lot of little ways. If we're given enough time to test our abilities, we find out we can move like the secret and anatomically impossible offspring of Baryshnikov and Jackie Chan with the strength of, oh, rough estimate? A *lot* of people. That's the best I can do on that score.

The woman—blonde hair, athletic, small like a gymnast—was coming at me with one of the pool cues in her hand like a javelin, and I respected her for at least trying to wield a weapon in her own defense. She moved like molasses, though, and I swept the cue aside and put the flat of my left hand against her nose so hard her whole face caved in. The small bones of her nose carved her own brain to pieces. She never even landed on the bubba at my feet. She simply turned to ash in mid-air. I wasn't breathing, of course, and I was very glad that I didn't have to. I bet it tasted just awful, all that greasy dust.

One second and a half. I was getting better.

Roderick had driven the legs of a stool through the chest of one of the two guys who'd come after him then used it to pin the second one against the wall behind the first one. They were both tiny, angry sorts, skinheads from the look of it. They both had that Small Dog Complex quality to them. I figured they were buddies. One of them probably turned the other after getting turned, himself. Roderick's scrawny little arms had no difficulty holding the two of them in place and so I took the time to look around for a convenient weapon to behead the bubba from before. He was gurgling and struggling on the floor, trying to heal his own wounds but doing it painfully slowly.

"You got a knife? Machete? Anything?" I was glancing back and forth around the room. Roderick didn't look at me; he was studying the faces of the vampires he held pinned. The one in front, with the stool through his chest, was grunting and straining and his eyes were bulging out. The one behind was—well, I was surprised again, as he was crying and pleading. His arms were pinned to his sides by the legs of the stool and whatever he was saying came out in a liquid burble, confused and incomprehensible.

Roderick kept staring at them, fangs descended. He leaned forward with his neck craned impossibly so that he could strike with his teeth. He finally said, very evenly, "No, Cousin. I didn't think to bring anything of the sort."

"Oh well," I sighed, "Nothing for it." I heard one of Roderick's guys scream after I turned my back again. I lifted one boot and brought it down square on the bubba's forehead. He tried to raise his arms to stop me, but his wrecked chest wouldn't let him: his muscles pulled his chest cavity even farther apart. I imagine it hurt like hell. He started to shout but he didn't get the chance. His skull cracked like a walnut and he was a pile of dust before I'd even lifted the boot again for a second blow.

I turned around and dusted my hands off. That made twice in as many minutes. Not good if I wanted to avoid a reputation as a showboating prima donna. "Right," I said. I sniffed once and looked over the one Neo-Nazi still pinned to the wall by that bar stool Roderick was holding. There was a cloud of ash in the air but I didn't have time to wonder why. Instead I felt a little sorry for my cousin, that he had scored so many fewer kills than I had. On the other hand it was my state to defend, not his.

The vampire being held in place by Roderick was wide-eyed and babbling something about his friends. He seemed terribly weak, like there was hardly any fight in him at all. I wondered if he'd even been a vampire for a year. "Alright," I said, "Now let's do some talking."

The skinhead didn't want to say anything coherent at first, so I decided to test Roderick's abilities in another way. "Just Jedi Mind Trick him," I said, shrugging it off. It was an easy thing for me to do. I wondered if he would be the same way. He looked at me for a second with the guy squirming ineffectually as two of the four legs of the stool poked through his chest at odd angles. Roderick had missed the guy's heart by a mile and I suspected he had meant to do so, that if we were really going to keep one of these jerks alive to talk to that he had intended to score the honor of having bagged our interview.

Roderick blinked at me twice and said, "Did you just say 'Jedi Mind Trick?'"

I frowned and crossed my arms. "Yes."

Roderick laughed suddenly, three quick chuckles—*huh huh huh*—and then looked back at the guy. He screwed up his face, closed his eyes, then opened them and said, "You want to tell me your name."

The guy just kept wiggling around. Roderick tried it again with no change. Very rapidly he descended into saying, "*Tell me your name tell me your name tellmeyourname,*" faster and faster, so that I put up a hand and stopped him by touching him on the shoulder.

"Here," I said, "Watch and learn." I reached over and took the guy's chin in my hand to turn his face towards me. He tried to get away but it was futile. I looked deep into his eyes, reached down inside myself for the hoodoo, and spoke. "Tell me your name."

"James." He growled it between gritted teeth, pushed out like pasta from a machine in one of those late night infomercials. I nodded, smiled a little, and considered what to ask next.

"How many of you are there?"

He paused for what was an unusual length of time. "Seventeen." It physically pained him to speak, not just from the wooden beams shoved through his lung, but, I guessed, also because the information was being dragged out of him against some sort of inner defense mechanism. I thought briefly of Marty Macintosh, of the way he'd not said anything to me about the map of disappearances in Transylvania County, how he'd simply said I should see it and then shown it to me and had been as nervous as a cat in a rocking chair factory the whole time. Ah, yes. So their maker wanted to stay hidden.

Gee, I wondered who *that* could be.

"Why only seven of you here tonight?" He didn't want to speak, but I was drilling down deep into his psyche and everywhere I could feel something push back I simply split it in two and kept going. We don't usually have to be like this—people, like the bartender, are easy to work the mojo on as a rule—so I had no idea what I was doing to his mind by being this rough with it. It didn't matter, though. I had already decided I couldn't let him live. I'd decided that before I'd known who he was, decided it when I'd said that *kill him too, of course line* to Roderick in the elevator. At the time it had felt like cheap but effective machismo and now, standing here, I knew I'd meant it deep down in a way I'd not even been conscious of when the words came out my mouth like so many *how are you*'s.

"Emergency meeting," he grunted. "Only ones who made it."

"About what," I said with a hint of a smile, "Was the emergency meeting?"

He didn't get proper grammar like that for a long moment, or maybe he was still fighting me in some way I couldn't detect, but finally his eyes closed and he tried again to twist away from the wall. Roderick mashed harder on the seat of the stool so that the guy groaned long and low, like a wounded bear. "You," he whispered.

I leaned in close enough to smell the terror on his skin and whispered, "And who am I?" He tried not to answer, tried to snap at me with his fangs but I was two feet away before he could blink. I laughed. I laughed right in his face and then leaned in again. "Who am I?"

"Withrow," he finally managed.

"No," I said. "I'm the *boss*. Who made you?"

He fought so hard against telling me that I started to lose my grip on his will. I had to put both hands against his face and hold his head steady against the wall so that he looked me in the eye. His own were wide, mad, yellowed with fury and terror. He was like a rabid animal being shocked into exhaustion so it can have a collar squeezed on and a shot administered. What I was doing was an act of cruelty and I relished that about it. James closed his eyes in defiance so I reached up and pulled them open with my finger tips on his eyelids. He groaned again and I heard one of the legs on the stool start to splinter.

"Cousin Withrow," Roderick said very casually, "I think we might need another chair in a few moments."

"Tell me," I growled at him and I felt his will snap a moment before the chair did so that he gasped, strangled, then blurted out the name: The Transylvanian. It wasn't much of a surprise, but it was nice to have it confirmed.

When the chair finally split down the middle, Roderick didn't spare a half of a second driving his fingers through the guy's neck and grabbing him by the spinal column from the wrong side. There was a snap and then a cloud of dust and we both stood there blinking for a moment.

"Cousin," Roderick started to say, voice oddly light, but I squeezed his shoulder with one hand and shook my head.

"Not now, Roderick," I sighed. "I need a drink."

The urge to drive straight to Brevard in the middle of the night, kick in every door and challenge The Transylvanian right then and there was pretty strong. Roderick and I slipped out the back door just in time to see the bartender and the DJ coming back looking confused. The hoodoo I put on them to get them and everyone else out of the club would wear off sooner or later, I knew, because I hadn't had the time to do something that would really stick. I guessed from their return that it was sooner. The bartender looked at me for a moment like he might recognize me then shook his head and kept walking. At least I'd gotten that part right.

The guy checking IDs, the one I'd punched, had been slapped awake by Roderick and I hoodoo'ed him, too. I figured we were pretty safe. He didn't get much chance to look at us, but still: better safe than sorry, as they say.

That is, actually, why I refrained from going after The Transylvanian right then. If that vampire back there was telling the truth—and from what I'd seen of breaking down the barriers in his head, he was—then there were at least ten more vampires somewhere in Western North Carolina, plus The Transylvanian, plus Cliff if he'd already been turned. I had, at this point, to assume that Marty Macintosh and Carla Van Buren were among those ten, so really there were eight that we needed to find. Marty had told me once that his maker was a vampire who lived in Philly now, but I'd never bothered to check; I had to assume he'd lied. Thing was, all those other vampires could be anywhere, and if there had been an emergency meeting called then they were all aware that I was out and probably looking for them. They were going to lay very low for a while was my guess. Either that, or The Transylvanian's hold on them was strong enough that they'd go there to protect him. Somehow I doubted that, though. If he'd been spending years populating this third of the state with his own personal brood just to have muscle around then he would have shown it all off when I got there instead of the one I'd seen. No, he probably wanted to keep them out in the field to keep their eyes on me and maybe for the same reason I'd turned down Roderick's initial offers of assistance: he didn't want to look like he *needed* the help.

Another good reason to wait was this: if there'd been a meeting, The Transylvanian knew about it. He'd be waiting to hear from them. If he didn't hear from them, he'd get nervous. I wanted him nervous, maybe a little frightened. I wanted him to know that death was coming for him.

None of this, however, explained away the old murder from back in the day. Sure, The Transylvanian was going to turn Cliff so he'd killed off his family. Very traditional, like I've said. Maybe a little overboard. Maybe *too* traditional in the end: after all, I'd never have gotten involved first if he hadn't done that. Still, there was some connection to the old murder, I felt certain. It was too much to claim that it was coincidence The Transylvanian would go after the kid of my last living friend when he was also somehow wrapped up in the guy's first case. With enough leg work, maybe—*maybe*—someone could independently figure out that Clyde and I knew one another but no, it would be a lot easier for The Transylvanian to have found out by virtue of being interested the whole time, ever since the murders happened, keeping an eye on Clyde and thus finding out that he and I knew one another by witnessing the times we met out there in that old field.

Well, whatever. These were questions I could ask him when I saw him. I wanted to wait just a night or two for that, but no more. I wanted to talk to him real, real soon. Roderick and I split up again after we walked back to his hotel. I went on home and sat out on the back porch with Smiles curled up on the back porch beside me. It was cold, but I didn't much mind. I didn't turn on any lights, didn't even try to do a crossword or play with the little sudoku gadget I'd gotten. I didn't check my email. Nothing. I just sat and listened to myself listening to the woods.

Around five in the morning, I went to bed and lay there while the sky turned from black to purple and then purple to blue. At that point I closed all the blinds, climbed into bed and read a book for a few minutes. The next thing I knew, the clock read 5:33pm and another day had passed in the land of the living.

CHAPTER 2

"He'll probably turn Cliff tonight," I said to Roderick on the phone. Yeah, yeah, electronic bugs, whatever. They listen for other stupid stuff these days. The way I reckon, the only vampires that ought to worry about telephones anymore are the ones speaking Arabic. That's people for you: always worried about the wrong damn thing.

"Why tonight?" Roderick's voice was wispy and wistful. It was easy to imagine him staring at nothing in his hotel room, talking on the phone, legs crossed, sitting hunched forward on the bed as though there were a spiritual TV only he could see, hovering in space three feet to the left of the physical one.

"Just a hunch," I finally replied. "He didn't hear from anybody after the little tea party they were having about me last night. He would have tried to get hold of them somehow. When that failed, he'd have to decide they're dead or flipped, sooner or later, no matter how he went about looking into it. He'll be wanting all the loyal allies he can get. My guess is he's putting out calls to the others right now. If they're all in Asheville already, which is a little unlikely what with there not being enough people for them all to stay hidden all the time, some of them will take a while to make it to Brevard. I figure he'll plan a big headcount affair tomorrow night, giving him tonight to turn Clyde and get him somewhat ready for his coming-out tomorrow." I shrugged, sitting on the porch again, talking quietly. Smiles was prowling around the back yard, sniffing at leaves and then taking a leak on them.

"Okay," Roderick said, "So what do we do?"

"Well, let's play a little what-if. If he tells Cliff tonight's the big night, what's the first thing he's going to want to go do?"

There was silence on the line and then Roderick chuckled. "Look at the world. Look at what he just lost?"

"Exactly. I figure Cliff gets one last visit to mom and dad's, either before or right after. Right?"

Roderick had always lived in the home where he grew up so to him it was all hypothetical, but I knew exactly where I'd gone the night I was turned. I went to my parents home and just watched it from the trees.   My family had been there at the time, but of course I didn't show myself to them. I'd chosen to say goodbye to all of that already. To be honest, the temptation to speak to them wasn't even there. I wasn't going to miss them very much. I hadn't known at the time what their fates would be, and I wouldn't have wished it on them had I known, but I wasn't exactly stewing over how to keep them in the dark, either. Roderick had been born by then, but just barely. I knew him as nothing more than a proxied signature in a Christmas card. It's funny how life works out, isn't it?

"Hmmmm," Roderick finally said. "Perhaps so. Shall I meet you there?"

"Nah, it's a pain in the ass to find," I said. "I'll be OK."

"But what if The Transylvanian decides to go with him? I wouldn't want you to face him alone."

I chuckled a little. "Don't worry about me," I said. "I'll worry enough for both of us."

As soon as Roderick clicked his phone shut, the door to his room opened. It wasn't kicked in, the lock wasn't shot out. The person at the desk had happily given a key card to the man who asked for one because that man was a vampire who had made the clerk do so by looking deep into his mind and telling him to do it. Now the man – a generic redneck thug, just short enough to carry a chip on his shoulder and just dumb enough to think he was clever – was holding a set of chains as thick as a tree limb and a tiny little revolver. They both knew its bullets wouldn't hurt Roderick in the least, but gunshots would sure as hell lead to some uncomfortable questions when the cops got called.

Roderick sighed a little impatiently and said, "Well, finally. I thought you would never get here. Are you going to tell me your name or do we skip straight to the kidnapping?"

I pulled into that little nook in the woods again and hid my car in the darkness between the trees. It had been a few nights since I'd been back to Clyde and Edith's place and I wondered if the cops would even still be watching it, looking for Cliff. Probably not. From what I've read and what Clyde told me, most of the motion on a case like this happens in the first few days and then drops off real fast. Leads either turn into an arrest or they dry up completely. Media saturation only buys them so much in the way of information from the public at large. It was probably safe, but I wanted to be stealthy anyway. I didn't want to alert Cliff to my arrival, if he were already there, any more than I wanted to alert the cops if they were there.

With Smiles silently padding along between the underbrush and the trees, me in my boots and doing my best Injun Tracker walk, we progressed up the hill and over it to stop about five feet back from the tree line. I was dressed more consciously ninja-fied tonight: black parachute pants, brand new black t-shirt without any letters or markings or anything, black trench coat, black gloves, black boots. I stopped and listened for a long time, able to see nothing moving in the house and nothing in the yard. No sign of Cliff yet. It was just barely past eight o'clock, and I doubted The Transylvanian could have turned Cliff so fast that he'd be up and about and here already. I hunkered down on my heels, gestured Smiles over and wrapped my coat around him so he'd stay a little warmer and keep me a little warmer while he was at it. The cold didn't usually bother me, but something about that night made me want to be warm.

Ten minutes, twenty, forty five. I heard a church down the mountains somewhere chime nine o'clock. Smiles stayed put right beside me, as loyal a companion as he could possibly be. There weren't any birds, no bats, no bugs, nothing in this weather, this far up the mountain. We just sat and listened to nothing for a very long time.

I was a little surprised, then, when I smelled a predator approach at the same time that I heard a car come up the gravel road, way down the base of the hill, half a mile or more away. I looked around, but still couldn't see anyone or anything. Smiles jerked his head upwards and I followed his gaze. Just barely visible against the clouded night sky was something reflecting some light back from that damned night light in the yard. It got bigger, very slowly, and I could see that it was Cliff trying to come in for the world's clumsiest landing.

So, that was that. He'd been turned and he'd taken a life and his Last Gasp was to fly in his own natural shape. Fuck me, I thought, It's really real. He was such a homebody no one really knows him who's left alive now that his mother and father are gone. I marveled for a moment. Takes all kinds. He wasn't very good at flying, though, and he was basically spiraling down, sort of backpedaling, trying to get a handle on landing without breaking both his legs. Maybe he'd do just that, I thought, and make it easier on both of us.

The crunch of gravel got closer and closer, slowly, crunching rocks together beneath its tires as it came our way. Light car, nothing big and old and heavy, so probably not The Transylvanian. Hell, I doubted he knew how to drive, the way he acted. That was no good at all, because that meant either a neighbor—harmless—or a cop. Nobody else in the world would be up here that I could imagine. I prayed to something, somewhere, that they didn't spot my car hidden back in the woods.

Clyde finally pinwheeled into place, more or less, on the ground. He stopped, looked around, blinked a little and then laughed a hearty, belly-shaking laugh that chilled me right to the core. Cliff wasn't here to remember a family he'd never see again. He was returning the victor, ready to piss on their graves.

I knew in that moment that Cliff had killed Clyde himself. He'd probably done something to cause his mother's heart attack, too, and sliced open the brake lines on his father's work partner's car. He'd killed them all so that he'd be free to become one of us. There was a time, it's said, when a human wasn't considered ready to make the transition unless they eliminated the survivors of their mortal life on their own. Cliff had lived up to that ancient tradition.

I stood up and walked out from between the trees, still hearing that car coming, and punched the palm of my left hand with the knuckles of my right, grinding them together. "Evening, Cliff," I murmured. He spun and stared at me, then recoiled a little and looked choked. "That's predator smell," I said, and I smiled. "You didn't notice it on The Transylvanian because he made you. Something about that cancels it out. Makes me wonder sometimes why more of us don't kill our makers since they can't see us coming, but then, all the other weird little connections probably provide some subconscious inhibition we don't even know we have."

Cliff was still staring at me, but he finally closed his mouth and hitched up his pants. "What do you want?"

"First, I want that amulet."

Cliff blinked at me for a minute and then said, "How'd you know about the bracelet?"

"Long story," I said. "I bet you're not wearing it anymore but you've got it on you. Am I right?"

Cliff was too stupid to defeat the reflex of putting his hand in his left pocket, which I could see bulged a little with a circle of some sort. If he'd brought it with him then it was important, maybe something he thought gave him power. If that was the case, he would be wearing it already. If he wasn't wearing it, he couldn't or he thought he couldn't. That was simple enough to work out in a hurry. Enough observation of human behaviors leads one to be able to think things through pretty quick and vampires have nothing but time to observe human behaviors.

"Second, I think I want to kill you." I shrugged. No reason not to tell him the truth. We both started when there was a crunch of metal back down the road and a horn went off for a second. I didn't know what that meant so I banked on it meaning a signal of some sort. That was all I needed. I swept forward, coat flung open and back like the classic vampire's opera cape—some things we do because, you know, we have to—and leapt up to come down on top of Cliff. He put his arms up to try to protect himself, but if a kid who's been a vampire for a decade still doesn't really know his own strength, like the skinheads in that goth bar, then Cliff was about as steady on his feet as a toddler. I knew what it felt like, the world just overwhelming his senses, everything made out of crystal and light, everything too beautiful to look at, and him feeling so strong in the middle of it all. No, he was too befuddled by the grandeur of what the world looks like to us to be able to put up anything like a resistance. I yanked his arms out of the way before we'd even fallen to the ground, landing with my knees pinning his upper arms to the dirt. He cried out—not good in the suburbs, even ones out in the country like this—so I reached down and put one fat hand all the way around the front of his throat and leaned down, very close, to hiss at him.

That made him shut up real fast.

"Did you know who I was, before?"

"Wh... wh..." Cliff's voice wobbled in his throat, strained, couldn't get out. He was panting, still in the habit of breathing, still half reacting with human instinct.

"Did your father ever tell you who I was? Anything about me?"

Cliff tried to shake his head but I still had my hand around his throat, the other pulled back and the fingers arched halfway to making a fist, halfway to looking like B-movie claws. "Nothing," he wheezed. "I don't know what you're talking about."

"Was it your idea or his to kill off your family?"

"His," he gargled. "His! He made me. The Transylvanian made me." Cliff was panting and struggling still but he was so very weak. He was like a paper doll. I did not feel sorry for him. I felt just a little embarrassed for all vampires, everywhere, that he might have lived long enough to represent us to someone who wasn't.

"Did The Transylvanian tell you why you had to kill them?"

"So I'd be free," Cliff managed. I saw tears of blood start to well up in his eyes. He stank of it: he had drunk himself fat on it after he'd been turned. I wondered what poor soul had given up their life to sate that first, awful hunger, when we feel like we're empty inside, like the only thing we'll ever be able to do, ever again, is drink. He started to sob, then, strangled and choked but he was crying, no doubt about it. "He said I'd be free to live forever, to find a way out."

I didn't ask out of what, or where. I knew. We were soaking in it: a dying town, no industry, no job but as night watchman for a factory that didn't even make anything more, living at home with his parents all his fifty long years. Maybe he'd had a girlfriend or two, maybe he'd fathered a kid or two, maybe he didn't even know about them. He'd been stuck here his whole life and always would be and then he'd turned the wrong corner, explored the wrong long, dark hallway at work—or maybe The Transylvanian had come to him, maybe he'd engineered the guy getting the job in the first place?—and there'd been someone ancient who could sound so strong and so wise and he'd said, Want to get away from all this stupid shit, kid? It had worked for me, hadn't it? No doubt it worked for Cliff. I'd had money, some talent as an artist, opportunities to go somewhere and study if I wanted. Cliff didn't have anything. He had two parents who'd gotten old enough they'd start needing care one day and he was the only one they'd ever have to give it. He'd been born and raised in their home, lived out a pathetic little life in their home and would watch them waste and die while he himself got old and started to follow their footsteps in that same drab little home. It probably felt like he'd never had a thing of his own and then all of a sudden there he was with an offer to have the whole world, all eternity, all just for him. All he had to do was kill a few people he'd started resenting anyway.

I didn't bother moralizing or lecturing or wondering whether I could train him better, make a better vampire out of him. I didn't think about any of that at all. I held him still and said, very slowly, "You killed my best friend. That's what I am. I'm the vampire who knew your father when he was young and strong and still capable of regretting his very few failures. I consider you one of them."

I pulled my hand back from Cliff's throat and punched him in it so hard I heard the firmer tissues, cartilage or whatever they are, splinter and collapse. That was just to keep him quiet, though, so I could separate his head from his body with my bare hands, one knee on one of his shoulders for leverage, and not have him scream bloody murder while I did so. I stopped, though, just as I started to pull so that he was straining and wriggling, and knelt back down beside him. I'd changed my mind. It was time to find out what I could do, what gift Cliff had inadvertently given me.

"This is what a vampire is," I whispered into his ear. I shot my fangs out and bent his neck roughly to one side. If he'd been mortal he'd have asphyxiated by then, but that's one of the nice things about being undead: try as he might to breathe out of habit, and as much panic as the failure to do so might cause in him just a couple hours after the Big Flush, he was still alive and kicking. Sort of. Alive enough, anyway. I drove my teeth into the thick flesh of his neck, hit the vein and started drinking as hard as I could.

Cliff was enough of a vampire to struggle when a mortal would have slipped into utter acquiescence and his hand came out of his pocket with the bracelet in his fingers. Something about it nearly shone in the dim light of the stars, something inside it that sang out at that moment. I paused and pulled my mouth away from his neck and some of his blood—much to my surprise—sprayed out and of course, because these things always happen, splattered right on the bracelet. For an instant it shone ruby red instead of white, and Cliff's fingers smoked a little even though he dropped it and gargled an attempted scream through that ruined throat. My teeth drove between the folds of his neck one last time.

The Last Gasp of a mortal gives us a rush of powers, an ability to tap into something unique to each of us—Carla's healing, Cliff's ability to fly. I had no idea if that was also true of draining the life from another vampire. If it did, see, that suggested something weird. It meant, well, by one interpretation of the Last Gasp—and there are a lot of rumors and myths, I assure you—that we have souls, or something like them, some spark of life. Maybe it's just what keeps us animate, I don't know. Most vampires' Last Gasp, according to the stories, expresses itself in some way directly related to the mortal they've killed. For instance, there's a vampire in Raleigh who told me once that when she drains the life out of a human she spends the rest of the night looking like them to anyone who knew them. It's something mystical and supernatural and none of us really understands how it works. None of us – or few of us, anyway – knows what happens, if anything, when we finish off a vampire the same way.

I felt Cliff's life slip away and into me and I tossed his corpse to the side and sat down on my haunches. Smiles whined once and then pitched his head to the sky and howled long and high, still sitting loyally just inside the tree line. It had driven him half crazy to watch this and he couldn't hold it in anymore.

There was a terrible noise somewhere, like boulders having a fistfight. Two seconds of listening and closing my eyes against the intense brightness of the night and that yard with a night light on the other side of the house told me that it was shoes on gravel. It was someone walking up the gravel road from whatever had happened to crunch the car so bad a minute or two ago, and I could hear it like it was being piped through a sound system and I'd gotten my head shoved into the speakers.

I stood up, wobbled a little, then ran for the edge of the tree line. I had to get back to my car and get to The Transylvanian fast because I knew, deep down, that he would feel the severing of some connection between maker and made when I'd drunk the last of Cliff's life. Everything was out of whack, though. Everything was too loud and too bright, even in the darkness. I felt disoriented and off-balance.

Then the world went away as something blossomed in the darkness: a light out of nowhere, my brain overloading, and I heard Smiles start barking like crazy.

Cliff Wilfred's last gasp – the final extinguishing of whatever might be the contents and substance of his mortal soul – overwhelmed me there in the darkness. My power, it turns out, is to watch the information making up the life of my victim unfurl and blow apart before me like the contents of a card catalogue hurled into the wind. Sharp points of blinding light emerged from the darkness that had blotted out the world of normal reality, like the stained glass of a bombed church as seen in freeze frame, each of them a topic available to be plucked from the maelstrom and examined. I knew, deep in my bones, at the core of the part of me that came from my maker and from her maker and theirs and theirs and so on, down from whoever or whatever was the first sick bastard to become this thing we call a vampire, that I could reach out as though with my physical hands to grasp any of those shards of the life that had been Cliff Wilfred's and instantly know everything about that topic – everything he had known and maybe a little other people had known, too. I could fully and totally realize all the details of a matter in which he was involved, from his perspective and possibly others, and also that I could only do so for one topic that in any way intersected his time on this earth. I didn't understand why or how it worked, what mystical mechanism operated in his blood or mine or in the world around us, but I knew – no, I sensed – I could learn a lot about any and only one of the topics in the vast index of his life that spun in the darkness between two moments of time.

I could become the ultimate detective of any one thing that had happened in a life I chose to take, anything in which they had been involved, but only in retrospect and it would always mean their death.

In that interstitial space between seconds, as Cliff's life drained away into the sewer system of my own veins, I reached out and took hold of the inexplicably crystalline shard of information I knew intrinsically to be the death of Cliff's father – my friend Clyde – and every detail of its planning, its purpose and his execution were revealed to me in a scalding rush of emotions: hatred, resentment, admiration, sorrow and something not entirely unlike love.

Cliff had told the truth, as he knew it. He'd been lied to, and not well, but he was a moron and the lies hadn't needed to be complicated for him to meet them halfway. He'd been working his rounds one night at the plant, doing a foot patrol around the back of the Chemical building, when he'd heard a twig snap and turned to see The Transylvanian standing there, backlit by a security light. He'd asked who was there and the big guy in overalls had told him he could ask the same; that the plant was his home and had been for decades. He told Cliff he'd had his eye on him for years and had been waiting for the opportunity to make his move. He filled Cliff up with stories of how he'd seen how wasted had been the potential of this "young man" and asked him if he enjoyed his little life in this microscopically tiny place. The Transylvanian already knew Cliff was unhappy and knew all the right things to say: that he could make Cliff strong, make him young again, give him a life of his own. It had been the bit about making him young again that made Cliff say yes: a lie, but one Cliff was so eager to believe because that's all he'd really wanted. Cliff looked back on his own youth, spent bouncing from one minimum wage job to another, not as a tremendous waste of time, but as the happiest he'd ever been. He'd had no steady income, no sense of stability, and he hadn't needed one. His parents were glad to keep him close and give him all the security anyone could want. They also gave him freedom, most of which had disappeared as the detritus of his dependency piled up between strata of their own rapidly increasing needs and concerns. One day he'd woken up to find his parents old and sick, needing a caretaker, and the next he'd looked halfway to joining them. That terrified him beyond belief. If this old bastard who claimed to live at the plant, who had remarkable powers Cliff could not deny once he'd seen them at work, could make that go away, could rewind the tape to some point before that, Cliff would do anything for that. Kill? Sure, no problem.

He'd do that and more if needed. The murders he committed were nothing, in his mind: victimless crimes, no more worthy of remorse than sweeping a dead spider out the back door.

Of course, it hadn't all been about Cliff. What Cliff didn't know was that it was about The Transylvanian tidying up before leaving the house. He'd slowly but surely spent decades building a population that knew to hide itself from the powers that be. The Transylvanian had a plan, one based on his ideas of how vampires behaved versus how they should behave and what might make one go off the deep end. The Transylvanian had built his own little fiefdom, up in the mountains, in defiance of the power structures and the inter-familial agreements and truces and cease-fires that had accumulated over centuries. He'd built a hidden kingdom running through these ancient forests, and now he wanted to come out of hiding to assert himself over the foolish and sentimental children who dared call themselves vampires in nights like these. The vampires down east had spent so long bickering and picking one another off that finally a child of the twentieth century – unthinkably young! – dared claim authority over the rest of them. The Transylvanian saw an opportunity to create chaos and then bring order, a means of conquest that's worked time and time again across the history of the world.

He'd taken notice of Clyde when he refused to give up the case of a minor murder – there was more there I couldn't get this way, and I didn't know why – and then quickly realized that the Others, the vampire power structures he'd escaped in coming here, the ones to which my maker and I belong, had taken notice as well. He was insulted to find one of them nosing around up here again after so long. He'd decided the time had come to take care of things once and for all: murder the last human who mattered to the sentimental idiot – that'd be me – and make his move once that put me off my breakfast. If I shut down and went into some sort of self-pitying regression, great. If not, I would probably start kicking in doors and demanding to know what happened and he'd have his excuse and his opportunity that way. All he wanted was to upset me so he could put me down and make it look like a reaction to what I was doing rather than an overt maneuver for power of his own. Real vampires, The Transylvanian felt, shouldn't act like big babies when mere mortal meat died. He counted on me being less than his idea of a real vampire. He'd told Cliff all this in his endless gloating, his ceaseless self-satisfaction with the plans he'd set in motion, and Cliff hadn't paid much attention to anything but the lies he'd wanted to hear.

And here I was, playing along nicely with The Transylvanian's aims.

I slammed face-first into the ground when the flood of information ended and I came back to normal time. My feet had flown out from under me in a great big tangle and Smiles bounded over. He was snuffling my face and neck. I tried to tell him it was okay, but I felt like I'd just gone on a three-week bender in the space between two seconds and now I had the hangover to deal with. Smiles grabbed my collar in his teeth and pulled so hard my shirt tore. I managed to get a couple of fingers around his collar and he backed away with all his strength, dragging me, half lifting me from the muck. I made some sort of moaning sound, then staggered to one knee and let go of Smiles. He skittered backwards for a moment, then came back and grabbed the hem of my coat to keep dragging. I ordered him off with something that was almost language, stood and blinked my eyes at the corpse on the ground back there. A vampire usually dusts pretty fast but Cliff was only a few hours old and it can take a long time – maybe minutes – for us to turn to ash when we're that new. Hell, parts of him were probably still technically alive, dying flesh being carried around in a vampiric sack. The transition is not instant like they show you in the movies. It can take hours or even several nights and it hurts like all hell in terrible spurts.

I fumbled around on the ground in his direction, got there and tried to grab the bracelet but my hand felt like I'd put it on a hot stove when I touched it. I'd soaked it in a vampire's blood and if that little poem Clyde had stowed away in his office meant what it obviously had to mean, I wouldn't be able to touch that thing ever again. I yelped and drew my hand back and heard the boots on gravel stop for a moment, then start running. Gods, I was blowing everything. The Transylvanian had to know what had happened, I'd activated some screwy anti-vampire magic thing and the cops were probably running this way. I finally just left it and took off at a ridiculously slow, drunken stagger back into the trees. Smiles and I made our way a few feet back into the shadows where things were darker and my eyes wouldn't hurt so much from how bright everything was.

The boots left the gravel road and tore through the trees alongside the house like a thousand drums beating in time to one another before they erupted into the yard. It was a stout little Asian woman. I figured she had to be that detective with the sheriff's department, Detective Bing, the cop I'd seen quoted in the paper. She had a gun out and she spun in a circle with it held out in what I regarded as a very professional but maybe not practiced stance, more like a cop on TV than I imagine cops are in real life, before running over to Cliff's very cold body and leaning down to feel his throat. I was too disoriented to think of licking closed the wound in Cliff's neck so her fingers stayed there for a moment and she studied him. She put her hands to his forehead, the sides of his face. She had to be thinking he'd been dead for hours, surely, as cold as he was. We're all basically room temperature.

She stood up and pulled a radio out of her belt and spoke into it, voice terse. "I need two units and an ambulance at the Wilfred residence in Kills River, immediately." There was some garbled, staticky response and then she said it again, louder. "There's been a murder," she said, and she said it that way, in total surprise, there's been a murder, two or three more times before slapping the radio back into its holster. Then she pulled it back out and shouted, "And I hit a deer on my way up here so watch out for my car, it's in the middle of the goddamn road."

I was feeling a little giddy from the blood, from drinking down another vampire like that, and I giggled a little then slapped my hand over my mouth. I don't know whether she saw me or heard me or what, but all of a sudden she jerked her flashlight in my direction and before I'd even thought about it, at the speed of my recovering instincts and not my still-reeling conscious mind, I'd slipped behind a tree. Smiles started growling, loud, and he sounded like a chain being dragged across the gravel road.

"I know you're there," she said. "I could see something move a second ago."

I could smell fear. I could smell it as rich and as sweet as an apple pie fresh out of the oven. It was pouring off of her the way it only does in our most secret fantasies. I closed my eyes for a moment and just let the smell fill me, then breathed out. I opened my eyes to find she was still standing there, still waving the flashlight around so that I could see it flicker madly between the trees.

"I know you're there!" she said again. "I know it!" That time, though, her voice sounded less sure, less certain. If I just kept my cool, she'd turn around and go back down to her car and forget all about how I was ever here. I could hoodoo her, sure, but in this state I didn't really know if it would work or maybe it would work too well. Maybe I'd squeeze her mind too hard and erase every memory she'd ever had her whole life. I stayed very still, Smiles beside me, and let the night just hang out there in the air between us in perfect silence.

She lowered the flashlight a little, took a step forward, paused and raised the flashlight. Smiles barked once, a sharp and instinctive warning to stay the hell back. I heard her gasp, saw the light hit him full in the face. He looked like he could murder an entire army on his own.

In that moment, I had a terrible decision to make.

CHAPTER 3

The thing was, I should have killed H'Diane Bing right then and there. I should have just swept forward too fast for her to see, broken her neck and left. That would have been the smart thing to do; the *vampire* thing to do. But here was a smart, young detective on a case she would very likely find impossible to crack all the way. All her leads had dried up days ago. She'd come out here tonight to watch the house, most likely, the way I imagined it was her who'd been here a few nights before. She probably came out here every night, after her shift, sitting and watching and waiting, hoping something would happen. Well, something had happened, alright: Cliff, The Transylvanian, me, we'd all *happened*. She was up to her neck in it and she had no idea. She didn't necessarily need to ever have an idea, either.

She reminded me of Clyde, standing out there in that field, going back every so often to talk to his vampire friend, wondering if he'd ever know the truth. He never would. She never would either, I knew that, but maybe it would be okay if I just... helped her along. I could step out and gamble that I could handle the hoodoo after all, try to make her forget we were here, and Smiles and I could disappear back down the hill while she wondered where the time had gone.

On the other hand, I could step out and introduce myself. If she reminded me that much of Clyde, maybe I should go all the way. Wouldn't hurt to have a cop acquaintance up here again, would it? I was drunk on the blood and the Last Gasp or I never would have even considered this idea. Look at how I'd walked away from Jennifer McCordy that night in the ÜberBargains. That had been stupid and sentimental of me but I'd done it because it felt right and I'd known, somehow, that I could trust her to live up to that promise to try to stay away from me. I had no such feeling about this cop. It was her job – her calling – to run towards trouble.

Still, the idea was there and part of me was enamored of it. I'd told myself after meeting Jennifer that I wouldn't have known what to do with a friend if I'd made one, but Clyde was all the proof I needed of how untrue that was. I had a friend and now he was gone and part of me wanted, deep in my mourning him, to reach out and make another. I didn't know whether it was a side effect of the Last Gasp or something deeper and more intrinsically me, but for a moment I felt a deep and aching loneliness that resonated with that of my mortal days. Across all those decades I could hear the same morose tolling of the bell of sadness I had tried to leave behind by becoming the thing I now am.

Detective Bing from the newspapers, this young cop, she could be seen to fit the bill some part of me had dreamt up. It would be good to have some eyes up here. Yes. That argument kept suggesting itself to me as a justification. I dug a lot of information out of Clyde in tiny flakes over the decades. Only seeing him every once in a while didn't put much of a damper on his usefulness for that, really. Most stuff with vampires moves real, real slow. So, if option A was to leave her ignorant or dead right that moment the way ninety nine out of a hundred other vampires would have done, this was option B: offer a hand and try to make nice.

She stood there, gun out, flashlight out, Smiles staring at her, but to her massive credit she didn't shoot. It would have pissed him off something terrible. I heard her draw a shaky breath and say, with tremendous fear, "Good dog." There was a rustling somewhere off in the woods to the side, yards away. She turned for just a moment, just long enough, and I swept Smiles up in my arms, holding all hundred fifty pounds of him in both arms, out of sight behind a tree.

Detective Bing turned back around, gasped at the sudden absence of a dog, and then took two steps back. I waited long seconds. She took another step, this time closer to the woods. *Gods no*, I thought, *Just give up, go back, get scared or think you were crazy or anything other than come stomping into the woods to find the dog that just disappeared.* The rustling off to the side reoccurred and a deer shot away into the night. It must have been standing, frozen, the whole time. I heard H'Diane gasp again, then produce an involuntary chuckle of nervousness: she thought Smiles was some neighborhood dog making a hasty retreat or something like that. "Stupid fucking dogs," she said to herself, and she turned and walked back to Cliff's twice-dead corpse. I eased Smiles back onto the ground, put a hand over his mouth and peeked out in practiced silence. If I breathed anymore I would have been letting out the one I'd been holding.

She started patting Cliff down, checked that he had a wallet but didn't pull it out, checked his pulse again, and then surprised me by picking up the bracelet with obvious interest, looking at it for long seconds, then fishing around inside her shirt to produce a little leather loop on a long string around her neck. The leather had a kind of new smell about it, like it'd just come from a store, and the leather—my eyes were this powerful after draining Cliff—had fresh tears and seams in it where it had been cut up, then sewn back together. There were tiny little teeth around the edge and two iron nails driven through it and sewn in so that they formed a cross. H'Diane compared it and the bracelet and though they weren't the *same*, they clearly had the same general design sense.

Curiouser and curiouser.

She knelt there for a moment and then produced a scrap of paper from a pocket. She unfolded it. I could tell it was a small and hastily folded piece of lined paper from a little flip-pad. She mouthed the words on it to herself and I could hear so clearly that the half-whisper of sound carried to me like a shout:

> *If danger's high and hurtful nigh*
> *This necklace will give out a cry*
> *No one shall hear it but you my dear*
> *You'll know the reason for your fear*
> *It warns you if there's bad around*
> *Do not ignore this silent hound*

Christ, but I hadn't counted on there being that much folk magic around. What was this, Pagan Pride Day at the state fairgrounds? I sighed a little to myself. I don't know what it is about us, but we draw out all the old ways in a hurry whenever we're active. H'Diane went on comparing the two and then looked like she might slip the bracelet on. If she did, if I didn't stop her, she'd be protected from vampires as long as she wore it. I was certain of that. She reminded me of Clyde, yes, but did she remind me of him that much? Did I see so much of my friend in her that I could let her not just escape but give her an unknown, unquantifiable defense against us?

That made the decision for me. I couldn't just be passive and hope for the best. I stepped forward, through the trees, and I didn't bother to be quiet about it. I'd expected H'Diane to turn and use her gun: point it at me, maybe even shoot at me, something along those lines. I would have been fine with those but instead she slipped the bracelet on without even thinking about it.

Hell and damnation.

I held up both hands to show I had no weapons and then spoke aloud, from memory, Clyde's poem:

When Sun is low and Moon is high
Cold on you and danger nigh
Drench in blood of what you fear
Wear on wrist or keep it near
It stops the danger keeps you whole
It helps dear Jesus save your soul

H'Diane blinked as she listened. "Where is that from? What is that?"

"It's old. It was written for the bracelet you're wearing."

"You..." She swallowed. "You made the 911 call."

I watched her and then slowly nodded. "I did." She didn't raise her gun so I kept talking. Getting a human talking is always the key to moving things along. Most of them can't shoot someone who's responding to them; even the ones who are trained to shoot people are trained not to shoot someone who's still talking. "Tell no one that you have the bracelet. It will keep you safe from... us."

"What 'us?' What the hell are 'us?' What are you? This thing my girlfriend bought me is itching like crazy whenever I look at you."

"I'm no one of consequence," I said softly. Smiles stood stock still beside me, ears up, eyes like two dark gems in the night.

"My..." H'Diane closed her mouth and reached up to wipe her mouth on her sleeve. She looked like she was about to puke. The charms she was wearing must have actually worked. "My girlfriend had this necklace made for me. She said that a witch-woman told her that whatever this was wrapped up in was old and dark and hidden in the hills so that people didn't talk about it anymore."

"She was right." I cleared my throat a little; I didn't need to stick around, I needed to go! Precious seconds, a whole minute, had gone by while I dithered and hemmed and hawed and put on this little show. "Be careful of us." I paused and added, "But know that I might come to you again in the future. I might have a favor to ask. I'll offer whatever I can in return."

H'Diane gave me a look of incredulity and I laughed suddenly.

"I don't mean a bribe. I don't know exactly what I mean, but I don't mean that. I just want you to get that I'm not your enemy. I was a friend of Clyde's. I could be a friend of yours, too. Maybe. If you're willing to overlook what the charms tell you when I'm around. We're not all bad." I reconsidered. "Not all the time, anyway. Now I'm leaving. I'm going to walk off with my dog and you're going to let us go. Think about what I said. I could have hidden Clyde from you or hidden Cliff from you, but I didn't. Let that settle before you decide anything in particular about me. Don't try to fight me. You'll lose. Please, get that: I could hurt you but I don't want to hurt you. I want something better for both of us."

H'Diane started to go for her gun again but I didn't care about that. I'd already let her have the bracelet. It wouldn't be any use to try fighting her, but she didn't know that. I wasn't sure what would happen if I tried so I simply wasn't going to try. I turned around and started walking back into the trees, Smiles plodding along beside me.

"I could arrest you," H'Diane called after me, somewhat weakly.

I called over my shoulder, "Maybe next time."

I stopped once I was well up the hill and out of sight and hearing range so that I could watch H'Diane. I wanted to see whether she came after me. I could get away, I was sure, but I wanted to know what choice she made. To my surprise, she gave up on me. She knelt again by Cliff, patted him down on the other side and came out with a little leather holster for a little steel knife. It was technically within the limits of what state law would allow Cliff to carry but the blade was wicked sharp, way sharper than it was when he picked it up at whatever gun and knife show he'd been haunting, waiting for the perfect weapon. I could see the blade's edge from there.

I could smell his father's blood on it, too, even though it had been wiped down. Cliff had carried it since the murder as a souvenir. I'd seen him use it, in my mind's eye, when I drank down the unraveling of that particular topic along with the last spark of his life: he'd walked up behind him in the back yard and drawn it across my friend's throat with one quick movement and almost no struggle. Clyde hadn't tried to fight. The boy I'd befriended in high school would have fought, but he'd been replaced a long time ago by a weak old man who simply died when a knife was dragged through his neck. H'Diane handled the blade very delicately, realizing that it was probably a clue. She'd have enough DNA samples from it by next week to know it was the murder weapon she obviously suspected it must be.

I felt such a tremendous sense of satisfaction in that moment that my mind was made for me: satisfaction that Clyde's murder would be resolved in the eyes of the world; that Cliff would take the blame; that this young mortal wouldn't carry that case around on her back the way Clyde had always carried his. I turned and walked away, silent as I could be, through the woods. Maybe she would be willing to befriend me over time, maybe not, but I was surprised at how glad I was to see that there in fact was not a new Clyde left to haunt her own first case in Hardisonville.

I walked back up to my car and my phone buzzed. I had a text message from Roderick. I flipped it open and read:

We have your cousin. Time to settle this. Be at the plant in the next thirty minutes if you want him to live. I demand satisfaction for the damage you have done to my family.

Smiles started growling. He'd sensed the shift in my emotions as I raced from something like acquiescent satisfaction to bristling rage in a moment. We both jumped into the Firebird and I threw gravel in every direction as I got out of there.

I drove thirty minutes, out 280 again, then turned onto 64, then up that long, lonely mountain road. When I roared into the parking lot of Clarke Industries' Brevard Operations Center I parked it across the handicapped spot in front of the gatehouse doors, got out and strode inside. There was no more need to be formal or stealthy or pretend-nice. As The Transylvanian had said, it was time to settle this.

Chapter 4

Iwas halfway up the walk towards the old factory's production plant when I heard The Transylvanian's voice about five feet to my left. "You've killed him," he said. "I can smell him on you."

It took everything dark and terrible every vampire carries inside just to keep from jumping ten feet in the air at that. Smiles barked at it once, like he had spotted a ghost. I stopped walking and looked over where the voice was. There was nothing there but empty space.

"You killed the others, too, didn't you?" This time he was ten feet behind me. I turned slowly; nothing but air.

"What purpose did you think that would serve?" The voice was twenty feet further up the walk, towards the building. The door in, the one I'd used when I'd first come here, was sitting there just like always. I doubted it was any more locked now than it had been then. I felt around with all my senses, still hyper-tuned from drinking down Cliff, and I knew there was nothing there but the voice. So that's what The Transylvanian could do, I figured; he could speak from afar. Weird, but probably very useful. I wondered how this related to the person he'd killed, what mysterious way this somehow reflected some facet of their personality.

"They were a disease, a cancer," I growled. "I am stamping them out. They endanger every last one of us."

"I don't think that's it." The sound of The Transylvanian's voice had moved again, closer to the door into the factory. "I think you *liked* killing them. I think you're the monster here."

I laughed. There wasn't much else to do, was there? "You want monster?" I laughed again and the lights in the parking lot flickered. "You've kidnapped and converted dozens of people over the years so that you could build a private army. Don't expect me to give much of a damn what you think."

The Transylvanian made a little 'tsk' noise that made my blood boil. "You've no respect for your elders, young man." His voice had moved towards the doors again. He was baiting me, I knew this, and I did not care in the least. My cousin was in there, assuming he was still alive, and I was perfectly willing to tear the building down to get him.

"You should see what I did to my elders," I muttered and in a flash few mortal eyes could have detected I shot in the door and was running down the hall and taking the stairs upwards three at a time.

"Do you dare to enter my domain and challenge me?" The voice stayed three yards ahead of me as I ran. I marveled, somewhere in some left over part of my mind, at the control he exhibited over this odd little power. I was practically floating from step to step. I hadn't escaped the bounds of gravity by any stretch, I was putting one boot down after another as I climbed, but I could feel the tiniest touch, just enough to catch a whiff, of Cliff's power of flight. Another secret of my kind I'd learned in one night, another to file away for later and wonder how many of us knew this: that we could super-charge our powers by draining one another, that we could take just a little of their own Last Gasp and use it as our own.

"I'm coming after you, aren't I?" Normally a big guy like me would have stroked out one flight up, but that's one of the many advantages of having a purely optional circulatory system. My voice was steady and even. I wouldn't sweat, wouldn't pant, wouldn't get tired for a very long time. Those are all the things we think about when we accept the Big Flush, all those flashy entrances by our makers-to-be, the effortlessness, the inherent grace. We don't think about the other 360 nights of the year. Now, though, I was perfectly happy to revert to those old tricks of showmanship if it was down to a head-on turf war between me and The Transylvanian. Maybe he'd kept in top form and maybe not. I didn't see him having a lot of excuses to stand around flexing the mojo in a factory full of mortals all those years; even less opportunity as he passed night after night hanging around an empty one.

"You are," the voice said. It sounded... pleased. Almost. That was enough to make me stop cold in my tracks. "Oh, there's no trap," he assured me. He'd dropped a lot of the drawl now and sounded more mature, more intelligent; to be frank, more cunning. "It's just a pleasant surprise. It's the old way, you know. From *before*."

"Before what?" I was annoyed at all this, suddenly, and leaned against the hand rail on the stairs—four flights up and he was still leading me higher—and let the silence stretch out as he considered an answer.

"Before vampires started laying claim to territories that weren't theirs. Before the Bobs started showing up in North Carolina, before *you*. You want rules, order, good behavior. You want safety and certainty. You eradicate my children because you can't control or cow them, because they don't recognize your..." He chewed the word unpleasantly. "Your *authority*. You don't even consider that there might be another way, a way just as safe if not safer for all of us, a way older than you or your maker."

I took a long breath and tried to look bored. "What way is that?"

"The way we lived for millennia before this modern era of cell phones and false identities and computer records and *fixers*." He said 'fixers' like it smelled bad. "To live quietly, to accrete power and wealth to sustain us, to create communities around ourselves that would rely on us as much as we relied on them, to make being chattel so rewarding to them that the mortals eventually can't imagine denying us our due." He tsk'ed again and it made me even angrier this time.

The voice had started drifting upstairs again and I followed it at an easier pace, watching warily the spot from which it seemed to emanate. I wasn't going to be caught off guard by him appearing out of nowhere. If he could throw his voice that was one thing; if he could turn invisible that was quite another. "I'm not sure I understand," I said, though I understood well enough: the village at the foot of Dracula's castle, perhaps? The peasants who refuse to look at Harker when he's leaving, the villagers who cross themselves at the sight of the Count's obsidian coach. The Transylvanian was training up vampires to be monsters like him who cowed and herded the humans around them—Carla healing up that old man so he'd leave her more of his wealth when he died, Blaine draining the Latinos dry because he didn't like them on his turf and hiring a cadre of mortals to staff his business and become addicted to his blood, both of them taking big actions that would start tiny rumors they could nurture and tend and groom as they grew into superstitions. They were creating a world in which locals got used to living in a town where the wealthy people clung to life just a little longer than they should and the undesired outsiders wound up dead in a ditch with a little booze splashed in their face and nobody got too stirred up about it.

"Of course you do," The Transylvanian said. He was practically purring by now. "Do you know anything about the history of this plant?"

I wrinkled my brow and then quietly but casually told him no.

"Most floors ran in darkness all the time as unpackaged, unprotected film would spool from one machine to another as it was made. There was a spoken code for going around on those floors: 'Watch watch!' The workers would all say that when they were about to turn a corner in the darkness. It was how they signaled one another so they wouldn't run into one another all the time. Walking down the halls, then, I'd hear that at every corner, say it at every corner, could hear it coming from other corners down other halls, a beehive of warnings flashing from one person to the next."

I sighed and kept walking. "Go ahead and spit out your tortured metaphor so we can get this over with," I said.

The Transylvanian allowed a small chuckle. "They—mortals—are like that. When there are unknown dangers, when something unknown and unknowable looms in the darkness, they shout warnings to one another. As you and your little friends in modern vampire society run around hiding behind he facades of legal identities and feeding in shadowed corners, they sense your presence. They sense that danger. They rush to investigate and then to warn one another. No, the better way is my way, where we build ourselves into the environment so that they have nothing special to fear from us. When you hide from them you still leave traces—a case of anemia that goes unexplained, a mysterious death, a scream heard drifting over the hills. You leave a blank spot in their view of the universe which the mortal mind yearns to fill. Look at how they live today, obsessed by fears known or otherwise. They create television channels that do nothing but tell them of new reasons to be afraid. They live in terror of terrorism. They live in angry fear of whole religions. On the rare occasion their leaders assert their cultural identity the mortal hordes quail and shudder and urge those leaders to back down after it's too late."

"And you and all your minions have fixed that?"

The voice was still leading me. We had walked up to the seventh floor and then down a darkened hallway only very dimly lit by an occasional red light fixture in a high corner. I could see perfectly well by that, but I could only imagine what it was like for human eyes, when the plant ran all the time, trying to navigate these halls by feel and, after enough years, memory. I could imagine them calling out this "watch, watch!" at every corner, warning others who might or might not be there that they were there, too. We had turned one of those corners and gone to a set of double doors that had CUTTER #9 on a large plaque on either door.

I pulled open the one on the right and stepped inside as The Transylvanian spoke again.

"We give them the solace of knowing what to fear." His voice was soft, almost wistful. "They know to fear the night, the darkness, and they have some idea of *why* they fear it—not a full conscious knowledge, nothing that would ever get printed, but enough subjective experience to come up with an explanation they can live with. We are the heart of their superstitions, their nightmares, but we are an old and careful race and they know, deep down, that their ancestors grew and thrived alongside us, and if they behave themselves, they can do the same. They stop searching for what plagues their sleep and makes those screams across the hills. They huddle together, yes, they find it unpleasant, yes, but they *stop searching for more to fear.*"

The room was almost pitch dark. I had my eyes as open as they could be but there simply wasn't much light here by which to see. I was almost as blind as a human in a tomb: I could see shapes in the darkness. Feeling around, I found a switch that turned on a light in a closet. The sliver that came out from under the door was enough for me to see again. The machinery of the cutter, whatever that is, was dusty but intact. I doubted any part of it could move anymore, sitting without maintenance for years by this point, but it was an interesting arrangement of interlocking contraptions nonetheless. I looked around a bit in the room, taking a few steps this way and then that to peer around various mechanisms and into corners. I pulled the door open on the lighted closet. I could smell dead flesh on the other side as I did so and found two recent corpses, one male, one female, neither of them anyone I knew or especially cared about. They, I imagined, had served to slake the thirst of Cliff after he was turned. The hunger in that moment is unbearable, the body's new need to feed at any cost overwhelming any other thought or desire.

There was also a much older corpse, desiccated, like the natural mummy of that guy they dug up in the Alps a few years ago. He was wearing a fairly modern outfit, though: chinos and galoshes and a heavy sweater and oxford shirt. He'd had gloves on his hands, but all I could see between the gloves and the sleeve of his sweater were exposed bones.

"The songchaser?" I said it aloud, though I hadn't heard much from the voice lately and so for all I knew The Transylvanian had gone away or his power had faded or something like that.

The simple "yes" came from a few yards behind me and was delivered, I could tell, by The Transylvanian himself. He was in the room. I was stunned I hadn't smelled him come in but maybe that was another part of this Last Breath ventriloquism he had going. I turned slowly.

"He was mortal."

"He was a hunter."

"A what?"

The Transylvanian smiled a little, hands in the pocket of his overalls. "A vampire *hunter*. We used to get them more than we do now. He was a vampire hunter. I could tell from the way he asked questions around town. Some of the people he talked to were loyal to me for one thing or another—a favor I'd done their family, a big buck I'd killed and brought and skinned and cleaned so their dear old grandmother would have something to eat in the winter, that sort of thing. He wasn't asking about songs, he was asking about disappearances, deaths, strange occurrences. I hunted him and his helpers, his local *guides*, and slew them to protect us all. You cannot possibly believe that's a bad thing."

I wrinkled up my brow at him. "So why all the charades about not being involved? Why keep his body here when someone from the plant might find it? That doesn't seem too smart, and being all smart about this vampire shit seems to be your biggest claim to fame."

The Transylvanian favored me with a luxuriously slow shrug that happened entirely in his shoulders and neck; his hands never left his pockets. He didn't otherwise move, except to speak. "He was a trophy. I'd hunted the hunter and won. That victory was *mine* and no one else's. I saw no reason to share it with anyone else. This was my territory and I acted within my prerogative within my territory. No one else needed to know and no one else needed to share that victory with me."

"A trophy?"

The Transylvanian smiled a little in reply.

"Christ," I said, holding up my middle finger. "Keeping a mortal corpse around to look at as a reminder of your skill as a hunter? That's what sport hunters do, not food hunters. That's the most human thing ever. Also, your metaphor—simile, whatever—about the dark hallway and the mortals saying 'watch, watch?' That doesn't make any sense. You, my friend are just super-attached to this idea of being the big, scary monster in the woods. That's what you get off on. I don't think it's really enough to call a philosophy or an ethos or anything, it's a *pose*. It is overt *posturing*. It doesn't hold up under the most cursory examination. You know why those mortals walked around saying 'watch, watch?' Because they worked in a building with rooms named things like 'Cutter Number Fucking Four,' that's why. They were on high alert all the time and adopted systems of warning one another *because they knew they were in danger*. Sure, maybe you and your brood have conditioned a few specific people to be accustomed to being in your presence. Do you think none of them will *ever* reject that? Do you think none of them will ever decide it's time to get that yoke from around their necks? You ought to meet a lady who lives in my neighborhood. She'd set you straight in about two seconds flat.

"You think all us modern vampires endanger the rest of us by living among humans in secret? You've created an even greater chance that some individual human being will take it upon herself or himself to hunt us all down, you moron. You said yourself that back then there were *more* people who hunted us. I think that, really, is why you hide this 'trophy' away and try to make people think you didn't have anything to do with that murder. You got up on your high horse and went out and murdered three people and left two of their bodies to be discovered and what did it get you? A couple of cops up your tail pipe for fifty years! Shit, man, you're clueless. You are beyond stupid."

That got to him. I could tell that The Transylvanian was starting to get pissed at me. He'd taken his hands out of that front pocket on his ridiculous overalls and cracked his knuckles one by one at his sides. I figured he was going to jump me while I was still talking so I drew another breath and kept going.

"You've been out of the game, out of human society, for way too long, man. You think they don't all carry cameras and telephones and video cameras in their pockets—and all of those are one device! Do you even know what a video camera *is*?"

But I stopped talking then, because I heard two shouts from another room and one of them was Roderick. Smiles started barking like crazy and I leapt at The Transylvanian with my fangs out.

Chapter 5

The Transylvanian wasn't completely ready for me, but he'd had a long time to hone his physical skills. He sidestepped my flying tackle and swung me around by one arm so that I went face-first into one of those big film making machines, bashing my face against it. I could feel my nose crunch when he did it but I didn't give him a moment of leeway. I bounced off the machine, pushed some blood through my veins to give me all that strength we always have on tap and pushed away with my feet to plant my skull in his abdomen and send both of us flying the opposite direction across the room. Smiles was in the air, too, on an intercept path, like a rocket made of teeth and foaming spittle. It was like playing pinball with those super-bouncy balls they sell in drugstores. The Transylvanian was slammed into the wall—I could hear his spine crunch a little—and all three hundred fifty pounds of me and another buck fifty of crazy dog sandwiched him there for a moment before he could push us away. I heard popping up and down his back as he healed—I was reknitting my nose already, myself—and he hauled back and landed a massive fist against my left temple as I tried to stand.

That sent me spinning around in a circle and rolling across the floor but I came up in a crouch as he started to charge after me. I drew a knife out of one boot and held it in both hands to get as much force behind it as I could.

We collided a moment later, and I planted both feet on the floor, pushing the knife against his neck with all my weight. He scrabbled to try to pull me away, off of him, as my momentum overcame his and started sliding him backwards. I thought for a moment that the knife had found a way through his skin, and I saw the tip disappear between folds of wrinkled flesh, but I didn't smell any blood and pushing against him didn't suddenly get any easier. Finally I had scrabbled him back across the floor to the machine he'd smashed my face against and I pressed his head against it then planted a boot on some other part of the machine for leverage. I kept pressing the knife just as hard as I could. Smiles was trying to bind up one of his arms but he could only get the one. With a desperate snarl, The Transylvanian tore a pipe or arm or something off that huge machine and swung it around to clock me good and hard on the right temple and send me flying.

As we both stood straight again, I reached into my coat and drew out a sawed off shotgun, then leapt back over the cutter and started firing silver pellets at The Transylvanian just in case he had that exceptionally rare weakness. Seth gave me the gun and the custom shells back in Raleigh, right after I took over, and I've never known quite what to think of that, but right then I could have kissed him square on the lips. The tiny beads of birdshot were sufficiently bright that I could see them cut The Transylvanian's skin and draw blood in thin and perfectly straight lines across his face. He didn't like that at all and the way he roared back at me made me wonder for a second whether maybe I'd hit the jackpot with silver after all. No luck: a vampire who's vulnerable to silver goes down in a heap at the sight of the good flatware; a face full of two shells of bird shot would have reduced him to ash on the ground before the smoke cleared. All this did was piss him off even worse.

As he came at me I gritted my teeth and tossed the shotgun into the air, flipping it, and caught it by the still smoking barrel then spun in a circle and clocked The Transylvanian across the nose with the stock like I was going for the home run record. I heard bones snap and shatter in his face and let the gun go so that it flew across the room and, more importantly, out of my hands. They would knit fast enough but the burns from the still-smoking barrels hurt like you wouldn't believe. I let the momentum of the spin carry me and on my second time around I put up one boot like a kung fu ballerina, catching The Transylvanian on the back of the head—the whack with the shotgun having spun him around—and heard bone give way to steel toes. I felt his skull crack open; something cold splashed out and hit me in the face and I could smell that it was his rank, revolting blood. There was another roar and he reached up to catch my boot in both hands and yank me off balance so that I went down in a sliding, sprawling heap as he tried to fall upon me. Smiles was leaping again, but The Transylvanian ducked and my old dog sailed right over in a clean miss like they'd practiced that move for a week.

I felt The Transylvanian's teeth graze my collarbone and something about that woke up every possible emergency reserve of panic in my system. Vampires don't operate much on our own hormones and such, what with all those glands getting shut down along with everything else, but the lizard brain is still back there doing its thing the whole time and all of a sudden I knew I had to do whatever was necessary to keep this monster from drinking my blood until I was really and permanently dead. I shot to my feet with him still wrapped around me and ran across the room and into another of these big-ass cutting machines. They were the size of a mini-van and built into the floor, with huge arms and levers and, somewhere, one assumed, blades on the same scale. I slammed The Transylvanian into it so hard that I actually drove his fangs into my shoulder—not on a vein or an artery but piercing my flesh and grinding against my clavicle which, it turned out, didn't help so much with the panic.

An unspeakably loud boom went off right in my ear and the teeth came out of me suddenly, tearing flesh as they went. I could smell gunsmoke and saw more silver pellets drift past as time slowed down in my panic. Roderick was standing there with blood on his shirt and the shotgun in his hands.

"Sorry to take so long," Roderick said, "But I had these giant chains to break." Handcuffs hung from his wrists and the chains dragged behind his feet.

"Any others around?" I shouted as The Transylvanian tried to recover from a shotgun blast delivered directly to the side of his throat, writhing wildly in my arms. He was trying to kick, but Smiles had managed to get both leg cuffs of his overalls and bind him up again.

Roderick shook his head at me, eyes searching mine for a moment. I couldn't believe the overconfidence of this vampire, to hide up here all by himself for so long, no lieutenants or offspring or agents to assist him: to go get my cousin all by himself, I guessed, and then take me on mano-a-mano. It was madly prideful, but then, that was The Transylvanian's whole shtick.

Something about that snagged in my brain, but I didn't have time to think.

Reaching down, I grabbed The Transylvanian around the waist by the belt loops of his overalls and lifted him up into the air. His cries echoed around the room and I could feel and smell blood spattering onto me from the damage I'd done to his nose and the back of his head. He'd be healing already, of course, and, in whatever tiny corner of me wasn't completely and senselessly terrified, I knew I had to capitalize quickly on any advantage those wounds and my cousin's escape gave me.

"The machine," Roderick screeched. "Shove him into the machine!"

I slammed The Transylvanian head-first into the nest of equipment that comprised a cutter and then, praying to all the gods that might be listening that these devices lived up to their names, I started pushing so that I was driving him bodily farther and farther into it. I let go when he started kicking and caught me one in the eye and started feeling around for anything that might be a lever or a button or anything I could use to make this machine work by my own hands.

Roderick was one step ahead of me, his hands wrapped around something that seemed like a handle. He tried to jerk it back and forth but it wouldn't move. *This plant was highly automated,* I could feel myself thinking from about a million miles away. *They probably made it a real bitch to do exactly this.* I started running around it, yanking levers, mashing buttons, kicking it, cussing it, whatever it took, until finally Smiles grabbed on with his teeth and the two of us yanked so hard on part of it I felt a hose of some sort give way in my hand. Foul, chemically sweet-smelling fluid started belching out from whatever pressure remained in the line.

That stuff was apparently fairly important because I heard the machine start to creak. It wasn't that I had turned it on, it was that whatever nascent hydraulic pressure it had holding it still was all running out around my hand. There was a long, slow groan of metal, then another creak. The Transylvanian was still in there, screaming, his feet kicking like wild. The creak of metal turned into a shriek as something big and very heavy started to win out against the pressure that had held it up. Roderick gave one fierce pull, roaring with the effort, and The Transylvanian's shrieking shot higher, then started to sound like gurgling as the metal—what I assume was a or perhaps *the* blade—suddenly gave out a wet, thick sound like *SHLIRK* before clanging against whatever track or shield or groove it was made to rest in before being raised again.

Now legless, with mechanically clean slices where they had been, the upper majority of The Transylvanian shot out the other side of the machine and practically into my waiting arms. My fangs were out, pure instinct, and

Roderick's eyes glowed with all the dark light of a blood moon as he nodded vigorously. "Do it, cousin," he breathed. "Do it!"

The monster that lives deep inside each of us, the animal that wants blood in endless arcing fountains, won. I drove my teeth into the fat between The Transylvanian's jowls and tore at them until I tasted something salty and cold and wretched well up into my mouth. Smiles threw his head back and howled like a wolf, like a hound on his prey, like some animal that had never seen a man and never would. I started draining The Transylvanian as his own shriek of agony and defeat rose again and stayed up there amongst the rafters, a steady siren that never wavered until I felt that tiny spark – whatever part of him had been human once – fly out and fill me with the chilly fire of the Last Gasp.

The databanks of the life of Phineas Abraham Rochester yawned before me like a door pulled open on a blizzard of light.

There were many topics I could have explored in that moment: his life as a failed farmer in the third wave of early 19th century settlers to come to this place, spent watching crops underperform as plank roads and then boats and then railroads came and made his efforts obsolete; whatever ancient wyrm had seen fit to turn this embittered little slug of a man into one of us and why; the ways he'd passed the years since. Instead I reached out with my mind and grasped the one of most immediate interest to me: this plan of making a brood of his own to populate the mountains of Western North Carolina and then trying to set me off-balance. I already knew his intention but I wanted to know who else knew, who else was involved, and anyone whose path had intersected his plan to move against me whether they realized it or not.

I saw myself and my own actions in that context, of course, and his. I saw him making many, many vampires over the years, some of whom were so unstable he killed them himself later. I saw H'Diane Bing, saw her standing in that same field in exactly the same pose I'd seen Clyde take a million times: slightly stooped, wondering to herself what was wrong with this world that it could cast off a shard of pain and suffering in a field like that one moment and keep going along like nothing had happened the next. I saw The Transylvanian watching her from the sidelines, sometimes in person and sometimes through minions he had under orders to do nothing for now lest it attract the wrong kind of attention. I supposed he was afraid of humans after all, at least to some degree or another. I saw Clyde standing there, years before, in almost the same posture. I could feel The Transylvanian's gloating over leaving Clyde broken – just a little bit – when the case went up in smoke. I saw Roderick arrive in Asheville, but it was many days before he'd told me he got there. He'd been spotted right away by more of The Transylvanian's brood and they'd kept tabs on him because he clearly moved with a purpose I wouldn't have expected. Knowledge blossomed in my mind that he had been sent there by Agatha, that she and her whole organization knew The Transylvanian was there and probably up to something, but that she knew if she was seen to assist me then I'd never truly rule this state again. A king who still needs his mother's help is no king at all. I could see that Roderick was Agatha's latest recruit, that she was trying to bring him into the organization, and that he'd lied to me about it – they'd both lied – even if only by omission. It was one of those flashes of information at an intersection of lives and intentions: those of Agatha and of The Transylvanian and of Roderick. I didn't know why I knew, how things The Transylvanian himself hadn't known could come to me this way, but it was all new to me still. I had little ability to steer the experience. I could just cling to the ride and see what I saw once I'd picked a topic to reveal.

Then I saw Jennifer McCordy out there in those woods, installing her cameras and hoping for the best or possibly for the worst, depending on one's perspective. I could scarcely believe her determination. I'd left her feeling like she'd woken up to something, somehow: to life or to opportunity or to a new sense of self-determination. I had no idea what to think of what she'd done with it by hunting signs of any vampire but me. She'd kept her promise not to go looking for me, but surely, sooner or later, this would mean some sort of trouble.

The most shocking part of what I found as reality unfolded itself in the hands of my mind was watching as Roderick crept through the shadows of the whole topic, eliminating vampires one at a time, here and there. I assumed he had a Last Gasp power, too, or would have if I'd stopped to think about it, but I hadn't even bothered to wonder. Just minutes before, I'd wondered to myself about The Transylvanian's bravado in facing me by himself, but he'd had a minion who showed up at Roderick's hotel to take him prisoner; before that he'd had several of them. I'd seen them here myself the first time I arrived. Roderick had killed them all by draining them dry and then they'd simply dropped out of existence and when I thought of them later, recalled seeing them with my own eyes, reality had corrected my "error".

There had been thirty-odd vampires here when I rolled into town, thirty of them The Transylvanian's spawn, but James the Neo-Nazi told us with absolute honesty that there were seventeen. The Transylvanian himself hadn't noticed the discrepancy. There were vampires missing and no one even knew. More of my favorite topic: the missing missing. It occurred to me that was probably Agatha's plan B for Roderick: whether I succeeded in facing The Transylvanian and asserting my authority or not, Roderick was to eliminate his brood in his own special, invisible fashion. My cousin must be the backup *me* in Agatha's plan. If I had failed utterly, at least Agatha would finally, after patiently passing the decades, be rid of the arrogant and old-fashioned vampire who had thought he could just up and claim some territory and overpopulate it for no reason other than to prove he could. I wondered how different that really was from how I'd taken on Bob Three and claimed his mantle once he was dead, but then, that was to Agatha's advantage, wasn't it? She's one of the bosses of Atlanta and by extension the state of Georgia. Having her own offspring rule a contiguous state was both a feather in her cap and a promise of having backup muscle close at hand.

Every vampire to whom I'd spoken in my time here, other than Roderick, was one of The Transylvanian's brood. I would have to find and kill all of them. After that, Asheville would be essentially empty of vampires, another Charlotte, a city to which no one would move for reasons no one could quite express. I didn't want that, not in my state, but I couldn't immediately imagine an alternative in that space between motes of time when all of this flooded into my brain.

In all of this, a phrase kept bobbing to the surface but the machinery of the Last Gasp didn't choose in its ridiculous whimsy to reveal it to me: *the last war*. That was something I simply had to take in along with everything else and hope to revisit later in some better, more sober, more rational moment.

Reality snapped back and just before I swooned and hit the floor I looked at Roderick with blood all over my face. "You make the world forget," I burbled. "When you kill someone. You make us all forget they even existed, don't you?"

Roderick didn't immediately answer, or if he did then it was while I blacked out for a few seconds. I came back around or just blinked, I don't know which. In the darkness I could hear a new sound with my renewed hyper-active senses: the sound of dust—ash, even—sifting down through an old machine and settling in piles on the floor, like sand running over the metal of the equipment. Smiles was licking my face and whimpering in concern.

I coughed a little as I drew a breath—I was sufficiently freaked out from having The Transylvanian's teeth touch my flesh that I was panting a little even though I don't have to breathe anymore—and sucked some of the swirling dust of The Transylvanian into my lungs. Roderick moved in silence to reclaim my gun and hand it to me. Then he pried an ancient dust rag from a worktable off to one side and started wiping down all the places the dust had been disturbed by a handprint or a boot or the outline of a face.

"Answer me," I said. "Or don't. I already know. Goddamn it, you should have told me."

"No, cousin," Withrow said, offering me a hand to help me stand. He knew I didn't need the help, but the gesture mattered. "You would have thrown me out of town immediately and I was here to *help*. I couldn't allow that. I came here to help you because you came to me in Seattle and gave me a part of my family back." He shrugged. "And because it sounded fun."

The smile he gave me was one of the cruelest expressions I've ever seen a vampire wear.

Two nights later, Roderick and I stood in a nameless little graveyard off Kills River Road. It backed up against dark woods draped over a sloping hillside and had a narrow, poorly-paved lane wrapped around it like the icon of a moat. Clyde's grave was here, buried hurriedly by the county once they realized there was no family to whom they could hand over the corpse. He'd had an insurance policy for this stuff and a gravestone he'd picked out and paid for a lot of years ago. It was big and silver-gray and had his wife's name on the other half. I held a single lily in my hands, a restrained memento to the dead that I thought Clyde might appreciate. Smiles was wandering the graveyard on his own, investigating all the other dogs brought here by mournful inheritors in recent days, or ones from the general neighborhood, or ones who'd gone wild and lived in those ever-present woods just a tree line away.

Roderick joined me a few minutes after I arrived, graciously giving me time on my own in case I needed to get emotional. I didn't have tears to shed, though. I'd wrung them all out that first night and then, as so many find on the occasion of another's death, that initial energetic anguish had been replaced with the viscous silence of sorrow and the fury of clenched fists. I studied every detail of Clyde's gravestone while I waited for Roderick to arrive because I had a feeling it would be many years before I would want to go back to it.

Roderick pulled up in that absurdly tiny sports car he'd rented, a soapbox derby racer wrapped in leather and lights. In contrast to my lily he had a bouquet of a dozen roses. If it had been anyone else I would have torn into them—perhaps literally, I realized—but with my cousin it's different somehow. It's easier to chalk it up to his being crazy or just not knowing better or maybe even thinking I'd see it as some kind of a welcome joke. He set them at Clyde's grave, stepped back and stood beside me in silence. We meditated together that way for a long while with nothing more than a glance between us. There was a smile on Roderick's face when we exchanged that look but it was not of mockery; it was of being glad to be together.

"So," he said after a time, that same weird little smile of his returning. "Tell me everything. Tell me about Cliff and what happened at Clyde's house."

So, I did. Almost.

For reasons I couldn't quite suss out at the time, I didn't tell him about the necklace or the bracelet I'd left with H'Diane. I didn't initially know why, I just left it out. It took a while to tell him about The Transylvanian, to describe the way my Last Gasp works. We did not immediately discuss his. He had never responded to my question at the old film plant and I knew that meant it was off-limits, at least in the state our relationship had been right that moment. I found myself leaving out my inexplicable awareness that Roderick was here at Agatha's behest, too. Something made me hold back from that, perhaps because there was no way to bring it up without sounding accusatory, perhaps because I wasn't myself sure how or why I knew. In truth, I felt like I might have done the same in her shoes. When I was done, Roderick looked away and at that blanket of trees for three solid minutes. We could hear all the little creatures of the woods rustling around, ignorant of us, unaware. Finally he turned back to me and lit a cigarette. "So what now?"

"I don't know. I need to find the rest of The Transylvanian's brood but I don't even know who they are or how many. Sure, we got told a number by that one guy we questioned up in Asheville but he was probably conditioned to lie about it. Plus…" Again I bit down on bringing up Roderick's Last Gasp and the way it made the numbers iffy at best. Instead, I let it drop. Not yet. Something told me to wait.

Roderick nodded and sighed. "Does that mean you're going home to Raleigh? Are you just going to visit more?"

There was something in the way Roderick asked that question. I shut my mouth again before I could give a simple and mindless answer. We let it sit there for a few seconds and then I spoke. "I guess."

"Hmmmm." He just made a little noise like that and then looked away again.

"Why? What's it to you?"

"I have…" Roderick smiled again, still not looking at me. "I have an idea: a proposal."

I knew this was what I was waiting for: why I'd left out the necklace and my knowledge of Roderick's mission here.

"I would like you to give Asheville to me," Roderick said. "I would like to stay here and keep hunting The Transylvanian's minions. I would respect your authority over the state, but Asheville would be my jurisdiction, like… like a deputy sheriff. I would use it as a base from which to patrol the western mountains and search out more of The Transylvanian's spawn. I would report to you on a regular basis but I would have a great deal of power to use my own discretion in matters related to The Transylvanian's brood so that I might decisively act when I encounter one of them." Roderick turned and looked back at me, smiling weirdly again. His speech was so precise, so unlike him.

"I..." That was a genuine stunner. I didn't really see Roderick as being the middle-management type, you know? Were things that bad for him in Seattle? "Why?"

Roderick thought that one over for another minute or two while he smoked in silence. Finally, he replied. "Agatha, your maker, has offered me a role as one of her lieutenants. I haven't yet given her my answer. I've lived long enough in Seattle. My Last Gasp came and went decades ago. I have no reason to stay there and everything to gain from moving somewhere the talent pool is a little more sparse. I wish to do that under your tutelage, but I'll take what I can get." Roderick swiveled his eyes around and stared at me, no smile on his lips any longer. "Do you accept?"

I had to think about it. I knew the smart thing would be to sleep on it and see how I felt the next night but there was no time, I could tell. "Give me five minutes," I said and walked away from him, away from Clyde's grave, and took a quiet stroll between the dead to think about it.

Three minutes later I walked back up and took exactly the same position, but facing him instead of the remains of Clyde. He looked at me without distraction or movement.

"You would be loyal to me?" It was an honest question and my voice was low but my arms were crossed. I realized the defensive body language and tried to drop my hands to my side but instead just sort of fiddled around with my elbows.

"I would submit to you as a knight to his liege. You would be the ruler of this state but I would be your agent in Asheville and its surroundings. I would act to enforce and represent your rule."

"Once we find all of The Transylvanian's brood I doubt there will be any vampires to whom you could represent it." As I spoke, Smiles wandered back up the row in which we were standing and bumped his nose affectionately against Roderick's left leg.

"Perhaps, but perhaps not."

I squinted at him but I couldn't read his mind any more than he could mine. Finally I sighed. "And if I don't accept?"

"I go to work for Agatha, yes, but not against you if trouble ever broke out. You, meanwhile, are left without a helper in Asheville and The Transylvanian's minions retire to lick their wounds and plan for revenge. You'd be dead before you knew it." Roderick was so matter-of-fact, so sane, it made me shiver a little. "There's also the matter of your own soul and future to consider."

I blinked at that. "What?"

"You, your future, who you are." Roderick licked his lips, perhaps unaccustomed to speaking this much all at once and with so much *presence* in a conversation. "If you just act like none of this ever happened, what will you turn into? You'll turn into The Transylvanian. Not literally or anything, not at first, not for a long time, not in every single way. However, I know you. You would recede from the world. You must choose, cousin, right here and now, to accept that you are giving up a little control over your surroundings to someone you are choosing to trust. You must be a little vulnerable in some way so that you can still be a little *human*. Cousin Withrow, that is what makes vampires become The Transylvanian: an unwillingness to let life happen around them, a desire for predictability, the urge to leave nothing to chance. We are strong and fast and we get fun little powers and we turn all of them, in time, to our attempts at control over the world around us. We try to stop the passage of time because it's so meaningless and terrible from our perspectives and that's when we become the monsters. You must give up some of your power, give up some of your surety, so that you can live like a human does in some way. I am offering you that, right now. I offer you a chance at uncertainty so that you can still be alive inside. Don't try to turn the whole state into your personal Transylvania County. Relinquish something now so that you can stay connected to someone and something by caring what they do with it."

I stood in dumbfounded silence and turned that over in my mind. Roderick watched me very closely as I swiveled to gaze out at the woods myself, reflecting, considering. Finally, I spoke. "Where would you live?"

"I would buy a place, or rent a nice condo. I have money, that's not an issue. You saw my home in Seattle."

"When would it go into effect?"

"As soon as I could have the movers take everything from Seattle and bring it here; about four days."

"You've already been calling around, haven't you?"

Roderick smiled thinly and shrugged. "Covering my bases."

"Okay," I finally said. "You've got a deal." I held out my fat, sausage hand to shake and Roderick took it in his tiny little paw and that was that. I ceded to him all the control I had just fought hand-to-hand, fang and fur, to assert.

Roderick spoke again, only a little tentatively. "Now, the first request of your new lackey? Visit more often. Once a year is not enough. You cannot keep up with what's going on. Shoot for once a season, if not every month."

"Why? Aren't you going to be my eyes and ears here?"

"Because," Roderick said, shaking his head a little at me, "I would like to see you more."

I let out a long, ragged sigh. "Roderick," I said. "When I came out of the Last Gasp from The Transylvanian, I knew a lot. I knew that you were here on Agatha's orders. I figured you were here to clean up behind me and around the edges, to help without being seen to help. I'm glad you told me yourself about Agatha sending you here. That you brought it up is the only reason I'm willing to agree to this at all. Thank you."

Roderick blinked. "Of course, cousin," he said. "I'll always be straight with you." He paused. "You're not the first vampire I've heard of who has your power, by the way."

I raised both my eyebrows. "Really?"

"Yes." He nodded eagerly, as though we were kids sharing a secret. Perhaps we were: cousins, on our own, heads bowed in whispered conversation in a country graveyard at midnight. Talking about this stuff – the mechanics of our state, the things we do and how we do them – is all seen as a kind of dirty talk by the more respectable of our kind. "The others—the old ones, the ones who've seen lots of powers manifest in their time—they call it 'hindsight'."

I nodded at that and thanked him for the tidbit of information. Now was the time to ask about his Last Gasp again or forever give up. "And what is yours called?"

Roderick physically receded a little, shrinking back and shying away from answering, but he didn't force me to order him to tell me. I opened my mouth but he put up both hands and sighed. "It doesn't have a name, at least not one I know. No one ever even whispers about it for obvious reasons. I suspect lots of us have it, though, or at least more than just myself."

I set that aside for a moment. "How does it work?"

Roderick took his time answering. When he did, he started out in left field. "Do you ever see posters for missing persons on the Internet?"

I wrinkled up my brow. "I don't follow."

He smiled. "I look at social media sites sometimes and I see these digital missing-persons posters: a teen who has disappeared, a father who never came home from work, a child gone missing from the park. They usually have a photo and a physical description and the clothes they were wearing the last time they were seen."

I nodded. "Like on a milk carton." Roderick didn't eat food so he didn't grocery shop—hell, he had a butler, he wouldn't have been shopping anyway—so he shrugged that off.

"The online handbill gets seen, yes, but is the subject ever actually found because of it? No. A tiny fraction of the world sees the flyer and forgets it immediately; then they remember it when they see it re-posted a few days later. When they see it a third time, days after that, they wonder why their friend thinks it's worth the effort. Slowly the importance—the *value*—of that person fades from a world that cares less and less about her. In a few dozens of hours a missing child is worth less than the moment it takes to scroll past her picture in a web browser: just that quick!" He snapped one finger very lightly, as soft as a heart breaking. "Her family remembers and they weep for her in front of cameras. This makes good television if she's rich and white and pretty, but eventually the cameras go away because there is a new child who's disappeared and new rich, pretty, white parents shedding new tears. New photos are being posted to different social media sites. New circles of friends are wondering why they're being spammed with an image at which they've already heedlessly glanced. One day, one bright spring day, even her family forgets to think of her. At that point, it doesn't matter if she is alive somewhere or has been dead since the moment she was taken. The question is moot. The child is gone from the world, forever, and anyone who once truly cared for her and sees her photo will forget it again out of guilt—but not just guilt: perhaps also a little gratitude. Time sweeps her from the stream of life, dear cousin, and those who remain find their burden just slightly lightened. She is just one thread in a tapestry and time unravels her from it."

"Your power is like that?" I could barely speak.

"Yes. That person is removed from reality – I can feel it take place – and forgotten. It would happen anyway, eventually. I simply help the world at large arrive at that inevitable conclusion and no one has to endure experiencing it."

I left the next night. Roderick saw me off from the house. He was staying there while he looked for a place of his own. He knew a fixer from Seattle who could take care of his property there and his dog and all the arrangements with a moving company. His butler was going to take care of a lot of the daytime shit. In the meantime, he was reading real estate ads. If I knew him at all, he would wind up with one of those water-guzzling, overpriced mega-mcmansion things I hated so much. That's just how he is: no sense of tradition.

I've thought, ever since then, that maybe I should have told Roderick about H'Diane and the bracelet and the necklace, but I *still* haven't told him. I've never even hinted at it. I'm not sure why that is, but I guess it comes down to feeling like I've still got a card face-down on the table. I sincerely hope that they never run into one another and freak one another out, but I am not quite ready to leave my cousin alone in Asheville with absolutely nothing there to serve as a counterweight.

On my drive back, I stopped in Greensboro to pay a social call on Sarah. She wasn't thrilled at the idea that someone would have Asheville and all its surroundings all to themselves, but I got her to stop focusing on that and start focusing on The Transylvanian. She'd keep her eye out, she said. She wrinkled up her brow in a funny way when I told her what he'd said, the way he kept talking about *before* territories and allegiances. I didn't press the issue but I could practically see by the way she went blank every now and again after I mentioned that, standing perfectly still and her eyes flicking around, that some part of her was erasing any mention of those *before* times every time I brought them up.

I made a mental note to call Agatha and ask her when I got home but I never did. I just sort of forgot about it until now. I should call her tonight. On the other hand, writing all this down has kind of taken it out of me. Maybe a day of sleep would be good, clear my head, make me better able to focus on it all.

I guess we'll see.

Epilogue One

Roderick crept around the perimeter of the Shady Spot Assisted Living Estate. Despite the name, there were no trees immediately surrounding the small building—small for a hospital or rest home, anyway. It had room enough for a couple dozen tiny rooms and a miniscule "living" room for the "guests" and a microscopic kitchen where prepackaged meals could be reheated. Roderick smelled and saw all of this from the line of older trees that ran around the outside of the property. The building was probably thirty or forty years old. It had been built by cutting down all the trees around it, then bulldozing it flat, then putting down grass seed and a building and leaving again. It was wretched and weak and it smelled terrible. Roderick would have gagged when he was human, but he wasn't so he didn't. He smiled at that terrible smell. He was going to help this place get better. It would have to, wouldn't it? When he was done?

Carla Van Buren didn't keep him waiting for very long. She would be a bad nurse, he had thought to himself. She would be lax in her duties. She would hate these people, these mere mortal insects on whom she waited hand and foot while plotting for them to die and make her rich. Why she didn't simply kill them, well, Roderick couldn't fathom that. It simply made no sense. He had pondered this for a few minutes, maybe twenty, from inside the trees, when Carla came outside and lit her cigarette and started puffing on it.

Roderick had been very careful to stay downwind of the back yard of the building. Carla should not smell him; she did pull the cigarette from her lips and sniff the air a couple of times but no, she did not smell him.

She would already be running away or towards him if she did.

Roderick smiled at this. He liked knowing things that were happening and how they should happen and being able to compare the two. It was remarkably more... He stumbled for a moment, in his mind, looking for a word.

Together, he thought. Yes, that was a good word for it.

He would need to make sure that Carla Van Buren did not cry out or attract attention, so the butcher knife would need to be held at just the right height and position to disable her voice without cutting her head off.

Carla Van Buren was standing there, smoking her cigarette, worried that she hadn't heard from Blaine or any of the others at the meeting in over a week. She skipped the meeting because Mr. Wilson was in a bad way. She had to watch him very carefully these days to keep him alive. She could always have put him in better health but she liked walking that fine line, the balancing act between breath and the grave. Besides, when she used her gift it felt... wrong. It felt like something was coming out of her that shouldn't, like she shouldn't be able to do something "good" like that. Of course, she'd given up on things like right and wrong, good or bad a long --

She did not see who sped past her in a blur but she did feel her throat gape open with a ragged wound. She put her hands to her neck and tried to scream but nothing would come out except a wheeze of air.

Roderick shot past Carla, felt the knife bite down and then break free and kept going. At the tree line he held out one arm and wrapped it around a tree trunk to swing around and face Carla again. Her hands had just started going up to her neck and he watched to make sure she didn't scream.

She didn't.

Roderick shifted his position, planted his feet against the tree trunk and then shot back through the air towards her by pure momentum so that he tackled her to the ground, tumbled head-over-heels with her for three lengths and then came up so that he was on her back and her face was buried against the ground.

"My cousin does not take kindly to such liberal definitions of territory and loyalty as were enjoyed by your many siblings and yourself," Roderick whispered. "I apologize for what is about to happen but look at it this way: I could have been much, *much* crueler."

Then Roderick sank his teeth into her throat and took his time with it.

It was amazing, as it always was: as Carla turned to dust and ash and began to drift away in the breeze, he stood and closed his eyes and felt unravel and disappear her thread in the great tapestry of reality, her place in the high school yearbook of consensual reality. He could feel people forgetting – the people who had known her least, first, but it would work on anyone who had known her well soon enough. She might be remembered long enough to be reported missing, but no longer. The police would ignore the case if one were opened. Her patients would forget she existed. The rest home would wonder how they ever covered the shifts when they were already short one nurse. Nothing would be tracked back to him or to her or to vampires in general because there would be nothing to track back. It wasn't like Withrow's Jedi Mind Trick, which he said could be overcome by time or effort or coincidence. It was a fundamental rewrite of the world. It took a little time but that time was enough. No one remembered; no one except Roderick, who remembered them all.

The silence around him was exquisite.

Roderick took a moment to review his plans for the rest of the evening. He had hours and hours before sunrise.

Marty Macintosh proved to be quite easy to find. Roderick drove around the apartment complex with the window down, frigid winds carrying the scent of another vampire to him. He stopped his car, got out and let his senses reach out to touch all the apartments around him. Roderick smiled a little, to himself, like a kid with a stolen candy bar in his pocket.

Marty eventually answered his door after Roderick said all the right things from outside. He gawped at Roderick standing there, leaning against the door jam, looking as casual as Saturday afternoon.

"I am the cousin of Withrow Surrett, the boss of this state," Roderick said with absolutely zero otherwise in the way of niceties. "My name is Roderick Surrett. Withrow has allowed me the honor of assisting him in the eradication of the minions of the vampire you knew as The Transylvanian." Roderick watched Marty's face closely.

"You're here to kill me." Marty's voice was small and terrified and resigned and, Roderick realized, a little glad.

"Heavens no," Roderick said with a chuckle. "I'm here to ask you if you would like to be adopted and protected."

Marty blinked his wide eyes once, then again.

"If I take you as mine, my cousin will not harm you." Roderick smiled still, but it was growing a little brittle. He had been unaware Marty might require a visual aid to comprehension. "I am offering you that."

"Why?"

"Because you helped my dear cousin in his quest," Roderick purred. The smile was a little more natural now. "Because I wish to see you spared unnecessary harm. You tried to do what you could against the progenitor's sway The Transylvanian would hold over you. You also have useful skills. My time in this city is not at an end and I will need a great deal of assistance completing the work that remains to me."

"The maps." Marty was no great conversationalist and Roderick was already kind of tired of this.

"Yes. I wish you to map things for me. Notice things for me. Warn me of things. Assist me in identifying targets." Roderick licked his lips. He lacked his cousin's hoodoo but he had something like a very light ESP: he could sometimes get just a whiff of the motivations behind another's words. Marty was grappling with lots of competing influences but he didn't say enough to reveal any of them. Roderick pressed his case. "Do you accept? You will only have these moments in which to consider it. If you do not accept then I will eliminate you without pain or suffering. If you do accept, you will be protected and taught how to live in vampire society. If you accept and then betray me then I will kill you in some way that causes great anguish, starting with your mind."

"This can't be about maps." Marty simply said it, like the most obvious thing in the world.

Roderick sighed softly. "I'm also offering this because I need to sandwich myself somewhere between burdensome and helpful. I am soon going to be making a request of my cousin. It will help me if he sees me as more responsible. If he finds out about you then I can play you as the puppy for whom I've successfully cared all this time."

"Mr. Surrett," Marty finally said, "You're lying. You're not going to tell him about me one way or the other, are you?"

Roderick shrugged and tried not to look too incapable of something like guilt.

Marty blinked again, more rapidly. "I accept, Mr. Surrett."

Roderick held out a hand to shake. "I'm so glad to have you on board, Marty. Please, call me Roderick."

EPILOGUE TWO

H'Diane and Lavonde were sitting at home watching a DVD of a show they'd both missed when it aired a few years before. H'Diane wasn't that into it but LaVonde was and H'Diane didn't want to be the downer. During a break between episodes, she got up and went into the bathroom and stopped halfway to the toilet when all of a sudden the pendant around her neck *ached.*

It hadn't done that in a year, since the night Cliff had been found dead.

The night The Caller had talked to her.

She stopped, turned around, walked into the bedroom and grabbed her gun and her badge from the nightstand. Quietly, she walked back up the hall, crouched and peeked into the living room.

A swarthy guy of thirty-five or forty had LaVonde by both arms and had his mouth open, grotesquely long canines dripping with saliva, ready to bite the neck of the woman H'Diane loved.

Without thinking, without a moment's hesitation, she stood and pointed the gun and shot him in the mouth so that his jaw shattered and blood and gore splattered the wall behind him. He made a noise, a horrible noise sort of like a strangled growl, and tossed LaVonde aside to come straight for H'Diane. All she could do was throw her arms up over her face at the last second.

The guy touched her arm, touched the bracelet, and screamed bloody murder, flinging himself backwards, away from H'Diane, away from LaVonde, towards the front door. H'Diane stared for a second as he scrabbled with smoking hands at the door knob, trying to get away, then raised the gun again and shouted that he was under arrest.

He didn't comply, and he was clearly dangerous, so she pulled the trigger.

One shot, two shots, both directly in the abdominal region, precisely as her training dictated, but they didn't seem to stop him the way they should. The front door flew open, banging him in the face, and a third woman was standing there. H'Diane knew her but couldn't remember from where. The woman grabbed the top of the doorframe, kicked the guy in his shattered jaw so that he landed on his back, then drew out a wooden stake – there didn't seem to be a better word for it – and a hammer. H'Diane barely had time to shout something meaningless before the woman had driven it into the guy's chest with three savage blows. With a fourth swing of her arms, she yanked some sort of sharp tool on a short wooden handle out of a sling on her back and brought it down across the guy's neck.

Four seconds later there was a pile of ash settling on the floor and the bits of bone and flesh that had sprayed around were simply gone in little puffs of dust.

The women dropped her weapons and threw her hands into the air. "Jennifer McCordy! North Carolina Para-Science! We met in the field last year!" Her eyes were squeezed shut. H'Diane's hands were shaking. Somehow she managed *not* to fire the gun. The woman was clearly waiting for that to happen, and when it didn't, when the silence filled the room, LaVonde finally relaxed enough to scream.

Days later, H'Diane and LaVonde and Jennifer met at a hotel bar out by the airport and had a very long conversation about monsters in the night and the things that might work against them.

About the Author

MICHAEL G. WILLIAMS is a native of the mountains of western North Carolina. He is a brother in St. Anthony Hall and Mu Beta Psi and believes strongly in the power of found families. Michael lives in Durham with his two cats and more and better friends than he probably deserves.

Michael earned a BA in Performance Studies at UNC Chapel Hill and works as an engineer. He has been a successful participant in National Novel Writing Month for many years and encourages anyone interested in writing to jump headlong into the deep end of insanity for thirty days. More information can be found at www.nanowrimo.org.

For more information on this work and others by Michael G. Williams, visit www.michaelgwilliams-author.com. For information on Michael's open-source marketing, visit The Perishables Project at www.theperishablesproject.com.

Also by Michael G. Williams

Perishables
"COMPLICATIONS"

Connect with Michael via the following sites:

The Perishables Project
Twitter
Facebook
Google+
Amazon Author Central
GoodReads
WattPad

www.ingramcontent.com/pod-product-compliance
Lightning Source LLC
Chambersburg PA
CBHW032000180726
48283CB00008B/2502